A WITCH'S LIGHT

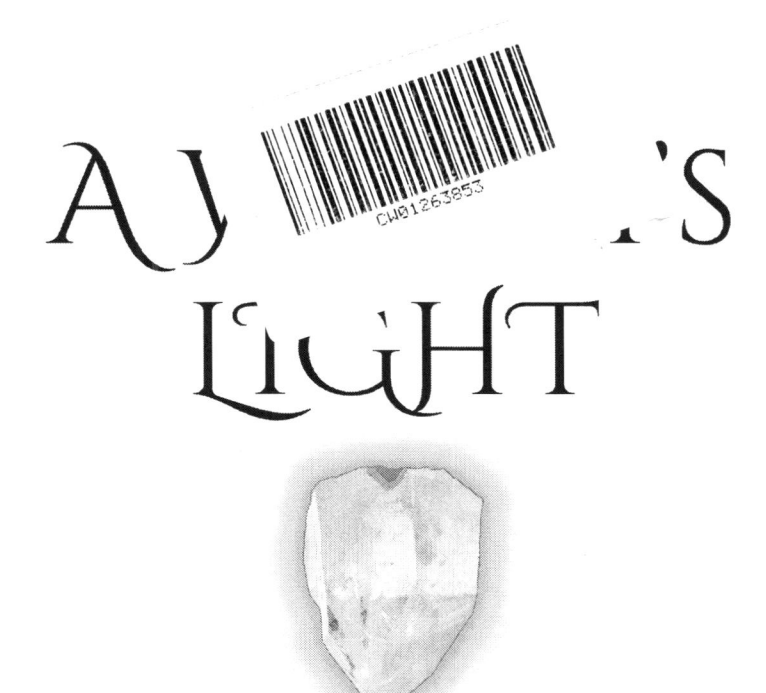

THE SALEM WITCHES - BOOK THREE

Cathy Walker
Author

No part of this publication may be reproduced, distributed, or transmitted in any form or by any means, including photocopying, recording, or other electronic or mechanical methods, without the prior written permission of the publisher, except as permitted by U.S. copyright law. For permission requests, contact [include publisher/author contact info].

The story, all names, characters, and incidents portrayed in this production are fictitious. No identification with actual persons (living or deceased), places, buildings, and products is intended or should be inferred.

Copyright © 2021 by Cathy Walker

ISBN 979-8753089496

All rights reserved

Book Cover by Cathy's Covers

Books By Cathy Walker

A Witch's Lament - The Salem Witches Book 1
A Witch's Legacy - The Salem Witches Book 2
A Witch's Light - The Salem Witches Book 3

The Witch of Endor – The Witch Tree Book 1
The Daughters of Endor – The Witch Tree Book 2
Coming in 2024
The Book of Endor – The Witch Tree Book 3
Coming in 2024
Sword Across Time
Solitary Cove
The Crystal of Light

PROLOGUE

The people of Salem grow complacent in the belief that they are safe. While they go about their lives, the darkness remains trapped within a sphere of light, roiling, spinning, looking for release. Fed by a hunger for destruction and death, it won't be long before intent comes together in a blinding streak and escapes its prison. The Light of Many Souls is the only hope of permanently destroying the evil. Be warned, Arch-Druid Seabhac, let not your ego rule you this time. You must relinquish control and accept the help you would not allow before your death. Look to the Holder of the Light, as salvation lies within the crystal she protects.

Excerpt from *Faerie Enchantments and Sorcerer Magick*

The air around Seabhac rippled and his heart skipped a couple of beats. A force of unknown roots intruded upon the peaceful surroundings created by him and Ainevar in this hidden corner of the Netherworld. Fear licked at his belly as his mind raced through a list of places Ainevar might be at this time of day. He ran for the door and yanked it open, only to find her already reaching for the handle.

Ainevar faced him. Her blond hair in disarray and blue eyes filled with fear. "What is happening? I feel a disturbance."

"I do not know, but I want you to sit down and relax while I figure it out. I am sure it is nothing to worry about."

Ainevar snorted in a very unladylike manner. "Don't patronize me. My abilities are just as fine-tuned as yours. Something is wrong and you will need my help."

It was Seabhac's turn to snort. He placed his hands on Ainevar's shoulders and looked her in the eyes. "This is not up for discussion. You. Sit." He pointed to a nearby chair and stared at his beloved until she complied. Albeit with some difficulty, because of her large belly.

Seabhac's gaze softened as he spoke. "You and the babe are more important than anyone or anything, and it is my responsibility to protect you both." Sadness weighed his words and hinted at past regrets. "I failed you once and I refuse to do so again."

"Seabhac, that was so long ago and none of it was your fault."

"I stole you from your family and took you away to live a life in a foreign place with strange people and then I died and left you to the dark clutches of evil."

"Shush. That foreign land became the home I loved, and those strangers were priestesses of Avalon. You fought with every bit of your soul to defeat that evil. And you managed it eventually. You have no reason to feel guilty."

A cramp twisted Seabhac's chest. "We have no time for this now. I need to figure out what is happening. You stay here."

With those words, he stepped outside and closed his eyes. Drawing in the air from around him, he cleared his mind and concentrated on the feelings that agitated him. It was simple enough to follow the sliver of energy that alerted him to a problem. It led directly to the outbuilding that acted as an altar room and protection for the knife and journal he had created back in Avalon so long ago.

Heavily spelled, the small wooden structure was virtually impenetrable to any person or force. Though, the chance of being discovered in the Netherworld was next to none, and that was why Seabhac and Ainevar chose here to settle when they fled Salem. They had brought with them the ball of light created in the church's basement. The ball of light that Seabhac had created from thought and a sense of desperation to hold the darkness captive. It had worked, but only by pure chance combined with the concentrated force of all those involved that day.

With a wave of his hand, he cleared the spells from the door and stepped into the room. An everlasting ball of druid light floated near the low ceiling and lit the room. Shadows danced across the dirt floor and into the corners. The knife and journal sat on a raised wooden dais, innocuous looking enough, unless you tried to touch either of them. The resulting jolt would send even the most powerful druid or witch into another realm.

That wasn't Seabhac's primary concern, though. He moved across the room to open a hidden door concealing a recessed area in the wall. The sight of the ball of light still intact sent a rush of relief through him. He frowned. If the problem was not the encased darkness, it must be the knife or journal, but they sat untouched. Wait. A whisper drew him to them. Each step closer, raising a drumbeat in his head.

Clearing the wards, he reached out and touched the book. His journal. The book that his otherworldly self had used to communicate with Ainevar and, after her death, with chosen humans. His words marked the pages of the journal, which could morph and guide others as needed. The last entry would tell the story of how the humans, Samson and Cassandra, as well as Ainevar and himself, had defeated the darkness in a damp church basement.

His fingers flipped through the pages until he found that last entry. Heat and disbelief rushed through him as he saw a new and unknown entry. He read the words written in unfamiliar handwriting and blanched at the implications.

" ... *it won't be long before intent comes together in a blinding streak and escapes its prison.*"

No, that couldn't be. The darkness had remained imprisoned all this time, it could not be at risk of escaping now. Nothing had changed. He looked at the newest journal entry and realized that, yes, something had changed. Someone possessed the ability to write in *his* journal. That person, or entity, would have to be scary powerful to do such a thing. Seabhac did not think such power existed anymore. Over the years, any of the ancient bloodlines had weakened and dispersed with interbreeding and an ignorance

3

of the old ways. As far as he knew, there was no one left who possessed the power that he and Ainevar could wield.

Obviously, he was wrong. And the remark about him not letting his ego get in the way this time would mean that whoever was responsible for this must have known him before his death in Avalon on that long ago day. Since then, other than the brief foray to Salem, he'd spent his time in the Netherworld. A place no one frequented by choice, which made it the perfect place for Ainevar and him to reside as guardians of the sphere.

What was the *Light of Many Soul?* And who was the *Holder of the Light?*

He needed to talk with Ainevar. This was too vast for him to hide from her, and they needed a plan. Slamming the journal shut, he placed it back in its resting place, reset the wards, and strode with a purpose back to the house.

With shaky hands, Ainevar placed the teacups on the table and sat. "But none of it makes sense. How could anyone else use your journal for messages? What is the *Light of Many Souls?* And who, or what, is the *Holder of the Light?* I have heard none of those terms before. Would one of us not know something about this? Seriously. No one has lived longer or seen more than we have. Who could possess knowledge that we do not?"

Seabhac gently placed a hand over Ainevar's. "Sweetling. Relax. Think of the child and do not stress over questions which we cannot answer."

"But, Seabhac, even if we do not have the answers, what do we do now? The journal speaks of the darkness breaking free from the sphere. If we know that to be the case, can we not stop it before it happens? And, if we cannot stop it, what happens then? How do we even know where it will go, or what time in history it will return to?"

Seabhac sighed. Ainevar's questions were all valid and ones to which he had no answers.

CHAPTER ONE

A nwyn dusted the rose quartz globe and placed it back on the stand among all the other various crystals and gems. She loved this part of her day. Cleaning the crystals and soaking up their energy always gave her a lift and balanced out any imbalance in her aura. Her fingers tingled as she lifted the purple amethyst and enjoyed the sensations it gave her.

Mondays were typically slow days, and it gave her a chance to reorganize her store and take pride in the comfortable clutter of candles, crystals, books, incense, herbs, wands and all the other paraphernalia expected in a witch store in Salem, Massachusetts. Most of it seemed excessive to her, as her history had taught her that power lay within and a true witch did not need all these accoutrements. Of course, the words *true witch* said it all. From what she had seen in her short time in town, there were only a few witches of true bloodlines remaining. Most of the people who frequented her store were witch wannabes.

She smiled in amusement at the term she had learned just the other day. There was so much to learn, and Anwyn spent all day soaking up tidbits of conversation and learning from each person who came to *Avalon's Light*. When she had bought *A Witches Haven* from the previous owner, Verity Parker, she had changed the name to make it more personal. It seemed appropriate, and dispensing with the witch part of the title was better as well, considering her own past and the fact that she did not consider herself a witch.

Within days of taking possession of the keys for her new store, Anwyn had moved everything around and brought in new stock.

The glass cases, bright lights, perfectly organized books, and bare floors had been cold and uninviting. Anwyn worked a miracle in the few weeks she had owned the store. She packed floor to ceiling with jars of dried herbs, vials of essential oils, crystals, candles, amulets, brooms, cord, and divination tools such as tarot cards and runes. The back wall boasted a glass showcase of knives—athames for ritual and bollines for cutting and carving—as well as a bookshelf stocked with some very impressive books. Brocade wall hangings depicting the Green Man, witches dancing around, and other various scenes adorned various spots on the walls. Her thought was to make stepping into the store like entering the past. A world of enchantment, solid earth-magic, time-honored natural remedies, and a perception of one's own eternal cycle of life. She hoped she had achieved her goal.

A hint of the familiar broke her from her reverie and she felt a touch of nostalgia and a flashback to long-ago times. Earthy sounds and scents like sun-baked cedar, the whisper of a breeze and birdsong on a warm summer day, and the peaty smell of fires burning in winter. Anwyn sighed. Peaceful memories that made her long for home...before the slaughter that took the lives of everyone she cared for and flung her into an unknown future.

The familiar feeling overwhelmed her as it seemed to move closer. A flash of fear shot through her, but she realized the fear was unwarranted. The jingle of the bell signaled the opening of the door, and Anwyn turned to face the cause of her jumbled emotions.

What she saw sent a sharp jolt of awareness through her and left her pushing down a rising tide of warmth. Taking a shuddering breath, she fought to present an unruffled and calm presence. She achieved a semblance of control and a slight smile as she greeted the two women. The term *witch wannabes* did not apply to these women. In fact, ancient power radiated from them in a way Anwyn had not felt for a long time. No wonder yearning for times gone past had briefly taken her over.

She managed a greeting. "Good morning, ladies. Welcome to *Avalon's Light*. If there is anything I can do to help you, please ask for help."

The petite blonde woman turned striking blue eyes in her direction. "Oh, you startled me. I didn't see you standing there." She advanced, her hand outstretched. "I assume you're the new owner?"

Even though the woman's words were friendly, Anwyn felt the trickle of apprehension and distrust that the woman tried to hide. "Yes, I am." She awkwardly extended her hand to shake. Such a natural greeting, yet she found such pleasantries difficult with strangers.

The blonde dropped Anwyn's hand and gestured toward the dark-haired woman. "This is Skye and my name is Cassandra. It's so nice to meet you. We meant to come in earlier, but Skye has been rather busy the last few weeks."

Skye snorted as she tucked a wild curl of black hair behind her ear and reached down to lift a newborn babe from an apparition with wheels. "Understatement of the year. I was busy giving birth to this little bundle of joy."

Anwyn's heart melted. A babe. A sweet, gurgling, innocent, wide-eyed babe. Regret for her lost past almost choked her, but she hid her turbulent emotions. Or so she thought.

The women shared a glance and stepped toward Anwyn. Comfort came with them as soft waves of caring and concern.

Cassandra, the blonde, spoke first. "Hey, are you okay?"

"Yes. Yes, of course." Anwyn looked at the baby. "Do you think I could hold your child? I understand if you are not comfortable allowing it."

Skye hesitated only a second and then gently passed her baby over to Anwyn. "It's okay. I think Sarah would love to meet you."

"Sarah, such a lovely name." Anwyn took the baby into her arms and rocked back and forth in an age-old maternal tradition. "Is it a family name?"

"Yes. It goes back many generations."

A minor disruption in Skye's aura let Anwyn know that there was a story behind that simple statement, and it might be part of the reason she was here in Salem.

"Would you like to hold her for a few minutes while Cassandra and I look around?"

"Yes, please. Browse around all you want." Anwyn cuddled the baby, but watched the two women as they wandered around the store, oohing and awing over the inventory. Inhaling, she enjoyed the newborn smell and rubbed a finger over the baby's soft cheek. "You are the sweet one, are you not?" She whispered. "And you possess even more power than your mommy does."

"What." Skye put down the crystal she'd been holding and her gaze locked with Anwyn's. "Why would you say that?"

Fates. Anwyn flushed and cursed the good acoustics in the building. "It was just a guess." A time-worn mantra echoed through her mind. A voice from the past. *Do not let anyone know how powerful you are. Do not let anyone know how powerful you are.*

Cassandra and Skye shared another glance and moved to stand in front of Anwyn. Skye's hands were full with the baby, but Cassandra touched Anwyn's arm and said, "It's okay. You obviously possess certain abilities. You don't need to hide. After all, you own a witch store in the witch capital of the world and customers expect a certain amount of witchiness."

"I am not a witch." Anwyn realized that she'd spoken too harshly, so she softened her tone. "I mean, there is nothing wrong with being a witch, but that is not what I consider myself."

"That's interesting." Skye put Sarah back in the small vehicle with wheels and turned her piercing blue eyes on Anwyn, who shifted self-consciously. "What do you consider yourself?"

Why do these two women make me feel so awkward and say things that are better left unsaid?

Anwyn's mind raced as she fiddled with the crystal necklace she wore. It comforted and helped ground her. "I suppose, if I had to clarify, I am more of a priestess than a witch."

"Fascinating." Skye stared at her for a moment, as if deciding. She smiled and said, "I would love to find out more and get to know you better, but my husband, Jerome, will wonder what is keeping us. We're leaving this afternoon to visit my parents in Camden. They haven't met their grandchild yet and are waiting impatiently for us." She turned to the door, then stopped. "By the way, that is a lovely necklace you're wearing. It looks extraordinarily old."

Anwyn's heart thudded, and she was sure she flushed. "It is old. It has been in the family for generations." Had her voice cracked? She really hoped it had not.

Skye smiled. "I am sure that Cassandra will make you feel more than welcome over the next couple of weeks. When I'm back in town, I'd love for all three of us to go for lunch. In the meantime, best be on my way. Are you coming Cassandra?"

"Yes. Right behind you." Cassandra shot a warm smile at Anwyn. "I'll come back and have a closer look. I'm decorating a couple of houses and there are a few items here that I can definitely see complementing the style I'm aiming for."

Before Anwyn could reply, the women had left. She wrapped a shaking hand around her necklace and realized the events were in motion and there was nothing she could do except to fulfill her destiny. She only hoped she would have the strength to do what needed doing.

CHAPTER TWO

Memnon dropped the last box on the floor in the kitchen and grabbed a beer from the fridge before collapsing on his couch. Or, rather, Samson's couch. He surveyed the minimalist decoration of the condo and decided that he needed new furniture, rugs, decorations...basically everything. And he knew just the person to call to get the job done.

Pulling a cell phone from his jeans pocket, he pushed the first button on his contacts list and waited while the phone rang on the other side.

"Hey, you." The soft voice of his sister, Cassandra, reached through the phone and made him smile. "Are you all unpacked and settled into your new, temporary home?"

"Well, the boxes are in, but I haven't unpacked yet."

"Let me guess, you're taking a break and drinking a beer."

Memnon laughed. "You know me too well. So, since you're so smart, how about telling me why I called you?"

"Hmm, if I have to guess, I'd say that it's a call for help because you're lazy and unimaginative."

"Whoa, insults on my first day in town. I hope this isn't the precedent that you're setting. You are right, though. I was hoping for some design time from you. Your boyfriend doesn't have the greatest sense of style and I'd love a condo makeover."

Cassandra laughed. "Wish I could help, but I'm busy with a couple of other jobs and have no spare time for the next few weeks. If you can wait that long, then I'm all yours."

"Damn. But I'm happy to hear that your business is picking up and you're settling in so well. See, I knew this was the place you needed to be."

"Quit bragging. I've thanked you enough for forcing me to come to Salem, meet the man I fell in love with, battle an ancient evil that possessed my body, and having the audacity to give me a house."

"That's what big brothers are for, right?"

"Among other things. I'm glad you're here, though. I always feel better when you're close by, and I wasn't happy being so far apart. We've been through so much together, you know. "

Memnon heard the crack in her voice and was glad he'd come to Salem for a while. Cassandra's life had not been easy, and getting her to Salem had been his way of making her fend for herself and build self-confidence. That, and his strong premonition that this was where she needed to be. He hadn't been wrong. Turns out that she had helped to battle a dark force that had been haunting Salem on and off for a long time. As far as they knew, that force was in limbo where it should remain forever. Hopefully.

Cassandra and Samson were now living together and if Memnon trusted anyone to care for his sister, it was Samson. But familial ties were strong, and a rough childhood had created a bond between him and Cassandra that would always be there.

His stomach rumbled, and he realized he had done no grocery shopping. "So, how about you invite your big brother over for lunch. I could use some food sustenance to keep going."

"I suppose I could throw together a sandwich for you. Samson will be here for lunch in about half an hour. Come on over."

"Okay, see you then."

Memnon sat pensively and finished his beer. Truth was, he came to Salem to be close to Cassandra and make sure everything was good with her. But there was another reason, and as much as he hated lying to his sister, he couldn't ruin her happiness by telling her that his presence in Salem was as much because of another premonition he'd experienced, as it was to be close to her.

"Drive careful and say hello to your parents for us." Memnon watched Cassandra step back from the car and give a last wave to Skye and Jerome as they drove away. Their dog, Chance, stuck his fur face out the back window and he gave a loud bark as if saying goodbye.

He put his arm around her shoulder. "You'll miss them, won't you?"

"Yes. More than I could have imagined when I came here less than a year ago. They are awesome neighbors, wonderful friends, and the life-changing events we shared have created a strong bond."

"I guess it's a good thing I'm here to take your mind off them leaving. Now, your big brother is hungry. Where's my lunch?"

As if on cue, Samson drove into the driveway in his unmarked police car and pulled to a stop beside Cassandra and Memnon. When he got out of the car and stood his full height, Memnon felt the usual slight sense of intimidation. It wasn't very often that anyone towered over him, as he was six feet tall himself, but Samson beat him by about four inches. It was a strange feeling for Memnon to have to look up to anybody.

He thrust his hand out for a handshake. "Good to see you, Samson."

Samson gripped the offered hand and lifted his mouth in a half-smile as he squeezed. Expecting the move, Memnon was ready and squeezed back just as hard.

Cassandra rolled her eyes and shook her head. "Men. Always trying to one-up each other. I don't know about either of you, but I'm hungry and lunch is ready. See you both inside."

While eating his sandwich, Memnon watched his sister's face as she laughed with Samson about an incident at work involving a cat up a tree, a ladder, and an officer afraid of heights. He'd spent so many years after their parent's accident worrying about her, protecting her, and trying to build her self-confidence. She'd shut herself off from people and emotions, buried herself in her work and struggled constantly to battle the natural abilities she'd been born with. Coming to Salem had released those powers and enabled her to thrive in a way that made Memnon only a bit jealous. Not that his life wasn't great, because it was. It was just a lonely existence, and he was ready to share his life with someone. Especially now that Cassandra was so obviously in love and moving on with someone in her life.

"Earth to Memnon." Cassandra snapped her fingers in front of his face. "Would you like another sandwich, or are you ready for some fruit salad and whipped cream for dessert?"

Pushing his self-pitying pondering away, he laughed. "Doesn't the whipped cream defeat the health benefits of the fruit salad?"

"Sure. What's your point?"

Samson grabbed a bowl of fruit and scooped a couple of heaping spoonfuls of whipped cream on top. "Hey, this is one argument you won't win. Just eat and enjoy."

Cassandra filled a bowl for Memnon and then for herself and sat down beside Samson. "By the way, Skye and I finally checked out the new store where Verity's store used to be. You know, *Avalon's Light*."

Samson mumbled through his mouthful of fruit. "Mmm, hmm. What did you think?"

"The new owner has done an amazing job of fixing it up and making it much more welcoming that Verity's set up. It used to be so cold and uninspired, but now it's filled with warm colors, rich tapestries, and new inventory spread out in a welcoming manner. Anwyn did a truly inspired makeover."

"Anwyn?" Samson questioned.

"Sorry. That's the new owner's name. She is a lovely woman. I'm actually jealous because she has the thick, dark auburn hair that I've always wanted. Her skin is luminescent, and she has an ethereal quality about her. Quite gorgeous, really. Though, I have to admit, there was something not quite right about her."

Samson perked up. His police instincts in full-on mode. "Oh. In what way?"

"Nothing I can pinpoint other than she just seemed out of step with her surroundings. And her speech was stilted. She never once used a contraction the whole time we spoke. She was so formal. Also shy and unsure."

"Sweetie, I think your imagination is working overtime. Your description fits many people I can think of." Samson said.

"I know, it can all be explained, and she truly was warm and welcoming. It's just a niggle in the back of my brain. Skye felt the same. When she gets back from visiting her parents, she wants to go back to the store and get a better feel for Anwyn. I think I'll go back before that, though. I'm curious if I feel the same after a second visit."

She turned her gaze to Memnon. "I wonder if she's in a relationship."

"Nope. No way. I'm only in town for a brief visit. I will not get dragged into dating or any kind of relationship." Which sounded so hypocritical in his head because he'd just finished thinking how he *wanted* a relationship. But not here in Salem. He'd wait until he got back to New York before giving serious thought to a relationship. But wait a minute. Why not here? He might enjoy living in Salem. Especially since Cassandra looked to be on her way to being a permanent resident.

Cassandra waved a hand in front of his face. "You're doing it again, Memnon. What the heck is up with you today? You can't stay focused on anything." Cassandra frowned. "You're usually right on top of the conversation."

"I guess I'm just tired. I think I'll go start unpacking, then grab an afternoon nap." He turned to Samson, who was helping himself to a second helping of dessert. "Thanks again for letting me stay in your place. I appreciate the gesture."

Samson laughed and motioned around the room. "It's the least I can do considering that you provided the home I'm currently living in."

Memnon drove back to his condo, but found it interesting, and somewhat unsettling, that he had to tap down the urge to go visit the new store, *Avalon's Light*.

CHAPTER THREE

The past becomes the present as time swirls in waves of discord and harmony combined. What was thought to be quelled is close to its rising and will bring with it a final blast of fury and hate. Be ever vigilant in your intent as it feeds on the darkness within humankind. Already, it grows restless. With mighty force, it will awaken from its slumber and wreak havoc upon the innocent. Be faithful to the Light. To relax within your hopes and focus only on the future will allow the ancient darkness an escape.

Excerpt from *Faerie Enchantments and Sorcerer Magick*

Seabhac slammed his journal shut and cursed in vivid druid manner. Ainevar raised an eyebrow, set down the shirt she was patching, and waited for an explanation.

"I do not understand how words keep appearing in my journal. No one should have the ability to meddle with my spells. And how can we trust the words written? How can we know whether the force tries to help us or mislead us?"

"We do not know. But either way, it is troubling and we need to decide upon a course of action. Have you checked on the sphere yet today?"

"No." Seabhac looked down at the journal which sat so innocuous looking on the table. "I suppose that in light of this newest entry, I should make it a daily priority." He stood, but before leaving, he leaned over and kissed Ainevar's forehead. "I will do everything in my power to ensure the safety of you and the babe."

"Seabhac, my love. You do not need to feel guilty. You saved me in Avalon and allowed me to live out my life. If you had not put your very soul into your journal and provided the knife for protection, I would have died along with you and the priestesses."

"Ha. You lived a life on the run from an evil that I was responsible for and then died alone and afraid. I failed you before and I will not do so again."

Ainevar sighed and smiled, a smile that did not quite reach her eyes. "On this, we shall never agree. But I suppose it matters not as we have been happy and now we have one last task to ensure our future."

The newly penned words from the journal jumped into Seabhac's mind. *To relax within your hopes and focus only on the future will allow the ancient darkness an escape.*

"Yes, our future." He spoke the words, but for the first time in a long while, he doubted he had a future. Before Ainevar could see the desolation in his eyes, he hastened to the door. "I will check the sphere."

He performed the usual ritual to remove the protection spells on the hut and entered the cool, musty interior. His eyes adjusted to the darker light fairly easily, but the instant he stepped over the threshold, he knew the sphere was weakening and allowing energy to leak from within its spelled prison.

Fine, sticky threads floated about the room. Seeking. Weaving. Slowly rolling around and back onto themselves as if trying to form. Not enough to be a danger. But their existence outside of the sphere was enough of a threat to strike inevitable fear within Seabhac. Not sure how he'd even performed the spell to bind the darkness in the sphere in the first place, he did not know how to repeat the actions. And when it escaped, the darkness would return to Salem. At least, that's what his journal stated.

There was no hope.

He needed to return to Salem.

Chapter Four

Anwyn shook off the heavy feeling that had plagued her since waking first thing that morning. After all the preparation, expectations, and years of waiting, she did not feel ready for whatever awaited her. She had not been in Salem long, but had built a business and even enjoyed her days and felt as if she could make this her home.

Of course, that was not possible. Her life was not her own and all the trappings of *Avalon's Light* and her being a normal person was a facade. A necessary lie in order to be in the right place to complete her task. She knew that, but it did not stop her from aching for a normal life.

The door jingled, and she continued dusting the counter in order to gather her thoughts before slipping back into her role as a business owner. "Just look around, I will be right with you."

Anwyn heard the creak of wooden floorboards, and rustle of material as the customer wandered around the store. She took a deep breath to relax and a warm feeling of peace enveloped her, which she thought was strange considering she had performed no soothing spells on herself. She turned to face her customer.

And got hit with a hot flush of need.

Need for love.

Need for comfort.

Need for a life she knew she would never have.

"Are you okay?"

The man spoke, but Anwyn was not sure if she was capable of answering. Instead, she stared into his warm, dark eyes, barely registering his very dark, curly hair, muscled body, and nonchalant demeanor as he leaned against the counter.

"Oh, yes. Of course I am fine. Was there anything in particular that I can help you look for?"

"No. I was just passing by when I got the urge to stop in and have a look. You've done wonders with redecorating and creating the homey feel that this place was missing."

Anwyn felt her face go warm with the compliment. She tried to hide the fact by looking away. "Thank you. Just let me know if you need anything."

But she was not about to get away that easily as the man put his hand out. "My name is Memnon."

Anwyn looked at the hand as it took a second to realize what he was expecting. These social conventions were difficult to remember. She put her hand in his but pulled it back as quickly as she could without seeming rude. "I am named Anwyn."

"Anwyn? That is an unusual name. Is it a family name?"

"Yes."

There was a brief silence, then Memnon gestured at Anwyn's necklace. "That is lovely. I could see my sister Cassandra wearing something like that. Do you sell them here?"

"No." Anwyn's emphatic denial sounded harsh. "Sorry. It is one of a kind and a family heirloom."

"A shame."

Memnon's gaze lingered on the necklace and Anwyn grasped at a way to shift his attention away from the crystal and from her. "There was a woman in here a couple of days ago with name Cassandra. Petite, blonde, blue eyes, and exquisitely beautiful."

Memnon's laughter broke the tension. "Sounds like Cassie. She'll be delighted and embarrassed to be described as exquisitely beautiful."

"I am sorry. Is that too personal to describe someone who is a stranger? I meant no disrespect."

"Relax. You didn't commit a social blunder. You're fine."

Blunder? Another new word for her to figure out. If she just smiled and nodded her head, maybe Memnon would not realize that she had no idea as to the meaning of his comment. Anwyn's brain raced to find a new subject to discuss. "So, do both you and your sister live in Salem?"

"Cassie moved here about nine months ago, not planning to stay permanently, but that's how it worked out. I am here for a visit, but have been considering a more permanent stay." A glimmer lit his eyes causing Anwyn's breath to catch in her throat.

"I see." Anwyn was sure that this man was deliberately teasing her. Flirting was possibly the correct word, and she found it to be a somewhat enjoyable pursuit. If she engaged him in conversation, he might stay in her store longer and she could explore this tingly feeling that fluttered around in her stomach.

No! Heartache and disappointment waited at the end of those thoughts. *Focus, Anwyn. Focus.*

While Memnon wandered around the store picking up and browsing items, Anwyn kept herself busy shuffling and rearranging items that did not need moving. She fought the urge to sneak a peek at her attractive customer and found herself at the losing end of that argument. She lifted her head and looked his direction, only to find him looking at her.

She forced a smile and hoped he couldn't see the tightness in her lips. There was an awkward moment of silence while Anwyn's brain searched for something to say that sounded natural.

"So, did you know the previous owner of this store?" Anwyn tried to sound casual. Her question was an innocent one, but she also knew there was a history involving Verity Parker and her son. She needed to learn more about what had happened in Salem in the past, as it might help prepare her for what was yet to come.

"No, I didn't. From what I understand, she and her son dabbled in some dark magic that drove him crazy and, as a result, Verity closed the store and ended up renting an apartment closer to the institute where Matthew is a patient. A permanent patient,

I believe." Memnon sent a searching look at Anwyn. "Is there a reason you're asking?"

"No, just idle curiosity about the person who ran this store before I took over."

"If you're thinking about living up to her standards...don't worry. Most people in town didn't like her and, well, there is the whole dark magic thing."

Just the words *dark magic* sent a shiver down Anwyn's spine. Before she could react or reply to Memnon, an unknown shadow crossed her vision. The ground beneath her shook, her legs weakened, and she grasped for something to hold herself steady.

"Whoa, there. Are you okay?"

Strong arms wrapped around her and lent her the strength she needed. Acutely aware of the chest pressed against her nose, Anwyn fought the urge to put her arms around the welcoming warmth of hard-muscled man. Her traitorous body softened and melted into the contour of his body. Before she could embarrass herself too much, his deep voice sounded in her ear.

"Are you okay?" Memnon asked.

"Yes, the tremor of the earth scared me, is all."

Memnon frowned. "Tremor?"

Oh, no. He had not felt it. That could not bode well.

"By the way, your necklace is glowing."

Those words slammed into Anwyn and chased away all thoughts of warmth and comfort. Pushing herself away from Memnon, her hand flew to cover the necklace. "Your eyes play you for a fool. It may have reflected the light, but it is not glowing."

Anxious and worried, she gave Memnon a push on the arm. "I need to close early today. If you are not purchasing anything, I would appreciate if you would leave now."

Memnon resisted the light push, and Anwyn knew she could not force him to leave. She prayed he would be amicable enough to give in to her request. With a last glance toward Anwyn's necklace, which she still kept covered with her hand, Memnon moved forward. Anwyn followed closely so she could lock the door after him before he changed his mind or another customer entered.

Memnon stepped out the door, but before Anwyn could close it, he turned and pinned her with his piercing gaze. "I'll be back."

"Fine. I look forward to such a time." Anwyn slammed and locked the door, pulled the shades down, sank to the floor, and put her head to her knees while mumbling. "I look forward to such a time. Trite. That sounded so trite."

Then, suddenly remembering her necklace, she leapt up and rushed over to the ornate mirror that she kept on the wall for customers to model jewelry they were thinking of buying. With heart pounding and her hand clenching the necklace in a tight fist, she closed her eyes and sent a silent prayer to the Goddess Branwen. Sneaking a peak through half-opened eyes, she slowly unclenched her fist to reveal the finely honed crystal she'd worn for so long. The talisman that would warn her. The item that could prove to be the eventual savior of Salem.

It glowed.

Anwyn gasped. Blood pumped hot through her. Her heart raced with fear and remembrance as memories overwhelmed her. She sank to the floor, lost in a haze of the past.

Memnon stared at the door as if it had been the one to kick him out of the store so unceremoniously. The lock clicked into place, and he shook his head in disbelief at such unwarranted rudeness. But the haunted look of fear that had lit Anwyn's amber eyes worried him. Why had she been so afraid? She'd mentioned a tremor, but he hadn't felt it. Though there had been something. A knot of unease deep in his stomach that had tensed and disappeared at the same time as he'd seen Anwyn's necklace glow. Now that was a sight to see. Such a unique, well-crafted crystal that had flared into brilliant light and then faded to a warm glow. Stunning. Also, a bit worrisome.

Everything about his visit to *Avalon's Light* bothered him. Especially the woman with auburn hair, eyes the color of dark golden honey, and alabaster skin. With her graceful way of moving and soft speech, she seemed delicate, yet he'd felt her strength when she'd pushed him toward the door and out of the store. Determined strength.

Memnon dug in his pocket for his keys and walked to his SUV parked up the street. Anwyn intrigued him in a way he'd never experienced with another woman. She seemed out of place in the way she spoke. Even her clothes would better fit in a forgotten period in history. The long, flowing dress in such a simple style and delicate pastel color made him envision Anwyn walking in a field of wildflowers with the gentle breeze rustling her hair.

Yuck! Get a grip. Memnon shook his head to clear the corny image and climbed into his Mercedes hybrid SUV. Used to beautiful women pursuing him, he'd grown a bit of a thick skin and extra-sensory perception. Being rich often became a deterrent to a genuine connection as women often fawned over him in the hopes of monetary gain.

With Anwyn, he'd sensed no insincerity, but he'd also sensed no interest in him as an attractive, rich, single man. Of course, she had no way of knowing that he was rich and single. Either way, the experience was novel for him and he intended to find out more about the new owner of *Avalon's Light.* He just wasn't sure how to go about getting closer to her. He wasn't used to being the one doing the pursuing. This could prove very interesting.

Then he remembered the premonition that had led him to Salem. Even the thought of pursuing a relationship with a beautiful woman couldn't deter him from the knot of unease and the feeling that something was wrong.

CHAPTER FIVE

*A*nwyn stood by a blazing fire in the middle of a clearing. Woven reed and grass huts sat in a circular pattern around the main fire while women rushed past her in a fearful, hurried manner. She frowned. Her mind refused to tell her where she was or why she was there.

"Anwyn. To me, now."

A commanding voice echoed across the din of yelling and harried people. Anwyn tried to find the source of the familiar voice and was rewarded by the vision of a woman gesturing to her near one of the larger huts.

Brighid. Warmth and love filled Anwyn, and she fell completely into the reawakened memory of a long ago time. Fear gripped her throat and shards of anger pricked her skin. Danger had come to Avalon and threatened the priestesses who lived and trained in the misty, mystical land of legends. And it was that druid, Seabhac, who had led the danger into their midst. Even though Seabhac lay dead in one of the huts, Anwyn fought the urge to curse his soul for what would assuredly be the death of many that day.

"Anwyn, time is short. Come. Now."

Anwyn gathered her skirts in hand and ran toward her mentor. The din around increased as women built the fire higher and threw anything of value or knowledge into the raging flames. Brighid had instructed they leave nothing for the enemy to scavenge when he arrived and the ensuing wood smoke burned her lungs. That discomfort was minor compared to the terror she felt when seeing the resignation and tears on the faces of those she had grown up with and considered family. Her heart clenched painfully in her chest.

Breathless, Anwyn scurried to an awkward stop in front of Brighid. "Yes, my Lady."

Without answering, Brighid turned and walked toward her hut on the edge of the clearing. Anwyn followed. She was scared. The Priestesses of Avalon had never faced a force of such power, at least not to Anwyn's knowledge. She had a difficult time believing that the High Priestess of Avalon was not strong enough to conquer anything. But the chaos taking place around her shattered that theory.

Brighid parted the thin cloth used as a privacy screen and entered her hut. Anwyn stepped into the hut behind her, the cool interior a sharp contrast to the outdoor heat of sun and fire. She stood still, uncertain why she was here. Other than Seabhac, few ever saw the inside of Brighid's hut. It was beautiful and thrummed with energy. Crystals, journals, wall hangings that depicted the old Gods, Morrigan, Dagda, Cernunnos, thick rugs scattered on the ground. Luxury, beauty, ancient knowledge...all more than Anwyn had ever seen.

Brighid rummaged through a wooden trunk, tossing out clothes and books as she searched for something. The hut muffled the outside sounds surprisingly well, but did nothing to decrease the emotions that assaulted Anwyn. Terror, anger, despair, even hate...a very unusual and unacceptable emotion in Avalon. But circumstances were extreme and some of the novice practitioners would have difficulty controlling their feelings. Anwyn wished she could comfort them, but as long as Brighid wanted her here, she must stay.

"Finally." Brighid turned, clutching an object to her chest in triumph. "Anwyn, time runs short and there is much you must know. Sit."

She motioned to a table with a couple of chairs, but Anwyn hesitated. Years of training and respect dictated that she never sit in the presence of the High Priestess. Her eyes widened. "I cannot."

Brighid smiled a sad smile. "Child. Nothing is as it was. You may sit without offense to me. I insist."

Anwyn sat gingerly on the chair's edge and folded her hands in her lap, head bowed and heart thumping in her chest.

"Anwyn, you know Seabhac is dead and evil follows his pathway to us."

Anwyn nodded, not looking up.

"What you do not know is that he has placed his essence in a book, spelled a knife with magick, and given them to Ainevar for guidance and protection. Though his body is about to be burned, his soul lives in the journal."

Anwyn snapped her head up. "I have never heard of such a thing. How is that possible?"

Brighid laughed. A deep, belly laugh that made the tension in her face disappear for a moment, to be replaced by the stunning beauty that the priestess must have claimed in her younger years. "Dearest Anwyn. You have such a limited concept of everything that is or can be. You are still in the early days of your training."

Anwyn frowned. "I have dedicated my entire life to learning. So many years that I cannot even remember or count them."

A tear slipped from the corner of Brighid's eye. "Yes. And you are the most gifted of all my priestesses. That is why I have chosen you."

"Chosen me?" Anwyn whispered the words. Her senses screamed at her that something was wrong. Something she would not like.

"The druid has sent his protégée into the world with the journal for guidance and the knife for protection. Seabhac's words to Ainevar upon his death were, They are the balance of elemental and physical. Intellect and force. Druid wisdom and brute strength. You will need both. Ainevar, I love you dearly and one day we will be together again. You are now the *Guardian of the Druid* knowledge. It is your place to ensure the safety of these objects until you can find a worthy recipient. Only when druids again walk in light and freedom, will we be free."

Brighid's voice broke with unreleased tears as she recited the words. Anwyn knew that she and Seabhac had been close. Both of them the last holder of knowledge of a dying lifestyle. Both of them more potent than anyone Anwyn knew.

"Ainevar is gone. She holds the knowledge and strength of all druids, and Seabhac thought that would be enough to battle the evil if it ever catches up with her. It will not be enough." Brighid gave a rather unladylike snort. "Seabhac's ego would never allow him to believe that a woman could be stronger than he. He struggled so hard to master the ability to transfer knowledge into an object so he could pass it on to Ainevar in case of an untimely death. He managed, but what he did not realize, would not listen to, is that the Priestesses of Avalon have held this ability for generations. I tried to work with him, but his obstinance forced me to give up and let him find his own way. I had no way of knowing that circumstances would come to this or I would have insisted on sharing more and made him listen to me. If only I had known."

Anwyn's empathetic response to Brighid's pain overwhelmed her. "I do not understand then, if Seabhac nor Ainevar can defeat the evil, but you are stronger than them, why are we destroying everything? Can you not defeat the evil when it comes?"

"No, child. It is the combined energies of druid and priestess that must work together to defeat this evil. Once Seabhac died, our chance to work together died with him."

"But what of Ainevar? Does she not hold his power?" Anwyn felt desperate. "If the two of you work together..."

"No. Ainevar holds his power in the knife and book, but has not had the chance to transfer Seabhac's knowledge from the knife to herself. There is no time. But as long as the knife and book still exist and a priestess of Avalon exists, there is a chance."

"Then we need to flee with her, help her transfer his power and stand against the evil." She stood and made for the door. "Come. Why are we waiting here?"

Brighid did not move, and Anwyn's heart sank. It would not be so easy. She sat down again.

"Child. This evil sent from the skies is almost upon us, and I need to stay and fight it with as many of my priestesses as possible. Holding it back long enough to let Ainevar escape with the book and knife is an absolute necessity. Sending one of my priestesses to safety is the other absolute necessity."

"I do not understand." But she was afraid that she did.

Brighid placed the object she'd been clutching onto the table and took Anwyn's hands in hers. "You are my brightest and most promising acolyte ever, my dear. I have chosen you for what lies ahead."

Anwyn shook her head and tried to stand, but the strength of Brighid's grip held her. She inclined her head in acquiescence and took a deep breath to prepare for what was coming.

"You are the hope for the future. But the path you must travel will be very difficult and you must accept the challenge fully, heart and soul, or all will be lost."

"What must I do?"

"I am sorry, but you must accept this challenge without knowing the truth of it in full. The selflessness of committing to an unknown task will be part of what lends strength to your eventual victory."

Anwyn tried to swallow, but her throat was tight and the muscles refused to work. She nodded. "I will agree without knowing the full truth of the task."

The cloth at the hut doorway blew open and let in a smoke-filled wind that whipped around the interior of the hut. Anwyn heard music in the distance and a haunting voice that lifted in mournful song.

"Ahh, your answer pleases the ancient ones." Brighid smiled, but her eyes held sadness. "I shall join them soon."

"No!"

"Yes, Anwyn. Do not mourn. There is much to do. Seabhac thinks he has out thought the evil, but he is wrong. The future holds disaster as this evil takes root and unleashes its dark energy on an unsuspecting world. Your task is to wait until such time as

Seabhac returns to the world and realizes he is lost. Then, and only then, will he accept your help and together you and he can destroy the darkness once and for all."

Anwyn shook her head in denial. "But, no, I am not strong enough. Why send me? You must be the one."

"No. I must stay here to give Ainevar a chance to escape. You will go and wait for the right time. No worries, Anwyn, you will not be alone in your battle." Brighid ran a finger over the smooth, dark wood of the small wooden box she had set on the table. When she pressed down, the lid popped open to reveal its contents.

Anwyn gasped. She'd never seen such a luxurious display of wealth.

Brighid waved her hand toward the box. "In here are gemstones and gold coins. As much as we could gather from the entire village. This should enable you to fit in nicely in whatever situation you find yourself when you reawaken."

"Reawaken?" Anwyn did not like the sound of that.

Brighid leaned in and took Anwyn's hands in hers. "It may be many years before circumstances come together in a manner that is best for you to appear. Seabhac can be stubborn, the evil might hibernate for a long time. There is no way of knowing."

Anwyn frowned. "If it is too long, I will be dead."

"No. You will spend the time in a resting state in the Nether-world. When the time comes, you will reawaken and will not have aged at all. You will rejoin the world in the place that the evil and Seabhac will be, and find him."

Panic made it difficult for Anwyn to breathe. "But, when? Where? We do not know what I will face, how long it will be, or what the world will be like. How will I...?"

"Calm yourself, child. I have prepared you as best I can. You have riches enough to not end up destitute on a street corner, and you will have this." From the box, Brighid lifted a stunning white crystal dangling on a silver chain. Roughly hewn, it nonetheless held a quality of beauty and timelessness. "You will wear this around your neck and never take it off. Once you leave here..."

Brighid's eyes teared up and she cleared her throat. "...the rest of us will sacrifice our physical bodies and transfer our essence to this crystal. This is the power you will have at your beckoning to help defeat the evil. We will be with you, to help drown out the darkness with our light."

Shock slammed into Anwyn. Not only at the sacrifice of so many lives, but that such a feat was even possible. She glanced toward the entrance of the hut. "You cannot do that. To ask such a thing, to expect such a sacrifice." A sob burned in her throat.

"Anwyn. Listen to me." Brighid's voice deepened and took on the commanding quality she usually reserved for outsiders or recalcitrant novices. "When the evil comes, it will feed on souls, energy, knowledge, and people. We are already doomed and must leave nothing for the enemy. At least this way, we can use our essence to help you in your task."

With a swipe of her arm across her teary face, Anwyn straightened her shoulders. "Do they know?"

Brighid nodded, and tears filled her eyes. "I gave all a choice to stay or go. Knowing they would forfeit their lives, they all stayed. Each one of my beloved novices, acolytes, and priestesses are willing to give everything in this battle."

"Oh." Anwyn's voice lowered to a whisper. "Then how can I do any less." Reaching out, she took the necklace from Brighid and lifted it over her head. The clear crystal settled in place between her breasts and filled Anwyn with comforting warmth.

"When the deed is done, the crystal will glow and you will feel our presence protecting you." Brighid held out a small vial filled with amber liquid. "Once you feel us in the crystal, drink this. It will send you into the Netherworld and into a sleeping state. The necklace will awaken you when the time is right. Then, it will be up to you to adapt, assess the situation, find Seabhac, and, ultimately, defeat the evil."

"Oh, is that all? " Even to herself, her voice sounded weak and whiny.

"It is all right to feel fear and apprehension, but you must not let it rule your actions. Too much rests on your shoulders, and there is no time to help you adjust. We must do this. And we must act with haste. Evil approaches swiftly on the breeze."

Brighid thrust the box into Anwyn's hands and pushed her out the door toward the forest. "Run. Go to the cliffs at the highest point, and wait. It will not be long. Do not look back. Do not hesitate, no matter what you hear. Promise."

Events were moving too quickly. Anwyn did not want to leave her home and all the people she considered her family. Especially to the fate that circumstances had determined for them.

"ANWYN. RUN. Do not look back."

Brighid shoved Anwyn hard enough that she tripped. With a sob, she grasped the box closely, gathered her skirts in the other hand, and ran. As directed, she did not look back. Even when the screams reached her ears. Her feet smacked the ground, sounding out the words racing through her mind.

We must leave nothing for the enemy.

We must leave nothing for the enemy.

We must leave nothing for the enemy.

It seemed an eternity, but she arrived at the cliffs and sank to the ground, exhausted. Filled with loss and despair, she waited.

CHAPTER SIX

Anwyn woke from her faint with a pounding heart, bitter-sweet sadness, and tears on her face. The reality of her memories brought back long ago emotions as vividly as if she had just experienced them. It left her feeling weak, scared, and battling an overwhelming sense of loneliness. Aware of the hard floor beneath her, she struggled to her feet and stretched her stiff muscles. Curious about how long the dream state had claimed her for, she looked at the clock on the wall. Only ten minutes. She had re-lived the most intense, chilling, devastating period of her life in ten minutes. A sob caught in her throat and she rested her hand on the necklace that held so much within its crystal facets.

The last thing she remembered was pushing that man, Memnon, out of her store after the tremor. The tremor that he had not felt. But, he had seen her necklace glow, something Anwyn had never seen happen. And what could it mean? She had expected a much clearer sign if the evil was near. Yet, she sensed nothing. Nothing even remotely similar to the heavy, pervasive, choking energy she had felt in Avalon so long ago.

Dear goddess, she needed to find out what was happening, and she needed solitude to perform a scrying. She checked the curtains to make sure there were no openings Memnon could have looked through to see her lying prone on the floor. Of course, if he had seen her, she would like to think that he would not take off and leave her there. On the other hand, she was glad there was no sight of him anywhere on the street. Her fainting spell and journey into the past were private. They also signalled danger.

With shaking hands, Anwyn started gathering the ingredients she would need for a scrying ritual. Normally, she loved to light a fire and settle on the ground close to the comforting warmth and leaping flames, but in such a populated area, it was difficult to have a fire without arousing unwanted attention. For scrying, she needed uninterrupted peace and solitude, so she resorted to her second favorite form of scrying, which was using a small, black cauldron filled with water. Yes, a bowl would work as well, but the comfort of familiar items helped keep her rooted. Fires and cauldrons were a huge part of the life she had been forced to leave behind in Avalon, and Anwyn tried to keep her rituals pure and traditional. She had tried using a crystal ball at one point, but found that it offered more of a two-dimensional image upon the smooth, unmoving surface, whereas water or fire could undulate with her vision and offer a more three-dimensional perspective.

Normally, she would perform most of her rituals outside, in the garden, but absolute secrecy was necessary, so she chose the back room. When Anwyn had bought the store, it had taken her days of doing nothing but ferreting out the dark magic and performing spells, incantations, cleansing, and protection spells inside the building and in the back garden. It seems that Verity Parker was a powerful witch who had performed dark magic. The choking, cloying effects had lingered even though the building had sat empty for months.

Anwyn's cleansing and healing rituals had made the area a welcoming one for faeries and spirits. She felt their warm, thankful presence as she sat on a cushion in front of her water-filled cauldron and began a quiet chant. Candlelight cast a mellow hue around the small room and shadows danced on the walls, as if in accompaniment to Anwyn's scrying spell. As her mind cleared and energy settled, she sent a thought to the water to show her what she needed to know.

Nothing happened.

She focused on her necklace, and, concentrating on combining her energy with the soul-energy of the other priestesses, she sent out another request to the water. This time, the smooth surface moved in a gentle curving ripple across the smooth water. Anwyn's chest expanded in an unrestricted expanse of breath and she felt the floor give way beneath her, allowing her body to drift in the nothingness that existed between worlds. All sound ended with a pop and the quiet of the Netherworld surrounded her in the familiar embrace developed from time long spent in the misty depths of limbo.

Having expected a vision within the water, she was unprepared when her essence transported to an entirely different environment. Afraid that her return to the Netherworld signalled a disastrous end to her presence in Salem, she panicked. Thoughts of spending eternity in this place terrified her, and she fought to keep herself focused.

Breathe.

Breathe.

Anwyn relaxed and let the floating sensation take her over. That's when she felt a buzz. A slight vibration deep inside her belly that actually made her feel nauseated. Heavy and thick, the sensation seemed to weigh her down, yet it was an ineffable and sporadic feeling. It reminded her of waking up from a dream and almost remembering it, but not quite able to grasp the memory. She tried to pinpoint the source of the feeling, but it drifted and morphed too much to take solid form.

Just then, she thought she heard laughter, deep and rumbling. In a sudden movement, she jerked to awareness, only to find herself back in the shop staring at the water-filled cauldron. Eerie silence greeted her, and she shivered. What she'd encountered in the Netherworld's mist held the same heavy, pervasive sense that she'd encountered back in Avalon so long ago. Memories of almost forgotten friends and priestesses crashed back into her mind with such force that Anwyn choked back a sob. Suddenly feeling very alone and lost, she wrapped her arms around herself and gave into the bitter longing that had haunted her since being forced from Avalon and all that she'd held dear.

She sobbed until there was nothing left within her to feel or think. With her tears spent, Anwyn dropped her arms to her sides and stood. With a last look at the now still water, Anwyn clutched her necklace in a gesture of comfort. One thing for sure, the essence of darkness was slowly seeping into this world and she needed to find Seabhac. Without him, she'd never win the battle that loomed ahead.

After leaving *Avalon's Light*, Memnon had gone back to the condo and spent a restless afternoon and even more restless night. Tossing and turning all night in bed, remembering events from his life in vivid detail. Rolling over in his mind, past decisions, both business and personal. Debating if he'd done right by others, or if he could have helped more.

Why did he suddenly feel so dissatisfied with his life? He'd always been the strong one, the one to hold things together and help others keep their lives together. There were dozens of businesses still in operation today because he'd swooped in like a guardian angel and helped salvage them as they floundered on the edge of bankruptcy and having to close their doors for good. Most of those businesses had become multi-million dollar companies. Because of Memnon's business acumen, he'd become rich by helping others.

Then there was Cassandra. The years after the accident that had claimed their parents' lives, he and Cassandra had grown close and learned to rely on and trust each other. Though his sister had struggled and tried to deny her prophetic abilities, Memnon had slowly guided her into accepting herself and letting go of any guilt she felt about the accident. She'd warned their parents not to go out that night, but they hadn't listened and it had almost destroyed Cassandra when she heard the news. But she'd survived, and in helping his sister get through it, she'd helped him in the fight for his own sanity. She'd kept him grounded and on track. She just didn't realize it.

With a sigh, he rose from bed. Maybe these feelings of dissatisfaction hadn't happened suddenly. He'd grown weary and bored at work lately, leaving more and more of the daily routine to his right-hand man and friend, Jerry Moore. With all his spare time, he now had a hole in his life and faced the unusual chore of having to help himself.

With Cassandra's help, of course. She'd always been the one to keep him grounded and on track, whether or not she knew it.

"Okay, sis." He mumbled as he finished in the bathroom and pulled on some jeans and a t-shirt. "You're about to have a visitor."

With a purpose and a destination in mind, Memnon left his still near-empty condo behind and headed for Cassandra and Samson's place only ten minutes away.

CHAPTER SEVEN

Seated in the kitchen of the house he'd bought and given to Cassandra when she'd fallen in love and made her life in Salem, Memnon gulped the last of his coffee and held his mug out. "More, please."

Cassandra raised an eyebrow and reached for the pot of coffee. "Really, you don't often have more than one. Is everything okay?"

She poured hot coffee into the proffered mug, and Memnon inhaled the aroma. Steam rose, and he was sure he could see shapes within the ever-changing swirls. He contemplated the steam's motion as he tried to define his jumbled thoughts and emotions. Tipping his mug, he let the hot, smooth, slightly nutty-flavored liquid run down his throat.

"Well?" Cassandra set the coffeepot down on the counter behind her and fixed an expectant gaze on him.

"Sorry, Cassie. Just trying to figure out how to answer the question."

"Just let it out. You've never had trouble before telling me exactly what you think." She waved a hand and glanced around the kitchen. "Hence the reason that I'm now living in Salem, far from the 212 area code where I spent most of my life, in a house you sent me to design, living with..."

Memnon laughed and raised his hands in protest. "Fine, I get it. Honestly, it's not that I don't want to talk about it, I'm just not sure what *it* is."

Cassandra brushed a stray piece of blonde hair off her face and tucked it behind her ear. "Hmm. Big brother is confused and unsure of himself. That is a first and might prove very interesting. I say that we figure it out together."

"That's why I'm here, but where do we start?"

Cassandra grinned and sat on one of the bar stools opposite Memnon. Reaching across the counter, she patted his hand. "Why don't we start with why you left your business in Jerry's hands and moved here to Salem."

"I didn't leave the business in his hands. I check in daily. Well, every few days. And I haven't moved to Salem. I'm just here to assure myself that you're settled and happy, that's all."

"Uh, huh." Her blue eyes bore into him with an intenseness that surprised Memnon. And if he wasn't mistaken, he felt the spider-web warmth of energy trying to find a way into his mind.

"Whoa, dial it down, sis." He laughed and shifted on his bar stool. "Have you been practicing your powers?"

Cassandra smiled. "Yup. I'm working on focus and concentration and trying to read people's thoughts and emotions. Of course, I only do it on people with their permission. Samson likes to be my guinea pig, but sometimes his thoughts..." she stammered and blushed.

Memnon covered his ears. "Too much information. Enough." He looked at the glow that encompassed his sister and realized that he'd never seen her looking so beautiful. But, more than that, she looked content. The corner of his mouth lifted in a smile. "Happy to see you looking so good. It's about time."

"Life hasn't always been easy for either of us, Memnon, but you've always been there for me. It's because of you I found Samson and a home in Salem. I can never thank you enough for forcing me into the confrontation that changed my life."

Memnon waved a hand dismissively. "Don't mention it."

A frown creased Cassandra's forehead. "So, tell me, big brother, why aren't you happy?"

Memnon laughed. "Not happy? Come on. I'm rich beyond belief. Beautiful women throw themselves at me. I have you for a sister, and in case you haven't noticed, I'm kinda good looking."

"Exactly. So why aren't you happy?"

Shifting his butt on the stool, Memnon tapped down the uncomfortable feeling that rose within. "Dammit, Cassie, I don't know. I mean, I didn't feel this way until recently, and then..." His voice drifted off as he tried to remember when the nagging sense of self-doubt and dissatisfaction had actually crept into his life.

"Yes. And then, what?"

A vision of auburn hair and amber eyes flashed briefly through Memnon's mind, and he smiled. A small lift of his corner lip at first, then a full-blown, blazing grin. "I'll be damned."

"Well, that likely holds true for both of us, but why you in particular?" Cassandra asked.

"Cassie, I've been on automatic for so long that I didn't even realize what was missing in my life until I saw how happy you are. Love, my dear sister. That is what my life is missing."

"Gah! I could have told you that one, Memnon. All you had to do was ask."

Cassandra sipped her coffee and sent a contemplative look at her brother over the rim of the mug before setting it down and asking innocently. "So, is there anyone in particular that you have in mind to, you know, fall in love with?"

"No, of course not." He sent a silent request for forgiveness for the minor untruth, because even as he spoke the words, he knew he'd be going back to *Avalon's Light* to get to know a certain enigmatic woman.

Cassandra opened her mouth to speak, but her phone chose that moment to chime out the familiar tune of Beethoven's *Für Elisse*. She picked up the phone and shot Memnon a look that plainly said *you're not done yet.*

"Hello." Cassandra paused and listened. "Oh, okay. Everything is good here." She looked at Memnon with a frown creasing her forehead. "Memnon is here having a morning coffee because he still has to buy groceries."

Memnon heard Samson's chuckle and mumbled reply through the phone and Cassandra laughed. "Yes, I'll tell him. Goodbye. I love you." She put her phone back on the counter.

"Samson says that he's letting you stay at his place, but you have to feed yourself and quit mooching over here."

They both laughed, but Memnon picked up on the hollow sound of his sister's usual warm laughter. His gaze narrowed. "You know you can't hide anything from me, so fess up. What else did he say?"

"Nothing. Well, not much, other than they are having an unusually busy day."

"Yes? What else?"

Cassandra smiled. "Always so persistent."

"Just like a big brother should be. It's only because I care."

"I know." She replied and nibbled on a cold piece of toast as she seemed to contemplate how to best answer his question. "Samson said that it's like an average full moon day would be. You know how people get crazy during that time. But this is ten times worse. Everyone is calling to complain about their neighbor, brother, co-worker. And it's for things like littering, stealing a stapler, yelling at a dog. He said it is as if the entire town is PMSing."

Knots formed a heavy ball in the pit of Memnon's stomach. "Oh. Does he have a theory?"

"No, just a bad feeling. But I've learned that Samson's bad feelings are worth heeding."

Memnon debated whether to tell Cassandra about his main reason for coming to Salem. He hadn't wanted to cause any problems, but if trouble was coming, he needed to be honest. "I'm afraid that I need to add my *bad feelings* to this one, sis."

"What? Memnon, what are you talking about?" Cassandra pinned him with a stare, her ice-blue eyes unwavering.

"Don't give me that look. Nothing was for sure. It was just a feeling."

"*What* was just a feeling?"

Memnon ran a hand through his hair and sighed. Better to get everything out in the open, especially if trouble was on its way. "I was telling the truth when I said I needed a break from work and wanted to come and see for myself that you're settled and happy. But, the same premonition that led me to send you here also brought me here now."

Cassandra's jaw clenched and a hint of fear darkened her eyes. "And you just *forgot* to mention this premonition."

"No. I didn't mention it because it made little sense to me and I didn't want to cause problems where none existed. Come on, Cass, you know I don't get vivid visions like you. Mine are more of a gut feeling, or insistent pull that leads me where I need to be. I have no idea why I came here, just that I had to come. I had nothing to tell you."

His sister stood and paced the kitchen, a sure sign that she was thinking. Memnon sat silently while she stewed things over in her mind. After a minute, she put her hands on her hips and faced him. "You could have just been honest with me."

"I know. But, to be fair, I have spent most of my life taking care of and protecting you. It's a tough habit to break. I know you have Samson to protect you now, but I can't just stop being your big brother."

Cassandra threw her hands up in the air. "I don't need anyone to take care of me. I am fully capable of taking care of myself, dammit. If you'd seen how I handled being possessed, thrust into some misty world that doesn't even exist in any form that we understand, and helped take out Pastor Joshua while condemning an evil darkness to a small globe of light, you'd know that I am more than able to fend for myself."

"Okay, okay. I get it. My sister is a badass who doesn't need a man to take care of her."

A smile lifted the corner of Cassandra's mouth. "I don't *need* a man to take care of me, but it is comforting to know that you are always there to care *about* me." She reached over and gave Memnon a quick hug.

"So what do we do about Samson and your feelings of doom?"

He shrugged. "There is nothing to do. Neither one of us knows anything. We just have a sense of something. We can't fight what we don't know." He pinned Cassandra with an intent gaze. "Have you not had any visions lately?"

"No. Nothing. Not even a ripple of unease."

They sat quietly sipping coffee, both lost in thought.

"So, I suppose we wait." Cassandra suggested.

Memnon leaned over and kissed her on the cheek. Grabbing his keys, he rose to leave. "You wait, I have unpacking and grocery shopping to do." What he neglected to mention was that he also had a certain store owner that he planned on getting to know better.

CHAPTER EIGHT

S wirls in the mist, escaping from confinement that has trapped its evil intent for years beyond measure. Gradually, it twists and creeps until the entirety of it is free. Free to return to a place that beckons it. A place that echoes with past failure and future victory. It senses the return of others. The ones who defeated it before. Evil snarls in the dark and twines through the Netherworld to find a physical form in one who has been waiting to exact revenge. The outcome has not been written, and the darkness is unaware of all the players who await its return. Sacrifices from the past are the secret held only by one. The Holder of the Light. The Light forms the foundation upon which all the others will draw strength. The Holder possesses the uncertainty of an untried priestess. Combined with the ego of a druid, and the self-doubt of one named for a Saint, there forms a weakness upon which the darkness can feed.

Excerpt from *Faerie Enchantments and Sorcerer Magick*

The darkness slithered into existence. Finally free from the confines of a prison that had held it captive for so long, it expanded with freedom and the scent of familiar surroundings. If it had a mouth, it would have roared. If it had feelings, it would have exulted. Instead, it hovered. Dark, foreboding, hunting for the elixir of human emotions to feed upon.

In a slow awakening of primal understanding, it knew that this time was different and the battle would be a final one. Survival instincts dictated that a powerful vessel be found this time. It had been human weaknesses that had led to failure in the past, and the same mistake could not be made again. The choice must be made with care and an eye toward a human thirsting for revenge, driven by a deep abhorrence and loathing of others. Their reason did not matter, just their dedication and acceptance of malevolent acts.

Drifting unnoticed above the streets of Salem, many sights struck a chord within the darkness. Much had changed since its first visit so long ago that had sparked the witch trials. Memories of how neighbors turned against each other and terror of being accused held an entire town in its thrall. Twice more returned, only to be beaten back and ensnared by wielders of ancient magic.

The darkness throbbed with rage that one weak female on the run for so long evaded death and passed on the knife and book. Two items holding power from a time when magic flowed freely and strongly upon the earth. Two items lending life and a holding vessel for the essence of the arch-druid who would not die.

And the air was rancid with his presence again. A sound resembling a snarl escaped the dark smear of smoke floating across Salem. This time, the Guardian of Knowledge would not win. This time, the darkness knew the weakness of the ancient human. And no one else existed, had not existed for a long time, who could stop what was to come.

There. Among the gray auras, petty jealousies, thieving and covetous thoughts, came the scent of hate. Acrid and hot, the raw, putrid stench of someone aching for revenge. The touch of dark magic marked them and an aura strong enough to hold the darkness within surrounded them.

The darkness streamlined its wavering essence and shot itself toward that person. No hesitation. No second guessing. The vessel was ripe and strong and would ensure a solid foundation for the darkness to work from.

The final battle was about to begin.

The afternoon sun hadn't quite come around the building far enough to shine through the windows, so the room was dark and, as always, depressing. Of course, the depressing part likely had more to do with the purpose of the room and the occupant of the chair facing the window.

The squeak of wheels from the medicine cart rolling past in the hallway was the only sound that broke up the frustration of today's visit. Every visit. Once a week, the two of them sat in uncomfortable silence, broken only by sporadic conversation.

It hadn't been like that at first.

Verity once held hope that her son, Matthew, would recover and become the vibrant, intelligent man that she'd raised. Daily visits full of laughter and chatty conversation as she filled him in on town events and updates on her life. He sat, sullen and quiet through it all, but she had persisted, sure that her being there would help guide him back from wherever he'd disappeared.

She wanted her son back. But this husk of a human was not her son.

There were times she thought he was better off like this because if he ever came out of his state of non-awareness, he'd be on trial for murder and end up in jail. But at least she'd be able to talk with him and hold him. She gazed into his vacant eyes for what seemed like the millionth time, praying to see a flicker of life, or slight acknowledgement of her presence. Matthew's lackluster gaze stared straight ahead, looking out the window, but seeing nothing. Verity's last flicker of hope sizzled, and she realized that she'd never see his eyes light up or hear his voice again. They had sapped his soul out of him and it wasn't coming back.

Her heart clenched with loss, and the tears filled her eyes. But they didn't fall because anger came quickly on the heels of her grief. So hot and sudden that it burned the tears away. For almost a year, her only concern had been for Matthew. After a couple of attempts to call upon magic and restore him to normal had failed, she'd abandoned magic, just as it had abandoned her.

Now she needed it again, but for a different purpose. It didn't matter that she had started the course of events during a ritual decades ago, or that Matthew had followed in her path of dark magic and a force of evil had driven him insane. No. All that mattered was that someone had to pay for the loss of her son.

Without a backward glance at the body that used to be her son, Verity marched out of the sanitarium with the renewed purpose in life. Her purpose no longer entailed the return of her son. Instead, she felt driven to exact revenge on those who made him this way.

The building's door slammed behind her in a last farewell and she walked across the parking lot toward her car. The sun shone, and the birds sang, but all Verity could hear was the pounding of her heart against her rib cage. Her thoughts kept diving into the past and that final scene at Skye's house that had ended in such tragedy. Flashes of a pentagram, candles, blood, Matthew's face morphing into some distorted, monstrous vision. The faces of everyone present that fateful night had haunted her, taunted her, driven her almost mad with hatred. Her blood thrummed with the need for revenge.

Verity shivered and reached to open her car door, but before she could take hold of the handle, a searing pain shot through her and drove her to the ground. She gasped for breath, but the weight on her chest prevented even that simple task. Heat grew from within and raced through her veins to the point of feeling as if she'd burst. Panic took hold, and the adrenaline gave Verity a brief moment of clarity. She could stand, but then her brain refused to work properly. Where was she? What had she been doing? Far away memories of places she didn't remember melded with familiar, comforting memories. She grasped at those ones, not wanting to lose them, but they shimmered away and left her feeling empty.

The searing pain ended, and the heat faded. Verity stood beside her car in a daze, then glanced around to see if anyone had noticed her actions, but she was alone. A frown creased her brow as she settled into her car, her mind returning to earlier thoughts of revenge. After so long feeling weak and unable to help Matthew, she now felt strong. Better than she ever had.

Then she heard the whispers. Surrounding her, guiding her, entering her very essence as if they belonged there. Whispers of hate, revenge and eventual victory over her enemies.

Verity smiled and put her car in gear. There was much to prepare.

CHAPTER NINE

A nwyn tugged self-consciously at her sweater as she perused her surroundings to see which store to check out next. With her own store closed for the day, she decided to play the tourist role for the first time since coming to Salem. Until now, she had been busy acclimating to a modern society, selling some of her gold, buying a store, and setting it up to her own tastes. Today was the day to discover Salem and all that it offered. She also needed to learn the layout of the town, suss out witch wannabes from legitimate witches of ancient bloodlines. She had already met those women, Cassandra and Skye, but needed to know everything she was dealing with and who she could count on if needed.

Also, and most importantly, she needed to find Seabhac.

Since *The Light of Many Souls* had woken her and brought her to Salem, Anwyn could only assume that the battle would take place here and Seabhac would show up eventually, as his destiny included being part of the final battle. Or so Brighid had prophesied many years ago. In the meantime, alone and unsure, Anwyn truly felt helpless.

Without thought, she reached up to touch the ever-present necklace and felt warmth and comfort wend its way through her. With a deep sigh and renewal of purpose, she continued on her shopping and information finding spree.

Essex St. pedestrian walk offered so many options for the tourist trade, but she was looking for any store that might delve into a deeper understanding of the craft and ritual. Used to the energy ley lines in Avalon feeding her own energy, the stifling surroundings of modern-day city drained her. She could not rely on the necklace to energize her. She required that power to remain pure and strong for the final battle, so she needed to tune in to the subtle shifts of energy and search out a way to renew herself.

A tingle brushed across Anwyn's skin. *A ley line*. Excited at the unexpected discovery, she stopped and gazed around the cobblestone street specifically designed for pedestrians, with no vehicles allowed. Quaint and rustic design, beautiful architecture, niche shops, it had likely built with witches and magic in mind. And someone, intentionally or not, had built it upon a ley line rippling with power.

Looking around, she detected a shimmer in the air just to her right. Barely visible, the flicker of heat and light would go unnoticed by most, but she had been raised among strong and ancient ley lines. They had fed and shaped her powers. To her, bonding with the earth's energy was as natural as breathing. Her heart beat quicker as she moved a couple of steps to the right and stood still to allow a rush of healing, enriching energy to roar through her body. Ahh, the absolute wonderfulness of connecting nearly overwhelmed her much depleted system. The earthy fullness made her limbs melt, yet gave her strength at the same time. A smile lit her face and her worries disappeared amid the familiar, much needed flow of energy coursing through her veins. With the heat of the sun warming her face, Anwyn revelled in the surge to her own innate powers.

Realizing the spectacle she was likely making of herself, Anwyn reluctantly stepped from the flow of energy and took a quick peek around. Since the street had been close to deserted, she wasn't too afraid of anyone noticing her moment of basking in the ley line. But she would be wrong. A woman stood in the doorway of a nearby shop, her arms folded and eyes piercing into Anwyn. She gulped and gave a hesitant smile in the woman's direction.

Wavering between turning and beating a hasty retreat, or going over to see how much the woman had seen, the woman solved her dilemma by waving and calling out. "Hi. Beautiful day, isn't it?"

Anwyn nodded and smiled. She had yet to become comfortable with the small talk and pleasantries that modern day people seemed so determined to push on her. Yes, she was polite to customers in her store, as she had to maintain a certain facade, but she did not enjoy exchanging talk about the weather, where she was from, or probing questions from tourists about whether she was she a *real* witch. Aloof was her usual persona on most days.

"You look like you could use a cool drink. Come on over and I'll see what I can find."

About to decline, Anwyn realized she wanted to talk with this woman. Strange. She acknowledged the invitation with a nod and moved forward, taking stock of everything as she walked the short distance across the cobblestones.

The storefront was tasteful and welcoming, boasting a wooden sign with the words *The Magic Corner* carved into its grain. Cream colored sheers with ruffles decorated the windows and gave a semblance of privacy, yet were see through enough to hint at the contents of the store and pique a person's curiosity.

As Anwyn drew closer, the woman extended a hand. "Hi. I'm Nora."

Anwyn took the hand in hers, the touch immediately creating a snap and a brief spark of light. Anwyn frowned and inspected the woman in front of her. Middle-aged with hair the color of rich soil, eyes of golden honey, and dressed in the casual attire of jeans and a silken blouse, the woman gave a contrasting feel of feminine and practical.

"I am named Anwyn."

A flicker deep in golden eyes and slight straightening of Nora's shoulders were almost imperceptible. "Anwyn. That is an old name."

It was half question, half statement, and Anwyn felt the need to explain. "Yes. It is a name passed down through the generations."

Nora stared a moment at Anwyn. Then, with a smile, held the door open and with a sweep of her hand, motioned her forward.

She bowed her head as Anwyn stepped past her. "It is an honor to have you grace my humble store."

Entering the store was like going home for Anwyn. The deep richness of ancient power, otherworldly enchantment, and solid earth-magic. Packed with jars of dried herbs, crystals, candles, amulets, brooms, cords, divination tools, athames, books, and more. The store and its contents enthralled Anwyn. As well as the usual touristy stuff, Nora's store catered to those who knew the craft. Knew what to look for and how to use it.

She breathed deeply and mentally identified blue vervain, wood betony, and slippery elm. Their aroma brought instant relaxation and easing of the headache that had plagued her for most of the day. She smiled and turned to Nora. "It is as if you knew exactly what I needed."

Nora waved a hand nonchalantly. "I'm just trying out some new incense sticks. Glad to hear they're having a positive effect."

Words of dismissal. Yet Anwyn sensed the avoidance of an unspoken truth that shimmered below the surface of conversation. "Well, either way. Thank you."

A customer entered the store, and Nora left to take care of the woman. Anwyn wandered, paying little attention to the ongoing conversation. The woman complained about readings not working; not able to contact spirits; energies dissipating; happening all over town.

She frowned, but before she could give it much thought, an insistent tingle up her spine led her to the rear of the store. She perused the area until she could see what had drawn her. A wooden podium with a glass case on top. Equipped with lock and alarm system, the case was empty, but Anwyn knew something powerful had rested there at one point. She ran her hand over top of the glass and it hummed with a familiar vibration. Ancient and powerful as well. Merely an echo, yet the area still retained enough energy for someone to use. Without thought, Anwyn pulled the energy into her palm and imagined it rising up through her arm and down her chest into the center of her soul. Her entire body pulsed with the rhythms of life and magic.

Seabhac.

Stunned, she withdrew her hand and her gaze flew to Nora, who now stood questioningly beside her. They locked eyes and within that moment, a probing pulse pushed against Anwyn's mind. With a gasp, she closed her senses and broke eye contact.

Nora immediately flushed and stammered. "I am so sorry. I would never...I didn't mean to do that without permission. It's just that your energy is so overwhelming that it seemed to take me over. For a second, I had no control and the mind probe just happened."

Anwyn knew by Nora's white face and pleading voice, that the shop owner spoke the truth. Unfortunately, as unintentional as the probe had been, Nora had broken through Anwyn's defenses and seen into her mind. How much she had seen was uncertain, but it had been enough to shift Nora's stance into one of respect and humble submission.

"My Lady..." Nora opened her mouth to speak, but Anwyn threw her hand up, palm facing out.

"No! Do not address me as anything other than Anwyn." She softened the shrill panic in her voice. "Please. I know not what you saw, but I am Anwyn, recently moved to Salem and new owner of the store, *Avalon's Light*. Nothing more. And no one must know anything more."

"Of course." Nora bowed her head in agreement.

"What used to rest in this case."

"An old book called, *Faerie Enchantments and Sorcerer Magick.*"

Anwyn's heart raced in her chest. She barely managed to speak through the dizziness that overwhelmed her. "What happened to it? Please."

"I gave it to a woman who needed it at that time. Well, actually, the book compelled me to give it to her. I merely followed the urge."

"It compelled you." In a whisper, she said. "So, it is still active."

"The woman, Skye is her name, had it for a while and then gave it to another woman, Cassandra." Nora frowned. "I can no longer sense the book, though. I don't think it is around anymore, as its intended purpose was resolved."

Anwyn's mind raced. *Gone.* How could the book be gone? What did that mean? The evil still existed, therefore nothing was resolved. And if the book was gone, did that mean Seabhac was no longer around? Fates above, all of this was so frustrating and confusing. She needed more information. She needed to find Seabhac. Had the crystal brought her back at the wrong time?

Tears welled up in her eyes. She was so alone and silently wished that there had been more time for Brighid to explain what to do when she returned to the world. There had been no time for questions, and now it was up to her to figure things out. Alone.

The touch of a hand on her arm jolted her from her self-pitying reverie. Nora stood in front of her, eyes filled with empathy. "Please trust that I know you have ancient, powerful energy surrounding you, as well as a purpose in this time and place. You will endure and you will find what, or who, it is that you need. In the meantime, I have a gift for you."

Touched, yet confused by Nora's words, Anwyn wanted to ask exactly what the shop owner knew. Instead, she wiped the tears from her eyes and smiled. "Thank you, but no gift is necessary."

"Oh, I think you'll like this one. And I believe it is necessary. I'll be right back."

Nora disappeared through a doorway hidden behind a hanging tapestry depicting a stag running through the woods, and Anwyn took the time to admire the intricate design and rich, earthy colors woven into such a beautiful work of art. When the tapestry parted and Nora stepped into the room, she wasn't alone. Within the cradle of her arms lay a black ball of fur with a white patch on the chest and gold eyes lit with the warm glow and assurance of a kitten who knows that cuteness can win hearts.

Anwyn's heart filled to bursting, and then it melted. Without thought, she reached out and took the offered kitten in her arms and snuggled the feline close to her cheek. The resulting purr and lick of a rough tongue on her face sent her into a spiral of happiness, and tears started rolling from her eyes.

"Her name is whatever you want to name her." Nora said.

"But I cannot accept her. This is too much." Anwyn made a move to give the kitten back to Nora, but the kitten dug her claws into Anwyn's sweater and refused to leave.

With a laugh, Nora waved a hand. "No, she is yours. I've given away all her siblings and have been waiting for the right person for her. She is special and needs someone special. That person is you. You need her."

"Oh. I do not know what to say. She is adorable, and perfect." As she spoke the words, Anwyn choked down the bitterness of knowing that her life here was fleeting and she would not be around long enough to see this kitten to mature into a cat. Reluctantly, she unstuck the claws from her sweater and handed the kitten back. With a whisper tone of regret, she said. "No, I really cannot accept her."

Nora folded her arms across her chest and stared. "Please forgive my boldness, My Lady...I mean, Anwyn, but you need her. Trust me on this. I was born with a knowing, and when that voice speaks to me, I listen. It is screaming within me now that you are to keep the kitten."

Anwyn searched the eyes of the woman before her. Mysterious pools of swirling colors drew Anwyn into their depths. Dark, rich, earth colors circled within paler colors of gold and shimmers of ivory. Ancient roots of knowledge ran deep and strength ebbed and flowed within this woman. She pulled the kitten back into her chest and trusted that Nora knew what was best. Within that moment of giving and taking, a connection formed between them, and Anwyn knew she could rely on this woman if she ever needed anything. That feeling of belonging and recognition of a kindred soul warmed Anwyn and gave her strength.

"Thank you. I shall accept your generous gift."

"Wonderful. Any idea what you'll call her?"

Anwyn thought for a moment, but the decision was a simple one. "I will name her Ebony." The memory of her spirit animal, a black and gray fox, came rushing to her. Along with the helpless horror of leaving the fox behind when she fled, and never knowing what happened to her pet. "I used to have a pet named Ebony."

Nora laid a comforting hand on Anwyn's arm. "I am sure that the other Ebony would be honored to have you name this kitten in his or her memory."

With a frown, Anwyn questioned. "Do you think I should put her in a container or box? I do not want her to get loose and run away." As if to answer her, Ebony snuggled under Anwyn's sweater and purred.

Both women laughed. It felt nice to relax, even if just for that one moment in time. "I don't think you have to worry about her going anywhere, and your store is just a short distance away. I assume you are living in the apartment above the store?"

"Yes. It is the perfect size for me, so there is no reason to rent anywhere else."

"Well, Ebony looks to be asleep, so as long as you go directly home, I think you'll be fine."

Anwyn made a move to leave, but a thought crossed her mind. "Oh, I am in need of some teas. Is there somewhere you can recommend that may have a variety other than the normal black or green tea?"

Nora's smile lit up her face. "Yes, there is a place, and let me tell you, you are in for a treat. Tartleby's teas is just around the corner and I am sure you'll find a tea or more to your liking. Tartleby, the owner has a collection of exotic teas from all over the world. His store is small, but his knowledge and grasp of teas is amazing."

"I thank you." She glanced down at the bundle of fur sleeping in her arms. "I will take Ebony home first and maybe stop at the tea shop later."

As Anwyn moved toward the door, Nora touched her arm and opened her mouth to speak. Instead, she just smiled. Anwyn smiled in return and left, puzzling over the words left unsaid.

Bless her little heart, Ebony barely blinked an eye as Anwyn hastened back to her store and up the stairs to her small apartment. She slid her bags off her arm and gently placing the kitten on the couch. With a pat on the tiny, soft head, Anwyn left the kitten sleeping while she organized her purchases and the items that Nora had graciously given her for the kitten.

Food, a couple of stainless steel bowls for food and water, a plastic litter box, a bag of litter, and a scoop. Things like a collar, leash, and treats, Anwyn could pick up later. She set an area up for Ebony in a small alcove area in the far corner of the living room. Hopefully, well enough out of sight to not interfere with anything.

With a sigh of satisfaction, Anwyn looked around her living quarters and felt delight with how much of a change she had made since moving in. Much like the store, the apartment had been heavy with negative energy, filled with dark, ornate furniture with walls painted black. Cloying strands of long-ago spells wafted about the gloomy rooms and the suffocating sense of doom had nearly sent Anwyn into a faint. Cleansing rituals, scrubbing through grime, many layers of paint, and some furniture from the local thrift store had created a tiny oasis where Anwyn felt safe. Now, with the addition of her four-legged roommate, the apartment also held the spark of life and love.

Self-satisfaction helped relax the tight muscles in her neck and she thought about how tasty a hot cup of tea would be. As she moved toward the kitchen, a wave of heat wrenched through her body. Flaming and dancing, the unseen fire seared her from the inside and left her limbs weak. Sound receded into a distant roar and then silence struck her. She went down to the ground and tried to organize her thoughts and pull energy from the air around to strengthen herself enough to withstand whatever had attacked her.

But she could not focus. Darkness claimed her, and a small moan escaped her lips as she gave into oblivion. A rough, wet scrape on her check gave her a sense of grounding. It happened again, this time with more force and the accompaniment of a fervent *meow*.

Ebony. Anwyn locked on to the sensation of the kitten's tongue and the sound of her meowing. Grasping with desperation at anything solid that could ground her, she focused on driving the heat back and surrounding herself with a protective white circle. Sound and consciousness rushed back and Anwyn sagged with relief as everything returned to normal, as if it had never happened.

Positioning herself into a sitting position, she reached down and picked up the kitten. "Ebony, you sweetie, you saved me." Anwyn lifted the kitten to eye level and looked into golden eyes. A glimmer of light flickered in the depths of innocent eyes, then disappeared. Ebony pawed Anwyn's face as if to make sure all was well, then she jumped to the floor and wandered off to munch on the kibble that Anwyn had put out for her.

Anwyn remained seated on the floor while pondering what had happened and the ramifications of the power surge. Her senses were not on alert. Her necklace glowed, but not in a menacing manner. One thing was certain.

She was no longer the only ancient one in Salem.

CHAPTER TEN

Memnon shut the condo door behind him and leaned against it with a sigh of relief. Thank goodness he'd finished the unpacking and stored the extra items in the basement storage area allocated to him. Well, technically, to Samson. Now, to eat some of the food that he had bought on his way back from Cassandra's. He'd worked up a raging appetite. After that, the plan was to visit *Avalon's Light* and get to know its new owner.

He moved to the small kitchen that was set in an alcove off the living room. Small, utilitarian, it served its purpose, but didn't lend itself well to entertainment or large parties. A true bachelor type kitchen, which was fine for this stage of Memnon's life while he figured out a way forward. He grabbed a handle and yanked open the cupboard to peruse the food supplies. Hmm, he had bought his usual foods and snacks, so why was nothing appealing to him?

He snorted. His lack of desire for food mirrored his dissatisfaction with his life. Lately, he'd felt as if he was bobbing in the middle of a vast ocean with waves that constantly threatened to sink him. So far, he'd remained atop the waves, but every once in a while, he dipped under the water and felt like he was drowning.

Realizing that he'd spent the last five minutes staring into the same cupboard and was no closer to deciding on a snack, he closed the cupboard door with a hard crack.

Not being in control of his own emotions and daily life frustrated him. He'd always been in charge, the go-to guy, the one who had it all together. What the hell had happened to him? When had he stepped off the solid earth and into the damn roiling ocean of uncertainty?

And how arrogant was he to be this unhappy when he had so much in his life and others had so little? He needed to pull it together.

The fridge was his next victim as he roughly yanked it open and stared inside. The cold air smacked him in the face and he let it engulf him. Maybe it could freeze his feelings and he could get on with life.

"Are you going to stand there all day with the door of that contraption open?"

"What the..." Memnon smacked his head on the freezer door as he lifted his head from looking in the lower part of the fridge. He looked right into the face of a stranger and the clearest blue eyes that he'd ever seen.

Grabbing the nearest item off the counter, he held it between him and the man. "Stay back, or I'll use it."

The man raised a white eyebrow and gave a snort. "And do what? Flip me."

Memnon lowered his gaze and flushed when he saw a spatula in his hand. Great. Someone breaks in and all he can do is protect himself with a kitchen utensil. No wonder his life was a mess.

The intruder rolled his eyes. "I do not have time for your woe is me thoughts. I need to speak with the arrogant one who lives here."

"Woe is me...what? How? Who the hell are you and what are you doing in my kitchen?"

Memnon smacked the spatula on the counter and took a step closer to the strange-looking intruder. Strange, not only in how he looked, but also in his choice of attire. White hair to his shoulders, beard halfway down his chest, eyes of blue so clear and vivid that they bore through Memnon like a drill. He wore a floor-length robe sashed at the waist and looked to be hand woven, just slightly worn at the sleeves.

"There is no time to educate the uneducated. Where is the arrogant one?"

The voice of the intruder held power. Soft power that surrounded Memnon in a web of silk and bound him as in an invisible cocoon. He tried to swear and tell the intruder to stop whatever he was doing, but he couldn't form the words he wanted. Instead, the shiver of silken energy compelled him to answer the question asked. "He doesn't live here anymore, but he is likely at work."

The ensuing roar shook the room and broke Memnon out of the spell. Without a thought, he launched himself at the obviously upset stranger, thinking that he could take him out while the unwanted news distracted him. It was a good tackle. His footing on take off was strong and propelled him forward. His aim direct and focused. But instead of grabbing an armful of man, he ran into an invisible barrier that smacked him right in his face and sent him sprawling to the floor.

"Ouch." He grabbed his bloody nose before it could drip all over the place and stood to find a paper towel or something to staunch the blood. His mind raced through all the possibilities as he put the facts together like a puzzle. Appearing out of nowhere, his clothes, beard, piercing eyes, and ability to read minds and create invisible barriers. The identity of his intruder suddenly became obvious.

Holding a towel to his nose, he turned to face the person responsible for the bloody nose. "Seabhac, I presume."

Seabhac raised an eyebrow and studied Memnon. "Humph, maybe you are not a total waste of oxygen after all. Of course, it did take you longer than it should have. If I had been of a different mind, I would have just killed you to save me the inconvenience of having to deal with you."

"Yeah, yeah. All gruff talk, no action. I've heard all about you."

Seabhac raised a hand as if to cast a spell. Sparks of light danced in his eyes. Memnon backed off. "Okay. Only kidding. Samson said that you had a sense of humor. I guess he was wrong."

Slowly lowering his hand, Seabhac replied. "No, he was not wrong. But the severity of the situation prevents me from displaying my humorous side."

The knot that had formed in Memnon's stomach at Cassandra's earlier mention of Samson's bad feeling dropped like a rock in his stomach. If the great Seabhac had returned to Salem, then things were very dire indeed. "Crap."

"This modern English language still confuses me. I do not know what you mean, but I do need to converse with Samson and his woman, Cassandra."

Memnon barked out a laugh. "Samson's woman, as you say, is my sister Cassandra. And I guarantee you she'd skin you alive for referring to her in such an archaic manner."

Seabhac frowned. "She is a woman and they are together. I do not see the problem with my terminology."

"It is insulting, as it infers that she belongs to him. Which we both know is an absurd notion."

Their gazes locked and a moment of silence ensued as Seabhac considered Memnon's words. He chuckled, then broke out in belly deep laughter. "Yes, I see your point. Your sister is not one to belong to anyone. Fates alive, she stared into the maw of pure evil and beat it down. There is not a man alive who could own her."

They both sobered as the reality of the current situation crashed back. Memnon spoke first. "I don't want my sister involved again."

"The choice is never ours to make. Fates and the universe will set the players in motion and we will be naught but chess pieces upon the board. All we have control over is our own dedication and motivation. That will determine the outcome of what is to come."

"And what exactly is coming?"

With a tightening of his jaw and clenching of fists, Seabhac replied. "The final battle."

Chapter Eleven

Anwyn had pondered the meaning and ramifications of her earlier blackout, but concluded that she did not have enough information or knowledge to even guess at the specifics. What she knew was that it signaled the presence of another ancient. She had tasted that well enough. Felt it deep in her soul. But who, or what, was unknown to her. As was the location of the unknown entity. She also knew that she needed to strengthen herself in every way possible and that did not entail calling on the protective power of the necklace. She needed to save that for the final battle.

Pursing her lips and looking at her new kitten, she wondered aloud. "Where can I meditate inconspicuously? I cannot use the ley line I found, as that is too public. I need a high-energy place that is relatively private."

While Anwyn considered her needs, Ebony walked over and pawed at a pile of papers on the nearby table. With a loud meow, she hooked her tiny paw and pulled them to the floor, where they spread out in a mess. With a sigh, Anwyn watched the kitten shuffle the papers with her little paw as if playing. But when Ebony placed her paw on a brochure and pinned her gaze on Anwyn, she realized that there might be an intent behind the playful motions.

Anwyn walked over and sat on the floor by Ebony. She reached down and picked up the brochure. She eyed the tagline. *Oldest cemetery in Salem and among the oldest in the United States.*

At first, she did not understand, then she realized what Ebony was showing her and she smiled. "You, my little sweetling, have already made yourself useful. Thank you. The cemetery is the perfect place to sit and meditate and not raise questions or suspicions. As far as anyone will know, I am paying respects to a loved one or ancestor."

Anwyn was excited. Thanks to her new pet, she now had a place to recharge and since it was mid-afternoon and mid-week, the cemetery should not be too busy, which would allow her to enjoy the full benefit of such a sacred place.

Kissing Ebony on her pink nose, Anwyn grasped the brochure in her hand and closed the door behind her with an admonishment to her kitten to behave herself. Perusing the map on the brochure, Anwyn was pleased to see the walk should only take her about five minutes. She headed to Brown St., New Liberty to Essex St. and then onto Charter, which placed her in the Historic District. Anwyn had not played tourist much since her arrival in Salem, and likely would never have that advantage, but took the time to enjoy the architecture and other sights along the way.

As Anwyn approached her destination, the excitement within her grew. A burying ground always had echoes of the people buried there. A lifetime of struggles and emotions all focused in such a small area. She knew when she was close. Energy was interesting that way. Sometimes, you walked into it like walking into a brick wall. It smacked you hard. Other times, that energy seeped and crept, as if it could not be held in place. Tingling strands that wafted on the breeze, floating around, searching for a place to land.

That is what the cemetery felt like. An ancient, primordial feeling that pulsed with life, yet felt heavy with the combined experiences of everyone buried there. It could be a powerful ambrosia. Knowing the history of this particular cemetery, Anwyn mentally connected with Earth energy and grounded herself. She was not there to get smacked down with dark or negative energy left over from the witch trials, or any other life that had ended too early or violently.

Located in a secluded area behind the Peabody Essex Museum, the cemetery presented a beautiful, yet haunting, scene with low stone walls, gravestones scattered haphazardly and crumbling with age, huge, dark trees that reached out over the graves as if guarding them with their thick limbs and delicate branches. Anwyn's attention immediately focused on the Salem Witch Trials Memorial. Having read about the memorial, she had a general idea of what to expect.

Wanting to create a permanent memorial to the twenty victims of the witch trials, the mayor established a committee in 1986, which resulted in a design competition. Judges chose the winning design and the Witch Trials Memorial was built and dedicated in 1992. Anwyn did not know any of the names of people involved, but it sounded as if the organizers gave the project proper and due respect.

Set in a peaceful setting and part of the burying ground, the memorial provided a place for people to pay respects and, hopefully, a place to reflect on tolerance and understanding. Simple and attractive, the memorial was a horseshoe shaped alcove with stacked granite stones and stone benches inscribed with the names of the executed people accused of witchcraft.

What Anwyn was not prepared for was the suffocating, heart-wrenching sense of trapped energy. A stagnant blend of fear, indignation, unspoken frustration at the injustice and hatred that had led to so many innocent deaths.

She needed to protect herself.

With one deep breath, she sent out mental feelers to find untainted energy. She latched on to tendrils of white light drifting among the gravestones and brought it to herself. She wrapped it around her body and imagined it growing into a bubble of protection. When she felt the pulsing strength around her, she stepped onto the path that led into the very heart of the memorial.

She shivered. It felt as if it sucked all the air out of her and then washed back in full force. With a slight gasp, Anwyn plopped down on one of the stone benches to take a second to stop herself from shaking. As her nerves settled and senses returned, she realized that something wasn't right. A quick glance around gave her a very clear view of...mist.

She jumped up from the bench and spun about, frantically looking for the cause of her sudden change of scenery. She still stood within the engulfing u-shape of the memorial, but a familiar mist shrouded anything beyond that. The mist of the Netherworld.

Just the thought of being back in the place that had held her for so long in a suspended state struck fear within. Before the fear could escalate to panic, whispers floated toward her from the engulfing mist. Insistent, hypnotic voices grew from a quiet hum to a swirling echo of voices all speaking at once. Anwyn couldn't make out any specific words, just indistinguishable voices all rolling together. With insistent force, they surrounded and battered Anwyn until she threw her hands over her ears and shouted, "Enough. I cannot understand you."

Immediate silence and then a gentle return of voices. This time they were quiet, calming even. And they spoke slow enough for Anwyn to pick out words, even phrases.

Darkness...beginning of time...Salem...return again...knife...w itches...evil....evil...evil.

"Stop. Please. I need only one of you to speak and help me understand what you are trying to tell me."

Silence fell. The mist moved in closer and Anwyn felt claustrophobic, afraid of being trapped inside the cloying threads of familiar fog. Pressure built in her chest and she tamped down the rising panic. *Breathe. Breathe.* The mantra repeated in her mind until she felt the knots let loose and her chest could rise and fall without feeling crushed with anxiety.

A single, calming voice reached out to her, and Anwyn turned to face the wavering form of a person taking shape in the mist. *"I am Annie. It was I who was first given the knife and book and swore a blood oath to protect them. You are of the same place as the woman who entrusted my family with these items. You are of the same purpose as all of us. Since the darkness came to this world, many have suffered and died. Its presence returns again and again to wreak havoc and soak up fear, blood, and death. It is time to destroy this force. It is time for all of us to come together in an indestructible, irreversible force for light. You are the Holder of the Light. You are the foundation that we will build upon."*

A wavering, translucent hand lifted and motioned toward the necklace nestled low on Anwyn's chest. *"We will join the others within* The Light of Many Souls *and you will be the foundation and conduit for all to come together from within."*

With these words, the surrounding mist assumed twenty loosely shaped human forms behind Annie's wavering form, and, in a focused shaft of white mist, twenty souls shot into the necklace. Anwyn's ears rang with the force of the added power. The sense of being overwhelmed and the nausea deep in the pit of her stomach wrenched her back to the memorial at a dizzying speed.

Her chest burned where the necklace sat, then cooled quickly enough. Anwyn realized her fingers had curled around the stone edge of the bench and now cramped painfully. With a gasp, she released her death grip and rubbed her hands together to restore circulation. Birdsong, traffic, distant voices, and the blast of a horn honking, slammed into her and threatened to overwhelm senses that had accustomed to the silence of Netherworld solitude.

But it was the prickly feeling biting her skin that alerted her to a presence. In a fluid motion, she jumped to a standing position and spun around until she saw the person watching her. A woman stood in the center of the cemetery, her gaze pinned on Anwyn. Middle-aged or slightly more, the woman's blond hair was messy, but looked to have been expensively styled at some point recently, her clothes were designer, but hung off her frame as if she had recently lost weight, and her lips curved into a smile that could only be described as taunting and challenging.

Even across the gravestones and the distance of the cemetery, their gazes locked and swirling visions of the past overcame Anwyn. For a brief second, she was back in Avalon, reliving the panic, desperation, and ultimate death of everyone she held dear. Losing her home and life as she knew it. A sob escaped her throat, and she returned to the present only to realize that the woman had left.

Clenching her fists, she sat again to regain her strength. Breathed in the lingering, acrid stench that had haunted her through time.

Anwyn knew with a certainty that evil had returned to Salem. And she still had not found Seabhac. Panic and fear wound through her and nudged at the doubt that she could handle this alone. Unbidden, her hand touched upon the necklace and a warm feeling gave reassurance that she had help and was not alone for the dark times approaching.

It did not change the fact that finding Seabhac was number one on her list of things to do.

CHAPTER TWELVE

Memnon stood in front of the door and took a deep breath before knocking. With a nervous glance at Seabhac, he motioned for the druid to stand off to the side, out of sight. His presence would not make for a pleasant surprise, and Memnon wanted to prepare his sister. But, how?

"You hesitate?"

"Of course I do. I wasn't here when all this went down before, but I heard enough to know that Cassandra almost lost her life to this evil thing." Memnon fixed an angry look on Seabhac. "This thing that you are responsible for."

The arch-druid sighed and shook his head. "I was merely there upon the creation of the energy, near the beginning of time. Fates placed me on that cliff top as a balance for the negative energy that came into being. My task for centuries has been to contain and negate the worst of its force. As with anything, there must be a balance. Dark and light. Hot and cold. Day and night. Evil and good. For me to be responsible for this dark force would make me the Creator of All, and I am not that." A smile lifted the corner of his mouth. "Though, I am likely the closest you will find, as I am more powerful and all-knowing than any living being...save for this force. With that, I am equal."

Memnon snorted. "Not too full of yourself, are you?"

"No more than most humans I meet. At least I have reason to feel self-important."

With those words, Seabhac narrowed his eyes, puffed out his chest, stood taller and seemed to grow. His features wavered as if being seen through ripples of water, and Memnon could have sworn he could see through the druid's body. Light shone from him in a blinding, white glow that extended up and beyond as far as Memnon could see. The surrounding air pulsed with alternating light and heavy energy, and Memnon had trouble breathing as the force of the true essence of Seabhac pushed against him. Then, in an instant, Seabhac returned to his more mundane self with a snort and self-satisfied glint in his blue eyes.

"That, human, is a mere taste of my actual form, so I heed you to show me respect."

Properly impressed and somewhat chastised, Memnon replied. "Fine. And I don't mean to be disrespectful, but my sister means everything to me and I want to protect her. Even if she can protect herself. As her big brother, that's my responsibility. And the reason that I came to Salem in the first place."

Memnon lifted his hand to knock on the door, but Seabhac grabbed his arm before he could. "Wait. You came here to protect your sister? What would make you think she needed protection?"

Memnon pulled his arm out of Seabhac's grasp and dropped it to his side. He fixed his gaze on the druid and considered his reply. On the one hand, he really knew nothing about this being who'd shown up in his kitchen unannounced. Heck, as far as he knew, this person, or whatever he was, wasn't even Seabhac, but just pretending to be the druid.

On the other hand, that display a moment ago was not one that could be put on by just any normal person, or otherworldly being. Also, why would he have insisted on coming to Cassandra and Samson's, two of the four people who could identify him? Memnon trusted his instincts, and they told him that the druid was exactly who he claimed to be.

"I had a vision, more of a feeling actually, that I needed to come to Salem. I don't know why, but that need overrode everything else, and I had no choice but to come. Cassandra saw through me in no time and she also told me that Samson has the same sense, or feeling, that things aren't quite right. You know that heavy pressure you feel when there is a storm brewing in the distance. That's what I feel."

Seabhac stared at him. Long enough and intensely enough that it made Memnon uncomfortable. He shifted on his feet and cleared his throat.

"So, do I knock now?" He heard light classical music from the other side of the door, but was sure it wouldn't be long before Cassandra looked out a window and saw them standing on the front porch.

"No." Seabhac took Memnon's arm and practically sent him flying toward the car. He literally felt his feet leave the ground at one point, but it happened so fast that he couldn't protest or try to pull back.

"Hey. What the hell are you doing?"

"It would seem that this time, it will not be your sister who is the foundation for defeating the evil force."

Memnon dug in his heels and barely stopped himself from being pushed forward. "Wait. You mean it's me? I am going to have to beat the evil. How is that even possible? I don't have any powers. Sure, I get mild premonitions. I can usually get a good sense of what people are thinking or feeling, but that won't defeat an age old force of evil. I mean..."

"I plead with you to please stop your meandering string of useless words." Seabhac snorted in derision and stomped the last few steps to Memnon's vehicle. "The absolute arrogance of humans never ceases to astound me. *You* are not meant to defeat the evil, but you *are* the link."

Memnon climbed into the driver's seat and frowned. "The link to evil?"

Rolling his eyes and snapping the length of his robe out of the way of the car door, Seabhac replied. " No. You are the link to the *Holder of the Light*. And do not pester me with more inane questions. That is all I know."

A look at the stubborn set of Seabhac's face let Memnon know he'd get no more answers to his questions. Jeesh. Talk about stone-faced. The druid could have been the model for the term. "Okay, so now what?"

"Obviously, we must search for the *Holder of the Light*. I thought I already made that clear. Now, if you would please take me to one of those places that sells the round tasty things and liquid that warms my belly, I would be greatly appreciative."

"What? I...oh, a coffee shop. You want coffee and a donut." Memnon laughed as he put his vehicle in gear and drove off. It seemed the druid wasn't above human weaknesses after all.

Anwyn stood on the cobblestones in front of the small shop. Painted dark green with burgundy and beige highlights, the store-front was pristine with windows that shone clean and bright, elegant scrolled shutters, and a wooden sign swinging from thick ropes above the colonial style double doors that signalled the entrance of the tea shop. *Tartleby's Teas.*

After her experience at the cemetery, Anwyn decided to check out the tea shop that Nora had recommended and maybe find a blend that would help her relax when she got back home. Stepping onto the welcoming mat, which featured a green turtle painted on its rubbery surface, she reached for the shiny brass door knob, but before she could touch it, the door opened and she stood face to face with a short man beckoning her forward.

"Please, come in."

Anwyn hesitated briefly. What was it with this town and every-one seeming to know she was coming before she even got there? Nora had done the same. She smiled and stepped into the store, allowing her eyes to unfocus long enough to glimpse the aura of the shopkeeper, who stood aside as he held the door and bowed his head as she passed. Interesting. His aura was palpable, even without her senses open. Rich, thick, and woven with dark and pale green, pink, indigo, and even a hint of white, the aura was one that Anwyn would not have expected to see in such an unassuming person.

It impressed her. The green instantly put her at ease as she breathed a sigh of relaxation and enjoyed the peace that washed over her. A shimmering light pink mingled with the green and wrapped Anwyn in an embrace of love and acceptance. *Heart.* This man was all heart. With an inner knowing and intuitive gift. White meant that his soul transcended beyond most souls and attested to experience gained through lifetimes of learning. Grounded, balanced, loving, compassionate, and almost beyond this world.

Her eyes filled with tears as she felt connected to such an old soul. It left her lonely and aching with a bittersweet longing for home. She felt awkward as she faced the shopkeeper, whose bald head only reached to her shoulder. He stood with a slight hunch in his shoulders and had a round nose that stood out prominently on his face. His small, slightly elongated eyes fixed on her and watched. Waited for her to speak. His calm smile gave her leave to take a moment to collect herself.

He shut the door behind her and Anwyn inhaled the wondrous scent of teas and herbs, some of which she had not smelled in a long time. Floral, fruity, simple, and complex scents. Her nostrils quivered as she identified lemongrass, chamomile, and vanilla, which was one of her favorites.

"It can be quite intoxicating, can it not?" The shop owner spoke softly.

"Yes, it can be." Anwyn extended her hand. "Hello. My name is Anwyn."

"Ah, such an ancient and regal name. Please, call me Tartleby." He took her hand in a gentle grip and held it briefly. "It is an honor, My Lady."

Anwyn flushed. "Please, Anwyn is my name."

"Yes, but your presence dictates a more respectful designation."

Tartleby swept a hand to encompass his shop. Each movement was slow, graceful, and deliberate. "I bid you to peruse to your heart's content and anything I can do to help would be my honor, My Lady. I live only to serve."

Anwyn sighed. Such a determined man, quite intent on his own path.

"Your shop came highly recommended, so I came to see what you offered. I need tea for relaxation and one to aid with cognitive thoughts. Clear and focus my mind, I suppose."

"Follow me, I have just the teas for you." Tartleby waved her forward as he set a slow, shuffling pace toward the back of the store.

The soft lighting that accentuated the apothecary-type setting of the tea store impressed Anwyn. Worn wooden counters held old-fashioned glass jars and colorful blends of loose leaf teas with names like *Dark Chocolate Peppermint Pu-erh, Peach Cobbler Guayusa, Caramel Chai, Ginger Cardamom*. As well as the usual *Oolong, White tea, Earl Grey, Chamomile, Rooibos, Lemongrass*. Too many for Anwyn to memorize, and many she'd never heard of before. Off to the side were some plump and comfortable looking lounge chairs with low tables beside them and thick braided scatter rugs dotted the gleaming pine plank floor. The gentle sound of rolling ocean waves sounded in the background to complete the ambience.

Tartleby had come to a stop beside a container filled with reddish brown and honey colored leaves mixed with dried lavender flowers. He smiled. "I believe this will suit your purposes. It is our *Salem Sleeps* blend with honey bush, chamomile, and lavender, mixed with just the right touch of caring to enhance relaxation and bring about a peaceful state of slumber."

Anwyn loved the tea's hues of brown, gold, and lavender that filled the glass jar. She also detected the barest hint of magic. *Just the right touch of caring*, she assumed meant a mild, magical spell to enhance to properties of the tea. The spell wrapped gently around the tea and infused the leaves in such an innocuous manner that it had obviously taken a true practitioner to achieve the desired result. So subtle that it would go unnoticed by even the most advanced witch. She smiled at this confirmation to her original thoughts about Tartleby.

"I will take some and thank you for knowing exactly what I need."

Tartleby lifted the lid, scooped the aromatic leaves into a small brown paper bag, folded the top down, and secured it with a turtle embossed sticker. "My Lady, you will come to find that I know you better than you realize. It is my duty."

Before Anwyn could ask exactly what that cryptic remark meant, the doorbell jingled a merry tune and a group of people came into the store, their laughter and lively conversation interrupting any further talk.

"How much do I owe you?" She asked.

Tartleby shook his bald head. "Nothing. It is my honor to help in any way that I can. No matter what you require, I am here to help." He laid his hand on her arm and squeezed. "I mean that. Call on me for anything."

His gaze seared into Anwyn with such intense focus that it raised goose bumps on her arms followed by a blanket of comfort over her entire body. Nostalgia, warm and shimmering, pulled at the corners of her emotions. Before she could question Tartelby about his cryptic remark, a customer called to him with a question about one of the tea blends.

As the customers continued to monopolize Tartleby, Anwyn knew she would return to Tartleby's Teas to unravel the enigma that the tea connoisseur presented.

Memnon held the door open for Seabhac with his foot as his hands were full of takeout bags and a couple of bottles of wine. The druid sauntered into the condo with his box of donuts in one hand and a donut in the other. Oblivious to Memnon's wavering, one-footed stance, Seabhac brushed past him as if he wasn't there. Cursing his unwanted guest, Memnon dropped his foot and released the door to slam shut on its own. "You're welcome." He mumbled on his way to the kitchen.

"Tell me. Are you always so inhospitable?" Seabhac brushed donut crumbs off his robe to the floor.

Memnon bit the inside of his cheek to remain calm. "Inhospitable? *Inhospitable?*" He forced himself to stop and take a deep breath before continuing. "Look, you show up in my condo uninvited, tell me I'm a link to some light holder, drag me around town, force me to fill you up with donuts, don't even offer to help me carry all this up from the car, and insult me constantly. And you call *me* inhospitable. I'm afraid my good graces have reached their limit."

Seabhac sighed and placed the box of donuts on the coffee table. "I see. Why are modern people always so sensitive? That Samson person was the same. Always complaining."

Memnon let out a snort. "I am sure that Samson would have a different view of events." He frowned as he unpacked hamburgers and fries from paper bags and arranged them onto plates. "Speaking of Samson, you do know that he has an uncanny ability to read people. Not to mention the fact that it's nearly impossible for me to keep a secret from Cassandra. We can't keep your presence a secret from them for long." He poured some red wine into wine glasses and pulled out a chair to sit.

"Hmm, you speak truthfully." Seabhac picked up his hamburger and looked at it as if he hadn't eaten for a week. He bit into the burger and closed his eyes with a satisfied moan of approval and a look of concentration wrinkled his face while he chewed his food. "We will avoid them. I do not want anyone involved and exposed to danger who does not need to be."

"I'm afraid that won't work for long. Cassandra will know something is wrong. She always does."

Seabhac took the last piece of burger into his mouth, followed almost immediately by a couple of french fries. Draining his wine, he put the wineglass down and rubbed his hands together. "Then, we must find the force of evil we seek, figure out the meaning of *The Holder of Light*, and end this entire fiasco before she comes looking for an explanation."

Memnon stared at Seabhac, not sure if the druid seriously thought it would be that easy. "And your suggestion to accomplish all this would be...?"

"My suggestion would be, sarcastic one, to have some of that chocolate ice cream in your cold box there." Seabhac gestured toward the freezer. "We will then get a hardy night of slumber and spend the day tomorrow scouting the town. It should not take any longer than that to find the source of evil. After all, I am..."

"Yes, I know, the most powerful druid who ever lived. No one is more powerful than you. You are the greatest, the strongest, the smartest." Memnon gathered up the now empty plates and glasses and put them into the sink. He'd wash them tomorrow.

"It is nice to know that you finally understand me. There may be hope for you yet. Now, where is that ice cream?"

Memnon rolled his eyes and grabbed the ice cream from the freezer. He hoped Seabhac was right and things would be over that quickly. He truly didn't want his sister involved in any of this again. She'd almost lost her life last time, and he would not let her risk herself again.

Verity pulled the box down from the shelf, set it gently on the floor, and looked up to see what else she would need for ritual. After leaving Matthew and feeling such a thirst for revenge, she knew she'd need her craft tools to attain her goals. Magic had not been a part of her life for a while, so she'd need to practice. After all, it had been almost a year since she'd put her store up for sale and packed up what she hadn't sold to help pay for Matthew's care. She honestly hadn't thought she'd want to return to her witchcraft or use her tools ever again. Matthew had become the primary concern in her life. He was her son, and she loved him. He deserved the best care she could provide and that meant financially as well as being there to visit him daily, so he didn't feel deserted.

Why?

Verity frowned. Where had that thought come from? She'd never questioned her resolve to help her son. He was the most important thing in her life.

Why?

The whisper slithered through the dim storage basement of the apartment building where she'd lived for the last months. Verity's heart pumped a swift staccato in her chest. She pressed herself against the back wall of the storage unit and peered in the direction she thought the whisper had originated. Nothing but piles of boxes, old Christmas trees, a couple of bicycles, and patio chairs all piled within various fenced and locked storage units.

Her breathing slowed, and she decided she must have imagined the voice. She really needed to get her altar set up and do some spell casting for protection. The usual circle of light that she mentally called upon to surround herself and her belongings didn't seem to work. Cold shivered down her spine and she grabbed another couple of small boxes until she was sure she had everything she needed.

The plan was to set up her altar and all her ritual tools, work on a spell of protection, and have the day free tomorrow to go visit Matthew.

He does not deserve your time.

Verity gasped and dropped the box she'd been carrying over to the stairs. That time, the thought had come from within. Her own sentiment. Is that how she really felt? A tremble started in her hands and worked its way through her entire body.

He failed you.

"No." Verity shouted into the dark.

Yes.

"But none of it was his fault. They ganged up on him and their magic was stronger."

It was his fault. How many times did you tell him to practice his spell casting and pay attention to the details? His arrogance ruled him and then he tried to claim the magic of the knife for himself. He did not tell you his plans. No, he just figured that he knew better than you, his own mother.

"Well, yes, but..."

No buts. You are the one who deserves the power, and he tried to take it from you. But I can give you that power.

Verity's thirst for power flared as she imagined achieving her goal of possessing unrivaled magical powers. Hope seared through her. "So, you have the knife."

You do not need the knife. There are ways to gain what you want without it. But you must be willing to make sacrifices.

The faces of everyone who had taunted her, looked down on her, snubbed her...all filtered through her mind like a movie. Amanda, Flora, Eldon and their snotty offspring. Jerome and Skye. Unfortunately, Amanda was dead and the rest of them out of town.

Do not worry, there are others who have earned the bite of your revenge. Others who have thwarted my...your quest for power. We will work together to destroy them. Once we do, no one will stand in our way. But, sacrifices. You must be willing to make sacrifices. We need the strength of many to defeat those who oppose us. I have already claimed many lingering spirits...they are so easy to suck into the dark, but you must claim the living for our cause. Kill. Kill. Kill.

Verity's blood thrummed with the thought of rising above all the people she'd envied most of her life. Having the ability to snap her fingers and make them pay for their holier-than-thou attitudes and constant diatribe to only use their powers for good. What fun was that? "Yes. I will sacrifice anything to become strong enough to destroy my enemies."

She meant what she said, yet a part of her cringed at making such a declaration. A vow without boundaries. Knots in her stomach tightened with fear. But before she could protest, the whispers started. Slithering, hypnotizing, encasing her with a need so strong that all her misgivings disappeared.

Then, the whispers told her what was required, and the part of her that remained human screamed in protest. But the screams went unheeded. Her agreement to the vow allowed the darkness to fully take over her will, her mind, and her body. Verity's consciousness became lost within a swirl of ancient anger and need for revenge. There was no escape.

Chapter Thirteen

A *s the dark of night falls upon the city, so falls darkness of a different kind. The deep desire for ultimate power drives the dark, which is fueled by instilling fear and grows with each death upon the hands of the human it inhabits. Whispering, prodding, guiding the human's thoughts with a never ending litany of vengeful words meant to fulfill a selfish purpose. Thwarted and imprisoned through the interference of humans, the darkness born upon the cliffs so long ago has had centuries to plan. This time, it will overcome any opponent who dares cross its path.*

Excerpt from *Faerie Enchantments and Sorcerer Magick*

The sun warmed Anwyn's face as she lifted it upwards to bask in the welcome warmth. Laughter from the circle of priestesses and novices that she had befriended echoed across the lake and filled her with a sense of belonging and peace.

She reached over and scratched her pet, Ebony, behind her black-tipped ears and ran her hand down a silver, furry neck. Silken soft and warmed by the sun. Anwyn smiled. She had rescued the kit from drowning in the lake 2 years ago. Pitifully small and mewling, Ebony must have wandered off from her mother and fallen in the water. Ever since then, the fox had followed Anwyn everywhere. Even defending her against the perceived threat of an attacking squirrel. Anwyn chuckled at the memory of the young hissing fox chasing off the surprised squirrel whose only crime had been to be looking for handouts from Anwyn. Not unusual, considering that Anwyn regularly handed out treats to the wildlife.

As Ebony rolled over and fell asleep, Anwyn relaxed and let herself feel the earth beneath her as she sat cross-legged upon fallen cedar leaves on the edge of the forest. Drifting, her mind blocked out sight, sound, and sense, and she felt herself become buoyant. Much as a wisp of smoke would drift, her soul reached out and danced about the shadows and light of the afternoon sun. The joyous feeling of belonging, yet being so free, filled Anwyn as she flexed her newfound skill of soul-dancing.

Sighting a passing butterfly, her energy floated over to try to communicate, something she had not yet done with animals while in this state of being. As she neared, she noticed the butterfly's wings turning black. Maybe they had flown into the shade of the nearby tree. But, no. The darkness spread and the butterfly grew in size. Turning to Anwyn, the butterfly morphed into a creature of nightmares. Huge, leathery wings, gaping maw filled with razor-like teeth, and eyes that burned through the daylight and into Anwyn's very soul.

She screamed. She tried to return to her body, but something held her fast. The creature came closer and opened its wings wide enough to block out the sun. Anwyn shivered in the shadow of the beast and screamed silently. She saw her body below her, still cross-legged, but twitching. She needed to return to physical form. Only then could she defend herself. The dark wings engulfed her and the fetid breath of the beast blew across her face. She gagged and screamed again, but the creature's grasp entrapped her.

Something hit her in the arm. Again. A solid smack with sharp stabs. It moved to her face, and she felt a solid tap and push.

Ebony. The fox urged her to awaken. Anwyn pulled away from the beast, who roared in triumph when she didn't succeed. A scream next to her ear forced her to try again. This time, she focused everything she had, everything she was, and shot it at the beast. Her effort was enough to knock the beast back and allow Anwyn to return to her body.

With a gasp and sob, she threw her arms up, ensuring herself that she truly was free. Heart pounding, Anwyn called upon the forces of Light to protect her. She saw no beast. It had disappeared, leaving no sign... not even a butterfly. Anwyn reached down to thank her fox for saving her life, but Ebony was not there. Well, she was, but she was no longer a fox. She was a cat. And Anwyn was not by the lake in Avalon. She was in her bed in Salem.

She swallowed the bitter taste of loss and nostalgia for the long ago time and took a deep breath. A warm paw tapped her on the leg and Anwyn reached down to scratch the cat. "Many thanks for saving me, Ebony. I do not know what would have happened had you not."

"Meow." Ebony sat on the bed and looked up at her so innocently. A tiny ball of black fur amidst the now rumpled covers of the bed.

Unease sat heavily within Anwyn. Nightmares such as the one she had just experienced, did not happen for no reason. It was a warning. She rose from the bed, ignoring the coolness of the wood under her feet, and crossed over to the window.

Parting the pale green curtains with a fingertip, she peeked out into the inky darkness of night. Usually a comforting time for her, a time of quiet solitude and muffled sounds of nocturnal life. This night held fear, pain, and death. A creeping darkness threatened the peace of the place that Anwyn considered home. Even if her time here was temporary, Salem was home. She loved her shop and enjoyed chatting with the customers who wandered in, hoping for a glimpse of a genuine witch or wanting a spell to entice a loved one. A pair of dark eyes and a handsome face jumped into her mind, and Anwyn shook off the unwelcome distraction. He was not for her. She had no future here, or anywhere.

The aching pain of loss wound around her heart and hardened her from thinking about anything other than fulfilling her intended task. She would die during the final battle with an evil that had travelled from a far off cliff top to Avalon, and across the ocean to Salem, leaving death and destruction in its wake. There was no life for her beyond that.

The glimmer of light against the curtains caught her attention, and she looked down to see her necklace glowing. Covering it with her hand, she looked down at Ebony and said, "I have to go out there. I might be able to stop whatever is about to happen. Besides, if I sense the evil, Seabhac will as well, so this is a chance to find him."

"Meow."

"No, Ebony, you stay here. It is much safer for you."

Without waiting for a response, Anwyn dressed quickly, marvelling again at the modern bra and how it enhanced her acceptably sized but not bodacious breasts. She pulled a summer dress on over her head and smoothed it down with a brush of her hand over the soft, flowing material. She loved the variety and simplicity of contemporary clothing. But she still could not bring herself to give up the feminine attire of a dress and wear pants. The idea was so foreign to her, yet it was a common sight to see women everywhere in pants. Maybe one day, but for now, dresses helped her feel closer to who she was...closer to a life that she had left so far behind.

Slipping her feet into sandals and grabbing a sweater against the cool October weather, Anwyn closed her apartment door and made her way down the stairs, through the dark shop, and out onto an eerily silent street. Beyond the reach of streetlights, the dark of a moonless night enshrouded the surroundings in shadows.

She paused long enough to breathe deeply. A quick glance around showed no one was out at this time of the night, so she was clear to do a simple finding spell, though she had doubts it would work. When she had first arrived in Salem, she had tried a finding spell to find Seabhac, but her crystal had just jumped around on the end of the chain and thrown off intermittent shafts of light. Seabhac's energy was so powerful and pervasive that she had not pinpointed a source. The druid possessed an ancient energy that had passed down within the confines of his journal and knife and seeped into the very foundations of Salem and the city's inhabitants.

Hopefully, she would have better luck looking for the source of evil. Clearing her mind and grasping the crystal within her fist, she closed her eyes, focused on the sense of chaos from her dream. The force that had woken her.

What I seek

Help me find

Heat warmed her palm, and the crystal vibrated lightly in her hand. Anwyn waited, willing the crystal to send her in the right direction. An image flashed within her mind, then the crystal became quiet and lay still against her chest. With a sigh, Anwyn thanked the Fates for that brief image, as she had recognized the gazebo at Salem Common as her destination. Tamping down the nervous queasiness in the pit of her stomach, Anwyn headed toward the Common, dreading what she might find once she arrived there.

Anwyn usually loved the night. It wrapped her in a comforting blanket of anonymity and muffled all sounds to a soft hum. But tonight, the silence was absolute. Heavy. Dull fear throbbed in her chest as Anwyn quietly made her way through the deserted streets toward the Common. Butterflies in her stomach fluttered a staccato beat against her insides. As the Common came into view, the butterflies grew into rocks which dropped to the pit of her stomach.

Darkness of the night should have been absolute, but it paled when compared to the black cloud that covered the gazebo in the center of Salem Common. Breath left Anwyn in a single whoosh of disbelief and she stood in shock at the sight before her, her feet frozen to the ground.

As she watched, the undulating waves of the thick cloud gradually parted and dissipated into nothingness. Revealed to the night was a cloaked figure on the steps of the structure, as well as a shape lying in the shadows at the feet of the figure. Frozen in time, much like Anwyn's current state.

She stood on the edge of the walkway that led to the arched roof pavilion and took a moment to settle her jumbled emotions. Fear, uncertainty, curiosity, and a sense of the inevitable all warred within her. She tried, but could not move forward.

She was about to face the centuries-old evil alone. If the most powerful arch-druid and his sorceress failed to defeat the force, how could she possibly succeed?

Anwyn clutched the crystal in a shaking fist. She was not alone. So many promising lives had ended amidst the threat of a violent attack, so many young women with a lifetime ahead of them had given themselves in order to be here. Now. With her. Not to mention the witches who offered their restless souls in service to defeat the evil that had been responsible for their deaths.

She was not alone.

Brighid had told her to find Seabhac because she would need his help. But with the evil within sight and what looked to be a person sprawled and helpless on the floor of the pavilion, Anwyn had no choice. She acted. Heat shot through her and set her pulse racing. A thread of white light moved from the crystal of the necklace and grew into a shimmering bubble of light surrounding Anwyn. Power surged through her and just as she was about to move forward, the figure raised a hand. Light flickered off what looked like a blade in the figure's hand.

"No." Anwyn screamed. But to no avail.

One straight and true arc sent the knife into the supine person. Again and again. The wind kicked up in a fierce, swirling mass of flying leaves and small stones that hit Anwyn and prevented her from moving. Pressure on her chest prevented her from breathing properly and quick gasps were all she was capable of to pull air into her lungs. Her ears rang and her head spun as she struggled to breathe.

Concentrating on the necklace, she tried to find the power that had filled her a moment ago, but found nothing. She felt powerless and could do nothing as the hooded figure turned to her and pointed the bloody knife in her direction. Even at the distance, Anwyn saw the triumph cross the pale features of what looked to be a woman's face.

With a snap of cloak and guttural laughter, the figure ran behind a couple of trees and disappeared into the dark clutches of the night. Anwyn felt weak and defeated. She sank to her knees and tears filled her eyes. Before she could recover her strength, gentle hands lifted her from the ground and she heard a familiar voice.

"Come, Lady. We must leave this place before the police arrive."

"Nora?" Anwyn peered through the dark. "What are you doing here? How do you know the police are coming?" Anwyn struggled to bring her senses back to normal.

"I am here to save you, and I know the police are coming because I called them." Nora pulled Anwyn's arm to lead her away from the Common, while sirens sounded in the distance. Approaching fast.

Confused and angry with herself for failing, Anwyn let Nora lead her through the streets of Salem. The siren sounds receded somewhat as they wound through the streets and ended up in front of *Tartleby's Teas*. Anwyn frowned as Nora rapped loudly and repeatedly on the door.

"Don't get yourself into a dither, I'm coming." Tartleby's muffled voice sounded from inside the darkened shop.

"Why are we here? And how did you know where to find me?"

"Shh. I'll explain everything. Let's just get you settled in a comfy chair with a piping hot cup of tea."

The curtains on the door parted and Tartleby's rather large, bulbous nose pressed against the glass. A muffled *oh* and sounds of a clicking lock preceded the opening of the door. Subdued light filled the doorway and cast shadows on the green turtle welcoming mat and cobbled stones of the walkway. Tartleby ushered them into the shop with a questioning look at Nora, who waved him off as she led Anwyn to the nearest chair.

With shaking limbs and confused thoughts, Anwyn sank into the chair with a sigh while Nora had a whispered conversation with Tartleby. She did not understand what had gone wrong. When she touched the necklace, power had streamed forth and lent her strength she needed to fight the evil. Then it just fizzled out and left her weak and shaken. Not only that, but it had left her vulnerable to some sort of psychic or otherworldly attack by the hooded person. Fear clutched her and gave rise to all sorts of speculative doubts.

What if Brighid had been wrong? What if all the Priestesses of Avalon had given their lives for naught? What if there was no chance of defeating the evil?

Panic made Anwyn feel sick to her stomach, and she was about to stand to flee outside for fresh air, but Nora thrust a cup of tea in front of her instead. Heady aromas of chamomile, lavender, and mint wafted up on a wave of steam, and Anwyn inhaled with a breath of relief.

"Perfect. Thank you, Tartleby." She sipped the tea and let the calming properties warm and steady her insides.

With the panic attack subdued, Anwyn looked up from her cup of tea and pinned her gaze on the two people sitting across from her on a loveseat Tartleby had angled to face her. Anwyn tried to read their expressions, but they gave nothing away. Tartleby's gaze wavered expectantly between Nora and Anwyn, while Nora watched Anwyn with concern and uncertainty in her eyes.

Anwyn spoke. Her voice cracking at first, then settling into a normal tone. "Neither one of you is who you appear at first. I believe tonight has shown that the time for secrets has passed. I need to know the truth."

CHAPTER FOURTEEN

*M*emnon *watched the woman sitting cross-legged on the edge of the forest glade. A wisp of auburn hair lifted by the breeze brushed across her face and settled back into place, while her golden eyes lit with innocent delight. His heart did a quick dance in his chest and he felt the urge to touch her, just to experience her perfection. When she reached out to scratch the strange looking animal beside her, Memnon marvelled at her gracefulness. Almost as if she was a part of the surrounding nature...flowing, dancing, beautiful. And so very familiar to him.*

Distant laughter drifted upon the sound of splashing water and windblown leaves, breaking Memnon from his slightly hypnotic state. With a frown, he surveyed his surroundings, but didn't recognize any landmarks. It must be a dream. Or maybe he was having a vision. But his visions usually came to him while he was awake, and as a feeling or certainty, rather than a physical sense of being in an altered reality. This was so real, right from the warm breeze on his face to the scents of lavender, grass, and sun-baked cedar.

A startled gasp jerked his attention back to the woman sitting with her fox. She no longer looked serene and content. Instead, her face twisted with fear and her body jerked awkwardly, while the fox sat beside her and yipped fervently.

Something was wrong. Memnon tried to move forward, but his feet wouldn't budge. Weight pressed down on him and he tried to claw himself free, but there was nothing visible to break free from.

The woman's struggle increased, and she waved her arms around as if fighting off an invisible attacker. Memnon's heart raced in his chest as he tried harder to make his feet move.

Something hit his shoulder. Hard. He struck out where he thought his attacker would be.

"Ouch. By the bloody veil, why did you hit me?"

What? Where had that voice come from?

"Wake up, man. There is danger."

Danger. Yes, there was. The woman was being attacked. He felt himself lifted from the ground and then let go to fall unceremoniously back to the ground. Except it wasn't grass he landed on. It was...wood? What the heck.

"Enough faffing about. We need to go. NOW."

Faffing about? Who talked like that? Memnon knew he needed to focus, but it was the stinging slap across his face that snapped him back to reality.

"Wait. What? Seabhac, what is going on?"

Memnon rubbed his face and pulled himself up from the cold wooden where he'd found himself upon being so rudely awakened. The dream state he'd been in receded, but the memory of it remained. Now that he was awake, he knew the identity of the meditating woman. He also remembered that she'd been in trouble and hoped that his dream hadn't been a portent.

While he was pondering the meaning of his dream, Seabhac threw some clothes at him and stalked from the room with a very direct command. "Get dressed. We need to go now."

Memnon watched the druid's retreating back while his clothes dropped to the floor at his feet. With a shake of his head and a whispered curse focused on the druid's arrogance, he reached for his clothes and tugged on the jeans and t-shirt. On his way out of the bedroom, he grabbed a pair of socks and a light jacket.

Seabhac paced by the front door, mumbling under his breath. When he saw Memnon, he stopped and clapped his hands together. "Come. Come. There is no time to dawdle."

With an exasperated snort, Memnon pulled on his boots and snapped at Seabhac. "Can you at least enlighten me as to why you've dragged me out of bed at this god-awful hour and where the heck we are going?"

Seabhac yanked the door open and strode through, his long robes snapping both sides of the door frame on his way out. "To save a life I hope."

Oh, no. Anwyn. His dream cracked back at him full force and with a surge of fear-lit energy, he ran after the druid, slamming the door shut behind him. He paid little attention to where their destination. He just followed Seabhac on a winding route around town while the druid mumbled, looked up at the night sky, or closed his eyes and stood silent. With nerves close to breaking level, Memnon hoped the druid knew what he was doing. But if Anwyn was the one in danger, why didn't they just head straight to her apartment above the store?

At one point during a brief stop, Memnon opened his mouth to ask why they were roaming the streets of Salem so late at night, but before he could speak, Seabhac silenced him with an impatient wave of his hand. Damn the power of druid magic, anyway. He stood silent but frustrated while Seabhac did his thing.

Suddenly, like a hound dog who catches a scent, Seabhac's head jerked up and his gaze focused on a distant point. Setting a course, Seabhac's ground eating stride forced Memnon to run just to keep up. Past the darkened windows of closed shops and past the Hawthorne Hotel, they ended up in Washington Square West and finally stopped at the northwest corner of Salem Common, just across from the Salem Witch Museum.

At first, nothing seemed out of place as Seabhac's gaze swept the Common, his nose twitching the entire time. Memnon's heart thudded and, with his senses on full alert, he squinted into the darkness of the still night.

Then he heard a sound.

Subdued voices drifted across the dark night and the sound of a stone skittering across the pavement as if kicked by a person.

Already alert and looking for anything out of place, Memnon snapped his head around. He stared, trying to see who was there. His gaze registered a flicker of movement at the corner, just past the Witch's Museum. A flash of what looked to be a flowing skirt and a hint of auburn hair. *Anwyn.* Or maybe it was his imagination, as the residue of his earlier dream still clung to his thoughts.

About to run after whoever shared the night with them, Memnon found himself unceremoniously jerked right off his feet and hit the ground running as Seabhac pulled him in the opposite direction. By the time he blurted out a word of protest, he and Seabhac stood in front of the gazebo in the middle of the Common.

Heaviness and a sense of dread pushed against Memnon so hard that he had trouble catching a breath. Seabhac stepped up a couple of stairs. Memnon followed. Those two steps up allowed them a better view of the floor of the gazebo.

In his entire life, Memnon had never seen, or even imagined, such a horrid display of deliberate and savage carnage. Arms and legs splayed in the center of the gazebo and nailed to the floor with spikes. Spliced down the middle and skin peeled back, lay what used to be a human being. Male or female was difficult to determine. Once Memnon's eyes adjusted to the darker recesses of the covered structure, he realized that the shadows on either side of the mutilated corpse were the person's organs.

He gagged. And gagged again. Pain and terror flared through him as he glimpsed a face twisted with evil and felt as if it was his insides being torn from him. Struggling to breathe and keep himself grounded, he turned from the sight and stumbled down the stairs. He knelt on the grass and threw up everything that remained in his stomach of his dinner. He heaved until his sides hurt and his emotions raged with the second hand memory of being eviscerated. He'd always known of his empathic abilities, but usually kept himself protected against daily assaults from depressed people, photos of animal abuse that ran rampant on certain social websites, and any stray emotions from people he did business with.

But the sight of this person, so horribly tortured and laid out in an obviously ceremonial, yet brutal manner, tore through all defenses. He felt the fear, the pain, the betrayal.

Betrayal? Why would the person feel betrayed? Unless they knew their killer.

The shrill scream of an approaching siren cut through Memnon's thoughts and brought him back from the mire of residual pain and emotions he'd picked up from the dead person. Wiping his mouth on the sleeve of his jacket, he looked toward the gazebo and saw that Seabhac was nowhere in sight. He whipped his head around, looking for him, but realized that the druid had disappeared. Memnon guessed Seabhac wasn't ready for his presence to be known, so he'd taken off and left Memnon to face the police alone.

How the heck was he going to explain being here? And who had called the police? It must have been whoever he'd glimpsed when he and Seabhac had arrived at the Common. A couple of police vehicles came to a screeching stop and officers jumped from both cars, guns drawn and yelling at him to put his hands up.

Memnon complied by thrusting his hands straight up, at the same time yelling. "Don't shoot. I'm unarmed and I only just got here."

"Down on the ground. Fingers locked behind your head. Now."

He dropped to the ground on his knees for the second time that night and put his hands up behind his head. Hands grabbed at him and yanked his arms down, locking his wrists into handcuffs.

"Wait." A voice boomed from the direction of the gazebo. "Turn him around."

Memnon groaned. He knew that voice and needed to think fast to come up with a reason for being there. Especially if he didn't want Seabhac's presence known, which would likely involve his sister.

The officer holding him lifted him up and spun him around to face the disapproving look on the police chief's face.

"Damn it, Memnon. What are you doing here?" Samson inclined his head to the officer holding him. "Let him go. I know him."

Memnon rubbed his now free wrists and frowned at the officer beside him. "Next time, maybe not so tight on the cuffs."

Samson raised an eyebrow. "There better not be a next time." With a glance back at the gazebo, which was now surrounded by yellow police tape, Samson said. "You better have a good explanation for this, Memnon, or your sister is going to kill me."

"I do. I mean, I don't, not really. I couldn't sleep and came out for a walk. I had only just gotten here and found the body when you guys showed up." He pulled his phone from his pocket. "I was just about to call you. Obviously, someone beat me to it."

Samson stared at him with those disconcerting blueberry colored eyes and frowned. He spoke to the officer beside Memnon. "Go see what you can do to help. Make sure no one, and I mean no one, gets anywhere near this crime scene."

"Yes, sir." The young officer left them alone.

"Memnon. I need the truth. What is going on? I'm sure you saw enough to know that this is a ritual murder. Did you see anyone? Hear anything."

Memnon hated lying to Samson, but Seabhac had been adamant about keeping his presence here a secret for now. And he didn't know if he'd actually seen anyone earlier, or if he'd been seeing a vision left over from his dream. For now, he had no choice but to give the answer he did.

"No. I swear, I couldn't sleep, was out walking and only just arrived when you guys showed up." With a Herculean effort, he looked Samson right in those purple-blue eyes of his and did his utmost to appear innocent. He must have succeeded, because Samson let out a breath and relaxed his shoulders.

"Okay. I believe you. But you need to try to remember everything. You may have seen or heard something during your walk.

It doesn't even have to be close to here. If the killer had already fled, you may have passed them or seen something elsewhere."

Memnon shrugged. "I'll do my best to remember anything I can."

"Good enough. Now, the question is, do I tell your sister that I found you here?"

The two men looked at each other and spoke simultaneously. "Nope."

"She'll only worry." Memnon said.

"Yes." Samson's gaze hardened. "But we may not have a choice if this is what I think it is." The police chief shook his head and spoke, arguing with himself. "But it can't be. Seabhac said it was over. He imprisoned the darkness and said we were safe now. If it had escaped, I'm sure Seabhac would have let us know. Maybe it's another dark force showing up. Or maybe it's just some crazy person getting off on this kind of torture. Damn it, sometimes I hate this job." He rubbed the back of his neck and sighed. "I best get on with figuring out what's going on."

Memnon bit the inside of his mouth, forcing himself to stay silent. He hated keeping secrets. It had never been easy for him and with people he cared about; it felt like a betrayal. And that took him back to what he'd felt during his empathic episode when he first saw the body. Betrayal. Once they found out the identity of the corpse, it would narrow down the suspects if the victim had known the killer. He debated sharing at least that tidbit of information with Samson when an officer waved the police chief over to the gazebo.

Samson signaled back. "Okay, I've got to go. Think about everything you saw or heard tonight and we'll talk tomorrow. For now, we tell Cassandra nothing." He glanced over at the morbid scene at the gazebo. "But I have a feeling this is going to blow up in our faces. Get ready, Memnon, my gut does not feel good about any of it."

If only you knew the whole truth, my friend, you'd know how right you are.

Lifting his hands and rubbing his wrists, he smiled at Samson. "Thanks for trusting me and getting those handcuffs off me."

"No problem. I know you aren't part of this. Now go home and try to stay out of trouble." Samson turned and strode over to the crime scene, his commanding presence parting the way through uniformed officers as he went.

Guilt tore a searing path through Memnon's stomach. Lying. He hated being forced into lying. When he found that darned druid, he was going to rake him over the coals for leaving him to face Samson and this situation by himself. And he also needed to pay a visit to a gorgeous, red-haired woman to find out what she'd been up to in the middle of the night. Other than haunting his dreams, that is.

CHAPTER FIFTEEN

T he restorative properties of the tea warmed Anwyn and gave her strength enough to repeat her demand in a firmer tone. "The truth. I need to know who both of you are and what's going on before someone else is killed."

Tartleby and Nora shared a look and Tartleby inclined his head. "You tell your story while I fix more tea."

The tea shop owner picked up the cups, moved to the counter where he plugged in the kettle and arranged the cups side by side. It struck Anwyn again how slow and smooth the small man's movement was. She understood how the preciseness and certainty of each move could soothe and bring structure to a cluttered mind. With a slight smile, she turned to Nora.

Anwyn was not sure she wanted to hear what Nora was about to say. This time period unsettled her enough, as every aspect of life as she had known it was now so different. She felt lost and somewhat fragmented. Even though hundreds of years had passed, her memories of her life in Avalon felt as if it had only happened yesterday. Add that to the burden of the crystal and its souls on a chain around her neck and her need to find Seabhac before anyone else was killed...well, it was rather a lot to deal with.

"I am ready to listen." She adjusted her dress, folded her hands on her knees, and sat back expectantly. Hesitantly.

Nora gave a somewhat wistful smile and laid a hand over Anwyn's comfortingly. "First of all, please be assured that we are only here to help you in any way possible. That is our task."

Anwyn frowned and was about to speak when Tartleby placed her teacup in her hands and said, "Patience."

Nora inclined her head in thanks to the little man and continued to speak. "To put it as succinctly as possible, I know your origins and purpose for being here, as my family has had the task of waiting for your return. Our responsibility is, always has been, to help you adjust to what would undoubtedly be an unsettling time for you in whatever time you appeared."

Heat slammed into Anwyn, and her hand shook enough to slosh tea over the edge of her teacup. With care, she placed the cup on the table in front of her as her mind struggled to understand what Nora had just shared with her. She cleared her throat and whispered. "How is such a thing possible? No one survived. No one knew. There is just me. It has always been just me." Tears threatened, but now was not the time for self-pity, so she blinked to clear her eyes. "Explain."

Nora sipped her tea and leaned back in the loveseat as if settling in for a long story. "It has never been just you. Brighid made sure of that after she sent you on your way so long ago. The youngest acolyte was only ten years old and Brighid felt the girl was too young to understand what was being asked of her. Or maybe she just couldn't bring herself to ask a child to give up her life in what could have very well been a futile cause." Nora shrugged and lifted the corner of her mouth in a half smile. "Whatever the reason, I am grateful she sent the girl home, as I would not exist today if she had not done so."

Anwyn gasped and leaned forward in rapt interest. "You are talking about Maeve. She was your ancestor?"

"Yes. And Brighid gave her an explicit duty to carry out." Tears filled Nora's eyes as she continued her tale. "Brighid implanted a genetic memory of all the events that day and sent Maeve home with instructions to pass the memory on to her child, who would pass it on to her child, and on down the line until such time as you appeared. Our duty was to help you acclimate to the unfamiliar culture that you'd find yourself in upon awakening. Also, to offer you the benefit of our ancient abilities to enhance the power of the crystal. The knowledge and memories have passed through many generations and have finally come to rest here in Salem. With your return."

"Genetic memory? How does that work?" Anwyn smiled at Tartleby as he placed a fresh cup of tea on the table in front of her and sat, then turned her attention back to Nora.

"Brighid captured all Maeve's memories and made sure she understood the magnitude of the events and sacrifices made that day. She then cordoned that knowledge into a section of Maeve's brain, along with the knowledge of the ritual to pass the memories down through each generation."

Anwyn shook her head in awe of what the Priestess had accomplished that day so long ago. "Brighid must have seen it all coming. The elaborate plans she carried out that day would have taken such thought. Think about it. She helped send Ainevar off with the knife and Seabhac's journal. Arranged for my trip to the Netherworld and, ultimately, the future. Somehow dealt with the sacrifice made by all the girls and women who gave their lives to ensure the defeat of the very evil that forced their deaths. Performed magic that melded all their energies into the necklace that I now wear. Sent your ancestor away so there would exist a connection to the past, so I would not be alone hundreds of years after that day. Such preciseness and forethought inspires awe within me."

Tartleby cleared his throat and leaned forward. The loveseat beneath him creaked in protest. "Those were not the only ways she set various destinies on their pathways. The previous day, she had sent a message to a nearby druid village asking for one of the younger druids to make the trek to Avalon, as she had a chore that needed doing. As the Priestesses of Avalon and Seabhac's druids shared a bond with nature's elements and similar purposes, there was nothing unusual about the request. Other than the fact that she requested him at a specific time...not too early, not too late."

The corners of his mouth lifted in a slow smile. "On that dusty road between Avalon and the druid village, is when my ancestor came across a young girl on her way home from the Temples of Avalon. Crying and scared, the girl told him everything and gave him a note written by Brighid to give to *the man she would come across on the road home.*"

Tartleby's usual monotone voice wavered and cracked. "My ancestors do not have first-hand genetic memories, but once Eoghan made sure Maeve was safely home with her family, he returned to Avalon." He cleared his throat and leaned back on the loveseat. "The spoken tale of what he found has passed down the years in vivid and terrifying detail. Enough so, that I don't think I would want the actual memory in my mind."

With a sad smile, Tartleby gave Nora's hand a gentle pat.

Anwyn tried to imagine the scene that Tartleby's ancestor had found, but realized she did not want that in her mind. Her stomach knotted enough with her own memories of that day. It was the day she lost everything and the day that everyone she knew gave their lives to help defeat evil on an unknown day in the future. A day that came closer as the minutes ticked. Her fingers touched the crystal hanging from her neck, and she choked back the emotions that threatened. The responsibility for all those lives, as well as the accused witches who more recently pledged their souls to help, now rested with her.

"You're not alone." Nora's voice broke Anwyn from her spiral into self-pity. "Tartleby and I still hold knowledge to power long forgotten and we have yet to find Seabhac. Brighid did well when she set her plans in motion to bring us all together when the time was right. We are all in this together and we will defeat the dark force."

"I truly hope so. I am stunned and fortified that I am not alone." Tears fell from her eyes. "We grow stronger in numbers. By the way, Tartleby, what did the note say that Brighid wrote for Eoghan?"

"It tasked him with caring for the young girl and making sure she returned home and remained safe until she passed her memories to her eventual daughter. His son would then become protector of the line of priestesses who carried the memories."

"So, your families have remained close through the generations. Was there ever the temptation to combine the two families?"

"I have no doubt, my Lady. But it could never happen. There needed to be one to carry the memories, and one to protect. If any of the preceding generations married each other, they would have created a single family and negated the structure set in place by Brighid. For the ultimate good of all, the memory holder and the protector needed to remain close, but only as friends. Therefore ensuring two distinct family lines."

Anwyn did not miss the wistful glance exchanged by her two new friends. She felt sad that they obviously cared so much for each other, but could be nothing more than friends.

"I see. So, what of you two? You must have married and had children in order to carry on the assigned tasks?"

Nora and Tartleby nodded in unison. Nora replied. "We were married. I am a widow and Tartleby divorced. I have a daughter and Tartleby has a son. Each of them is grown and living their lives away from Salem. There is no need for their presence for what's coming, as this is the final battle. Whatever happens."

Those words slammed home the reality of the present, and Anwyn sighed. "I am truly blessed to have found you both, but we need Seabhac. I am not sure why, but Brighid was very adamant that I had to find him before taking any action against the dark force. How can we find him?"

Nora replied. "Tartleby and I think he is cloaking his presence in order to remain unseen to the evil."

"But does he not realize that doing so keeps him invisible to us as well?"

"Lady." Tartleby frowned. "Seabhac died before any of Brighid's plans took place. He knows nothing of you, the crystal, or our family tasks. As far as he knows, he is in this alone."

"Oh. That does make things more difficult. But how can he not be aware of our presence? An arch-druid, such as he, should feel the undiluted ancient power that flows from me. From all of us. As well as the pulsing power of the necklace. His magic would draw it like a magnet. He should see the shimmering aura as it searches him out."

Nora replied. "My guess is that the oppressive, clinging vibration radiating from the dark force overwhelms him. And he does not know we're here, so anything he feels other than his own magic, he will attribute to the darkness."

"That makes sense. So, how do we find him?"

"We must find him soon." Nora looked from Tartleby to Anwyn and continued. "I hear rumblings around town that mediums are not connecting with their guides. The usual haunted places are suddenly ghost free. I think this evil is soaking up spirits and using them as an energy source. Nothing like this has ever happened, and it is causing quite a kerfuffle about town."

The three sat quietly, each lost in thought. Muffled sounds of the morning echoed outside on Exeter St. Laughter from a couple of people passing by the shop, the squeak of a door opening and closing across the walkway, a car horn honked in the distance, and the scrape of a sign being dragged across the bricks and set in place for the day.

Tartleby sat up straight, his glasses sliding down his nose with his unusually abrupt move. He pushed the glasses back up his nose and said. "Maybe we don't have to find him. He can find us."

Nora and Anwyn looked at each other and then focused their attention on Tartleby, who continued to speak. "If the three of us combine our magic and send it out, Seabhac will find us easily. He will assuredly recognize the root of ancient magic as it no longer exists, other than in a select few. He will hone in on it like a bloodhound and come looking for us."

A flicker of hope flared within Anwyn. The thought of finding Seabhac comforted her. Just as having two new friends who knew of her true past and reason for being here. The freedom from having to worry about every word she spoke, in case she said something wrong, the ability to speak of her upbringing and home with those who understood her. Nothing could feel better. Unless, of course, it was defeating the evil responsible for her being here. Out of her own time.

She smiled and nodded. "I believe your idea to be a good one, Tartleby. But the sooner the better, as there has already been one death."

"I agree." Nora said. "It's a new moon tonight, so perfect for activating a slightly altered summoning spell. I think that would be best for our purpose?"

Anwyn pursed her lips and considering the alternatives. "I believe you could be right. Though we will not be summoning a spirit from beyond. Instead, we want to summon Seabhac on the current plane of existence. The basic ritual will be the same, but a modified version of the spoken spell should suffice. Let me work on a spell over the day. Nora, can you supply the physical items needed and set up an altar at your place?"

"Yes, of course."

"So, we will meet at Nora's at dusk. Tartleby, bring yourself and some cinnamon tea."

The three of them stood and stretched. Anwyn felt stiff and sore from her earlier encounter with the dark force. And knots in the pit of her stomach reminded her that someone had died during the night and she had to ensure no one else died because she was too weak or slow in performing her one purpose for being in Salem.

"Until tonight." She lifted her hand in a farewell as she left the tea store and stepped into the cooling surroundings of the early morning.

Chapter Sixteen

Verity woke with a splitting headache and sore arms and shoulders. She was also still wearing yesterday's clothing, which seemed to be stiff and stained. Her nostrils twitched at the sharp, metallic smell that rose off her clothes.

Her eyes adjusted to the dim light of her bedroom as she slowly rose from the bed, where she'd obviously fallen asleep fully clothed. Disoriented and racking her brain to remember last night, she stretched and moved across the room to open the curtains.

Bright sunlight streamed into the room, and Verity flinched against the intrusion and put her hand across her eyes until they adjusted to the light.

That was when last night's memories hit her. With a strangled cry, Verity realized that the stain on her hands and clothes was blood.

Matthew's blood.

And she had killed him.

In her mind's eye, she saw the flash of a knife blade in the moonlight as it struck Matthew again and again. No wonder her arms and shoulders hurt.

Her shaking legs wouldn't support her, and she crumbled to the floor. Grief and loss overcame her as she tried to make sense of the shadowy memories. She loved Matthew. He was her son, and she'd do anything for him. Why would she kill him?

Well, because he deserved it, of course.

Verity sniffled and sat up straighter. Yes, now she remembered. She'd needed a sacrifice to show the dissenters her power. Make them fear her. She'd given up so much for Matthew and the time had come for him to give back. His life was little enough payment and he could move on, knowing that his blood would help bring his mother the power she so deserved. The influence and abilities that she'd craved her entire lifetime. It was the least he could have done for her.

She also remembered the one who'd tried to stop her. The woman in the shadows had reeked of earth magic. Ancient magic. The kind that passes through bloodlines. Nature-based. Not the watered down play magic that most people practiced these days. No. The magic force thrown at her last night had roots of the oldest kind.

Who in town would have knowledge of such arcane knowledge? Few enough, for sure. The people involved in entrapping the darkness twice before were the only likely ones. It hadn't been Seabhac as his magic encircled a person and wrapped them up tight. Whereas last night's magic had felt deeper. Richer, with an earthy scent. And it filled a person up and pulsed from the inside out.

Bah! Why will they not leave me be?

Lifting her chin, Verity stood, chose some clean clothes, and went into the bathroom for a hot shower. There was much to do today. She couldn't wait to bask in the ripples of fear that Matthew's very public, very sadistic, sacrificial murder, would set off among the people of Salem.

Anticipation and excitement rippled through her at the thought of choosing her next target. It had to be someone important. Someone who would be missed and mourned. The more fear, the more power she could fill up on.

Verity smiled as she stripped, stepped under the hot shower stream, and let the water cleanse her body. As she scrubbed the dried blood from her hands, the whispers filled her mind.

Chapter Seventeen

Seabhac cursed the Fates for being so temperamental and threw a pillow across the room. His third pillow. His third attempt at a finding spell.

Memnon chewed on the last of his toast and gulped down some coffee. He almost smiled at the druid's frustration, but the matter at hand was far too serious to take lightly. A murder had occurred last night and, even though he'd had no visions, Memnon knew the next murder wouldn't be far behind.

It was interesting how his usual prophetic feelings had changed since coming to Salem. Instead of being a thought or feeling that seemed somewhat separate from him, he now possessed a knowing. The understanding that came from deep within that told him of upcoming events. It pulsed within his blood and wound itself through his thoughts and emotions.

"So, Druid, what seems to be the problem? Is it anything I can help with?"

Seabhac snorted. "Bah! As if a human such as yourself could help the most powerful arch-druid of all time."

"If I remember correctly, *most powerful arch-druid of all time*, you had more than a little help from Cassandra when you defeated this thing last time. In fact, I would say that it's your fault it's on the loose again. So don't get all arrogant and egotistical with me."

Seabhac puffed up and raised his hand as if ready to shoot a blast of energy in Memnon's direction. His blue eyes sparked with pinpricks of light. Then, he deflated and plopped down on the sofa. "As much as it pains me to say so, you are correct. Your sister was almost solely responsible for defeating the evil last time, and that is why I need to be the one to recapture the evil this time. It is my battle and my responsibility. I cannot allow anyone else to risk their life."

Seabhac stood and paced the floor while Memnon considered the druid's confession. His guest was maybe not as uncaring as he seemed, and was only trying to correct a mistake he felt was his alone.

"Hey. None of this is your fault. It's not as if you allowed it to escape. I am sure you took all precautions and couldn't have foreseen any of this."

"None of that matters. The evil has returned to Salem. That is the truth. And I cannot even perform a simple scrying spell to find what I want."

"Okay, so why isn't it working? If we can figure that out, we might come up with a solution."

Seabhac ran his hands down his beard and hmm'd. "What I am attempting should be child's play, but I sense two different energies. Both of them are powerful, yet different. The darkness is clingy, invasive, suffocating. The other energy is potent and earthy. It fills me with familiarity and homesickness. The problem is that they are so strong that not only do they intermingle, but they spread over the entire city. There is no way to locate the source of either one."

"I think I should go talk to Cassandra. She has spent the last nine months developing her abilities and she might be able to help. Considering the darkness was part of her, she might have a connection and be able to locate it."

"No. This is not for anyone else to get involved and risk their lives."

"Oh, but it's okay for me to risk my life.?"

"That is only because you happened to be here rather than Samson. I thought I was coming to him for help. Now that you are involved, no one else needs to be."

"There's that ego again." Memnon walked to the front door and grabbed his jacked from the hook beside the door. "I'm going to talk with Cassandra. She doesn't need to know anything, but I can ask her a few pointed questions. You stay here and keep trying your finding spell."

Memnon slammed the door after himself and smiled a bit at the sound of the *most powerful arch-druid of all time*, sputtering and at a loss for words.

Cassandra poured coffee into Memnon's cup, put the pot back on the stove, put some bread in the toaster, and turned to face her brother. With arms folded, she fixed him with a stare until he shifted on his bar stool. Memnon gulped down some fiery liquid in an attempt to delay answering her question.

As usual, his sister had seen right through his reason for being there. In record-breaking time, she had him confessing to finding a murdered body in the middle of the night. So much for trying to keep her out of it. When Samson found out he'd talked, Memnon was likely to be the next murder victim. Now he had to explain to Cassandra what he'd been doing walking the streets in the middle of the night.

"Come on. Fess up. What were you doing out and about that late at night?"

"Would you believe if I said that I couldn't sleep?"

"Nope."

"Well, that's what happened. Honestly. I was restless, and it was a warm, quiet night, so I went for a walk."

"And just happened to end up at a murder scene. That's way too much of a coincidence, Memnon." Cassandra unfolded her arms, and her demeanor softened. "Look, after everything I went through less than a year ago, I'm worried about you. For goodness sake, the murder last night was almost identical to what was happening before. You cannot comprehend how scary that was. How horrible it was to be controlled by a force intent on destruction and murder." She shivered and rubbed her hands up and down her arms.

Memnon stood and went to wrap his arms around her. "Sis, you're right, I have no idea. But I promise I won't let you go through any of that again. Besides, it's likely a copycat killer or even totally unrelated to what happened before. I am sure that Seabhac has the evil force fully contained and we are all safe. Samson will find the murderer and we can all go on living our awesome lives." He crossed his fingers behind her back as he spoke.

Cassandra pushed him away and laughed as she wiped away a couple of tears that threatened to fall. "You always could spin a tale to make me feel better. But I'm still going to worry until I hear from Samson about what's really going on. He called to say he was on his way home. He was out all night so needs some food and sleep." Saving the toast before it burned, Cassandra slathered the couple of pieces with butter and honey and placed them on a plate between them.

Memnon realized he didn't have much time. No way could he hide even the most subtle third degree if Samson was here. He'd have to ask the right questions and try not to raise Cassandra's suspicions. He cleared his throat and spoke.

"That's good. I'll let you know what's going on and you'll be able to relax." He kept his voice steady and his eyes deliberately looking down at his coffee cup. If he so much as made eye contact, Cassandra would know something was up. "I mean, it's not as if you've had any visions lately or anything. And I'm sure you'd sense if there was any kind of ancient or powerful source of energy around."

Cassandra paused with her toast halfway to her mouth. "Why? Have you?"

Memnon frowned. "Cassandra..."

"Fine." She sighed and shrugged. "Nothing. Not really."

"Not really?"

"Not like last time. Then, I was right in the middle of it all and it was so intense. Thought, emotions, sensations...all amplified to near excruciating clarity. Now, I feel as if I'm standing on the outside of something. It's hazy, but it's there. Whatever *It* is, I have no idea. But something in Salem isn't right. So, yes, I'm worried."

She turned the blazing blue gaze of her eyes on him and raised an eyebrow. "Now you fess up. I know there's more to you being in Salem than just a visit. Why are you here?"

"Like I said, just to visit." Once again, he crossed his fingers, but below the counter so Cassandra couldn't see.

"Memnon. You can't lie to me, anymore than I can lie to you. What do you know?"

Memnon knew his sister and that tone well enough to know that she would not let it go. But he didn't want her involved, and he'd promised Seabhac not to mention his presence. His brain whirred, trying to come up with a reason that Cassandra would accept. But before he could answer, the sound of a car door slamming sounded from outside.

"Hmm, sounds as if Samson is home."

Cassandra pointed her finger at him. "That doesn't get you off the hook. You're going to tell me the truth."

Heavy footsteps sounded from the front of the house and back toward the kitchen. Samson stepped through the doorway, his gaze immediately seeking Cassandra. They shared a look, and Cassandra's face paled.

"It's bad, isn't it?" She whispered.

Samson walked over to the coffeepot, poured a cup, and turned around to face them. "Yes, it is. The victim was Matthew."

Cassandra gasped. "Matthew. Oh, no. That has to mean..."

Before Cassandra could finish her sentence, Samson put his coffee down and moved to give her a hug. She stood wrapped in his arms, her small size almost disappearing amidst the large frame of the man she loved.

While considering his next move, Memnon realized Samson was staring at him over the top of Cassandra's head. Easy to do, considering she was more than a foot shorter than him. Samson's blueberry colored eyes darkened and his gaze narrowed. Memnon swallowed. He had no doubt that the Chief of Police could intimidate most criminals into confessing almost anything. He needed to make a hasty exit before Samson got a confession out of him as well. He was about to stand when Samson stopped him with words spoken in a way that made Memnon think of steel wrapped in velvet. Soft, yet powerful.

"Why were you wandering around in the middle of the night?" Samson asked.

Cassandra unwrapped herself from Samson's embrace and faced her brother. "That's what I asked him as you were coming in. He was just about to tell me." She folded her arms and stared him down.

The two of them made quite a formidable couple, and Memnon worried he wouldn't get out without telling the truth. He hated lying to anyone, let alone his sister. This wasn't right. He owed his allegiance to her, not some out-of-time, ego-bloated druid. He was about the confess it all, when a knock sounded at the front door.

"Are you expecting anyone?" Cassandra asked Samson, who shook his head. She went to answer the door, and Samson turned his attention to Memnon.

"If you know anything, you better spill it. I will not let her get caught up in all this again."

"Look, just because it's Matthew, doesn't mean it has anything to do with past events." The denial sounded flimsy even to Memnon and obviously Samson didn't believe him because he clenched his jaw and flared his nostrils as if preparing for battle.

Cassandra chose that moment to break the tension when she came back into the kitchen with the person who'd been at the door. Verity. It was an awkward moment, but Cassandra was quick to introduce Verity and Memnon and offered coffee or tea.

"No, thank you. I just wanted to stop by and see if you've learned anything about Matthew's...death." Verity's voice cracked and tears filled her eyes. "Is it related to, well, you know, him dabbling in dark magic and doing what he did?"

"Now, Verity, we've barely had time to process the crime scene. As soon as I know anything, I promise I'll call you."

While Cassandra and Samson focused on Verity, Memnon slipped out of the kitchen before they could stop him. He had a couple of things to investigate on his own and then he was going to confront Seabhac and let him know it was time to let Cassandra and Samson know what was going on. Memnon refused to lie anymore.

With a sigh of relief at being out of the awkward situation, he decided it was time to visit *Avalon's Light* and check and see how the store's owner fared after her middle of the night walk.

CHAPTER EIGHTEEN

The window shutters were closed, the door shade pulled down, and the sandwich sign wasn't on the sidewalk. Memnon could only assume that *Avalon's Light* was closed. He also assumed that the closure was related to Anwyn's middle of the night stroll at a ritualistic murder scene.

Disappointed, he debated whether to knock on the door or leave and come back later in the day. The thing was, he wanted to see her, and not only to question her about last night. When he thought of her golden amber eyes and how her auburn hair tumbled over her shoulders and down her back, he wanted nothing more than to touch her. Revel in the warmth of the ethereal light that glowed softly around her.

Realizing that he was entering a full-blown fantasy right there on the sidewalk, he gave himself a shake. Not wanting to leave without at least seeing if Anwyn was as beautiful as he remembered, he fisted his hand and lifted it to knock.

Before he could knock, the door opened and a black ball of fur ran out from the darkened store and between his ankles. With a single fluid move, Memnon reached down and grabbed the cutest kitten he'd ever seen. Lifting the kitten to his face, he looked into gold eyes that blinked at him innocently.

"Well, hello, little one. What is your name?"

Meow.

"Her name is Ebony, and thank you for catching her. She can be quite energetic and I am not always fast enough to keep up with her."

Anwyn's slightly out of breath tone washed over Memnon like liquid honey on a warm summer day. A softly dulcet voice, yet spoken with unshakeable surety. As delicate as Anwyn may appear, Memnon sensed a deep-seated power and strength simmering below the surface. She intrigued him. The oddity of her formal speech interested him. Her beauty enthralled him. He wanted, no, he needed, to know more about her. Everything.

A frown wrinkled Anwyn's forehead, as if aware of Memnon's roiling thoughts and emotions. He cleared his throat and handed the kitten back to her owner. Anwyn reached out and took Ebony in her hands, the slightest touch of fingertips igniting a spark between them.

"Oh." Anwyn withdrew her hand and snuggled with Ebony. "Must be the static in the store. It tends to build up."

Memnon nodded in agreement, though his mind whirled with what he had felt when they touched. Even the briefest moment of skin upon skin and his entire body had reacted. His heart leapt in his chest, his pulse quickened, and the urge to step closer to feel her warmth felt like a punch to his solar plexus.

"The store is not open at the moment. Was there something you needed?"

Memnon watched her lips move, but had trouble focusing and giving an answer that wouldn't make him look awkward. When he managed to speak, the words that left his mouth were not the ones he'd intended to say.

"I was wondering if you'd like to take a walk around town and then maybe have lunch. I could show you a few of the local sights. That is, if you haven't seen everything already."

Anwyn hesitated and pinned him with a considering gaze. "I suppose I have time for a personal tour of Salem. Though, I have plans for later this evening and still need time to prepare."

Relief left Memnon feeling as if a giant rock had lifted off his chest.

She said yes. Awesome. Calm down, idiot.

Memnon chastised himself for the overreaction. It was just a walk and lunch, after all.

"Let me just put Ebony back in the apartment. I shall return in a moment."

Memnon wondered if she'd gone to some high-class finishing school that taught her to speak so formally. Hopefully, he'd find out more about her because he intended to ask all kinds of questions. For informational purposes that he could relay to Seabhac, of course, not for any personal need to know all about her.

Thinking of Seabhac prompted Memnon to pull his phone out and look for a message. The druid had warned him not to return until he messaged. His reasoning was that he'd be performing a ritual attempting to detect the dark force and the source of the archaic magic Seabhac sensed about town. As Memnon left the condo, there had been some threat of turning him into a pink toad if he returned before it was safe.

Anwyn returned and Memnon detected a hint of lavender scent. It suited her. As did the flowing dress that drifted around her legs like pieces of a feather floating through the air. Decorated with gold flowers that looked like watercolors brushed onto the chiffon-like material, Anwyn made Memnon think of regal elves and dainty faeries. Otherworldly. His heart performed another flip.

He cleared his throat, bent his arm and offered it to her. The gallant move seemed the right thing to do. With only the slightest hesitation, Anwyn placed her hand under the crook of his elbow and smiled.

"So where are you taking me first?"

Being relatively new to town, Memnon had just visited all the touristy sights and knew Salem's attractions well enough to recommend a place or two.

"Since our time is limited, why don't you tell me where you've been so far, and then I'll know where not to take you."

Anwyn laughed. A soft song of sound that lifted through the air and prompted a nearby songbird to sing merrily. At least, that's what it seemed like to Memnon. He had no doubt that magic flowed through this woman's veins.

"I have been so busy setting up my store and working that the only place I have visited so far is the Old Burying Point Cemetery."

"You're kidding. How long have you lived here?"

"Kidding? I am not sure what you mean, but I have been here about a month."

There. That was another of those slightly out of step characteristics that had Memnon wanting to know more about Anwyn. He stopped walking. "Kidding. Joking around. Fooling around. Joshing. Pulling your leg."

Anwyn flushed, looking embarrassed and uncomfortable. "Yes, of course." She mumbled.

Memnon instantly felt bad. "Hey, I'm sorry. I shouldn't tease you."

"It is fine."

She smiled, and Memnon's heart expanded with an unfamiliar emotion. In that one moment of looking into golden amber eyes wavering between innocence and caution, Memnon wanted, more than anything, to win her trust. All thoughts of grilling her for information about last night disappeared.

He smiled back and took her hand in his. "Let's say we head over to The House of Seven Gables. We'll grab some lunch on the way and if we have time, we can finish the tour with a visit to Ye Olde Pepper Candy Companie."

"I have not heard of the house you speak of, nor the pepper place. I have herbs for cooking and do not need more, so I think we can avoid that visit."

Memnon almost laughed out loud, but didn't want to alienate this wonderful woman. After her reaction to being teased about the word *kidding,* he'd be more diplomatic in this reply. She was definitely an enigma who he needed to understand before doing anything to distance her.

"The House of Seven Gables inspired a book of the same name by a man named Nathaniel Hawthorne. The story is a classic and if you haven't read it, I highly recommend it. I have a copy I can lend you."

"I would like that. I have not had time to read, but maybe...one day."

Anwyn's voice drifted off into a wistful tone that made Memnon wonder what path her thoughts had meandered down. Not wanting any amount of sadness or nostalgia to ruin the day, he broke her reverie with a soft laugh.

"And Ye Olde Pepper Candy Companie is not a place to buy pepper. No. It is a wondrous place filled with melt-in-your-mouth chocolate, sugary tasty candy, and savoury sweets."

Anwyn's eyes rounded and a spark of light took the place of sadness that had been there a moment ago. "Oh. That certainly sounds like a place worthy of a visit."

"Great. We'll have to drive, as it's likely too far to walk. But would you like to eat first? I have no idea if there are any restaurants near where we are going."

"I am rather hungry."

"Anything in particular you feel like eating. I don't know the restaurants well, but I assume most of them have a varied menu."

"Something light and non-greasy. Maybe a tasty salad."

Ten minutes later, they had settled into a secluded corner table in a small bistro on Washington St. The decor was simple and comforting with hanging pendant lights that cast a glow over round white tables, gleaming hardwood flooring, and cushioned wicker chairs painted black or white. Each table boasted a white vase filled with baby's breath flowers and delicate green ferns.

Glancing at the menu, Memnon saw that the fare was also simple, yet delicious sounding with offerings of fruit and yogurt, various egg dishes and salads, pancakes, banana bread, burgers, fries, grilled sandwiches, chicken pot pie, and more. He heard Anwyn's stomach grumble, and he chuckled. "I assume that means you've found something you like."

Her face flushed with embarrassment and she placed the menu on the table. "Do you not know it is impolite to mention a lady's appetite?"

Memnon's face dropped, and he opened his mouth to reply, but Anwyn laughed at him. "I am kidding with you. Yes, I will have the egg white frittata and a glass of ice tea."

Memnon watched the glimmer of satisfaction in Anwyn's golden eyes. He would guess it a rare thing for her to tease or relax enough to enjoy an afternoon not thinking about work. But he sensed more within her than just being a workaholic. His mind's eye flashed to an ancient stone well whose depths held more than the prerequisite substance of water. Deep within the shadows of the well, rested secrets of the ages. Wishes whispered into the well in playful, yet hopeful, abandon. Animals seeking water, yet trapped in the very place that supplied the life-giving liquid. Water, mud, intangible dreams...all swirling in the darkness within the well. That is what he sensed within Anwyn.

He shivered, and the vision disappeared as quickly as it had appeared. Unfortunately, the vision was as clear as the mud in it and left him with more questions than answers. Even though he had sensed no evil intent, there was more to this woman than the soft beauty that defined her on the surface.

"Memnon?" Anwyn prodded him. A frown etched on her forehead. "The order-taker is here. Have you decided what you are eating?"

Memnon wondered again where this woman was from. That *otherworldly* aura, strange mannerisms, and way of speaking surrounded her like a cloak. She fascinated Memnon at a visceral level. Memnon snapped the menu shut and handed it to the waitress, or order-taker, as Anwyn had called her.

"The three-cheese grilled sandwich and tomato soup, of course. The perfect American lunch for a perfect day." He smiled at the waitress, who blushed and beat a hasty retreat for the kitchen to place their orders.

"I think you are a bit of a tease. You embarrassed that young woman."

"Better that than to berate her for some small or imagined mistake. I always like to leave people feeling better about themselves rather than worse. I figure if I can put them in a good mood, then they'll pass that good mood on to others over the day."

"Where I come from, that is called respect and compassion. Is it not normal around here to practice that with others all the time? Is a special effort required?"

Memnon shook his head and gave a brief, cynical bark of laughter. "If that's how people treat other people where you're from, that's where I want to live." He blew on his coffee and took a sip. Placing the cup back on the table in a slow, deliberate manner. "So, since we're on the subject...where are you from?"

Anwyn was mid-sip in her iced tea and the question must have surprised her because she choked on her drink. Swiping her napkin across her mouth, she replied. "I am sure you would not be interested in such small place in the middle of nowhere. Even finding it on a map would be quite a challenge, so I am sure you have not heard of it."

The waitress interrupted Memnon's reply by placing their food on the table, her attention focused mainly on making sure Memnon had all he needed. As she set the crackers and ketchup down, she said, "If you need anything at all...anything...don't hesitate to ask." With a sway of her hips, she sauntered to the next table where the patron was waving his empty cup about, signaling for more coffee.

Anwyn raised an eyebrow. "Hmm. My feeling is, that she means *anything*."

Memnon noted the gleam in Anwyn's eyes and almost choked on his soup. He hadn't expected such a light-hearted quip from her. From their first meeting, she'd been aloof and serious. This more relaxed and teasing side of her attracted him to her even more.

They spent a couple of minutes enjoying the food, and Memnon watched the look on Anwyn's face as she savored each bite of her food. Almost as if she was eating for the first time.

In between bites and groans of delight, Anwyn asked questions about Salem. After what seemed to be a dozen questions, Memnon put up a hand. "Slow down. I've only been in town for a few weeks. You likely know as much about Salem as I do at this point."

"Oh, I did not know you were new here as well." Anwyn frowned. "I know nothing about you other than that your sister lives here. Are you visiting? Or have you moved here to be close to her?"

Memnon considered his answer. He could best describe his life as being in limbo at the moment. Along with being unsure about his professional future, keeping Seabhac's presence a secret from a sister who always knew when he was lying, the murder, and now being entranced by the woman standing in front of him, he didn't have an answer. He shrugged his shoulders.

"I don't know."

"You do not know if you are visiting or staying?"

"Exactly."

"Oh. You are trying to decide?"

Memnon hadn't decided whether to make his home in Salem or go back to New York. But now, the thought of going back to his old life depressed him. In fact, until now, he felt as if he'd been living life with a filter on and he needed a change in order to remove that filter and live life more clearly. With more of a focus.

"I am leaning heavily toward making Salem my permanent home."

"It is a wonderful place. I am sure that should you decide to stay, you would not be disappointed."

Memnon lifted the corner of his mouth in a half-smile and replied. "Oh, I am sure that disappointment is not what I'd feel."

Chapter Nineteen

Anwyn felt her face warm and glanced away. She knew she should have said no when Memnon asked if she wanted a tour, but when he asked, the acceptance had left her mouth before her brain could consider a more suitable reply. All thoughts of that evening's summoning ritual had left her mind to be replaced by a dizzying sense of breathless need.

Now, as she looked at the man with whom she'd agreed to spend the afternoon, she realized she did not want her time with him to end. Ever. She enjoyed his easy manner and light humor that made her laugh so easily. Not to mention his muscled body, dark eyes, and deep voice that entranced her when he spoke. Her imagination went to places that warmed her. Made her feel a sharp tug of unfamiliar emotions. The bitter sweetness of meeting this man and knowing that he could not be part of her future left an ache so deep she did not know how to bear it.

With a deep breath, she cleared her mind and masked her emotions, tamping them down to deal with later. For now, she planned to enjoy these few hours. She turned to face Memnon with a smile filled with hope and determination.

"I think I am sufficiently fortified now for a tour of this house you mentioned. Could you maybe tell me a bit about the author while we make our way there? I'd appreciated the information."

She smiled at and thanked the woman who came to take away their now empty dishes. While Memnon dealt with payment, Anwyn wandered outside to wait for him. The sun shone brightly and lit the street with a cheery sense of the warm day. Anwyn smiled at a passerby while her gaze took in every detail she could burn into her memory. Life here...now...was so very different from her life before. A life that felt as if it had only ended a few weeks ago, and not hundreds of years.

She startled when Memnon touched her arm. The warmth of his hand spread like wildfire through her body. Her heart beat quicker, her breath caught in her throat, and time stood still for a moment.

Then he smiled. "Let's go. My SUV is over here." He pointed to a black beast of a vehicle that reminded Anwyn of a panther. Built for speed and power, yet graceful and sleek looking.

The historic gardens at *The House of Seven Gables* were stunning. Anwyn stood in awe, her eyes alight with wonder at the abundant beauty that had come from careful planning over the centuries. A rose trellis, wisteria arbor, fragrant lilacs whose scent wafted over the area and made Anwyn inhale with delight. Cast iron garden furniture and meandering pathways lent the finishing touches to the garden that had Anwyn envying the person, or persons, responsible for maintaining such beauty. Birds and butterflies flitted about in dazzling displays of flying skill, and the musical birdsong gave an otherworldly feel to the lush gardens.

"So, the writer you told me about, Nathaniel Hawthorne, he used to live here?"

"No. He never actually did, though the house he was born in and lived for 4 years was moved to sit just over there." He pointed to a house visible through some shrubbery.

"Relatives of his owned *The House of Seven Gables* and would entertain occasionally. Something about the house itself pulled at Hawthorne. He felt it as if it were a living thing. In his book, he wrote, *The aspect of the venerable mansion has always affected me like a human countenance... It was itself like a great human heart, with a life of its own, and full of rich and sombre remi-nisces."*

Anwyn felt a shiver wend its way up her spine. "That's haunting-ly beautiful. And interesting that you can remember a quote from the book so well. I assume it must be one of your favorites?"

"When we read it in school, I fell in love with the book and have read it every couple of years since then. What about you, don't you remember the book from school?"

Anwyn's brain froze. School. Her only schooling had been in the ways of a priestess of Avalon. "Our school was rather unorthodox and I am not sure if I remember reading that book at all."

Attempting to distract Memnon from asking any more ques-tions, she said, "Let us go in to the house. I am eager to see this place so revered by a famous writer."

Not giving Memnon a chance to reply, Anwyn turned and walked toward the entrance. A tour was just starting, so their timing was perfect. She smiled at the guide and settled herself at the back of the small group while Memnon came up behind her. She felt the heat of his body close to her back. She resisted the powerful urge to take a step or two back and lean into him. In-stead, she directed her attention to the guide and listened intently as they made their way through the house.

The guide talked about the primitive standard of living of times gone past, which made Anwyn smile. The darkly panelled kitchen with its immense brick fireplace and cast iron ovens would have been the height of luxury back in Avalon, where they used to cook over open fire in a main fire pit. The responsibility of digging the fire pit, lining it with stones, and gathering wood to keep the fire burning, was a communal effort. And it became a gathering place at mealtime as well, where people could share events or news of the day.

Anwyn could relate easier to most of the amenities in the older house than the newer technology of today. If she had returned a few hundred years earlier, she would have fit in with the lifestyle and not been so out of step with everyone.

Of course, being a witch or even a priestess in those times was obviously much more dangerous than present times. Now, with everyone so open about their beliefs, it a much safer time to be in. Evil force aside, that is. Her heart lurched as her thoughts returned to the imminent battle and how she was going to defeat the age-old evil.

"Anwyn, are you okay?" Memnon had fallen back from the group and stood looking at her questioningly.

"Oh, yes, of course. I got lost in imagining what it would be like to live like this."

The guide's voice droned on somewhere up ahead, and Memnon motioned her forward. "He's about to show us the secret passage. Come on, let's catch up."

They entered the dining room just in time to hear the guide explain how the wood storage closet beside the fireplace contained the entrance to a narrow staircase that no one had known about until the 19th century.

In a hushed tone hinting at mystery and subterfuge, the guide explained. "The secret passageway leads up through the central chimney to a small room on the third floor. No one knows its original purpose, but we can guess that it might have hidden a family member accused of witchcraft, or a place to hide smuggled goods. It could even have been part of the underground railroad to hide runaway slaves. We will probably never know for sure."

Just then, Memnon's phone rang. He pulled it out and looked at the caller I.D. "I have to take this. I'll catch up in a minute."

He moved back into the dining area they had just left as Anwyn stepped through the small door into the secret passage. She shivered as she ascended the narrow stairs that curved up to the third floor. The ancient brick walls, chipped and discolored, wavered before her and morphed into freshly mortared, new looking brick. The wooden stairs of the stairway shone as if just polished, and at the top of the stairs, hugging himself and crying, sat a young boy.

A quick glance around showed no one paying attention to the boy. In fact, the guide walked right past him, impervious to the crying boy. When the next couple of people walked through the boy, Anwyn realized she was the only one who saw him. And she also noticed that though he was solid looking, the other people had become transparent. Stepping through the door into the winding staircase had somehow taken her into the past. Though she could see past and present, the past was where she stood more firmly.

She slowed her pace enough to let the others move on ahead. The guide's voice droned in the distance and the thump of shoes and boots echoed eerily in the enclosed space. Anwyn approached the boy and sat on the stair beside him. His sobs slowed, and he turned to her, his watery blue eyes rounded in surprise.

He whispered. "You can see me."

Anwyn smiled reassuringly. "Yes, I can. My name is Anwyn. What are you named?"

The boy looked at her as if deciding whether to answer. Anwyn waited, not wanting to rush him, but knowing it would not be long before Memnon finished his phone call.

Finally, he replied, "I am Thomas."

"Hello, Thomas. Why are you crying? Is there anything I can do to help?"

Her question elicited a fresh round of tears, and the boy's thin shoulders shook. Between sobs, he told her. "They disappeared and now I am all alone. I don't know what to do."

"Who disappeared? And when?" Anwyn was not sure if the boy knew he was dead. Sometimes spirits cling to the life that they knew and continue living their life, not realizing that they no longer existed on the earthly plane. But she did not want to shock the young boy until she was sure of his situation.

"Mother and Father. I don't know when but not too very long ago."

His little body quivered against Anwyn, and she gave him a reassuring hug. He sniffled and continued. "It should have been a white light. We waited so long for the light. Instead, a black, sticky hole came and mother made me run. They stood between me and the dark until I could get away, but it took them. Swallowed them right up and I just know I'll never see them again. Tell me what to do."

Anwyn's brain raced with possibilities, but she did not know what to tell the boy. Unease planted a seed, and as Nora's words came back to her, Anwyn thought she knew what had happened. If her belief was correct, the evil force had already entrenched itself firmly in Salem, and it was going to be more difficult to defeat than she had imagined.

Memnon's voice sounded closer, and she heard him say goodbye to whomever he had been talking to. Her heart quickened as she leaned close to the boy and said, "Do not worry. I am going to save your mother and father. You stay here and if you see the dark again, hide. I promise I will help. Can you do that for me?"

"I'm afraid."

"I know, but you have been so brave. Just think how proud your parents will be when they come back and you can tell them all about your adventure."

Thomas tilted his head as if considering Anwyn's words. "I suppose. Yes, I can do that."

Anwyn kissed his forehead and ruffled his hair. He giggled. The sound of the door opening from the dining room sounded, and Anwyn knew they only had seconds.

"I will be back. I promise." She stood and as she did, the dual vista of past, overlaid with the present, disappeared and become a single scene. Thomas was gone. She turned to face Memnon and smiled. "All finished?"

He moved toward her. The stairs creaking as he stepped. "Yes. My business manager had some questions about our latest acquisition. What are you doing here all alone?"

"Waiting for you and enjoying the ambience. I can almost feel the past seeping in through the brick and mortar."

Memnon's gaze swept around the circular stairway and then came to rest on her. His dark eyes questioning her words as if he knew she was not being truthful. Lying was not comfortable for Anwyn. The very act went against everything she learned as a priestess of Avalon. But telling Memnon that she had been conversing with a child's ghost was not an option.

"We better hurry and catch up or we might miss something interesting." Memnon's gaze burned into her back as she turned and walked up the stairs to join the rest of the group.

The rest of the tour passed in a haze for Anwyn. Her thoughts raced with the implications of what she had learned and her suspicions about what the disappearance of Thomas's parents could mean. Memnon attempted to converse several times, but Anwyn couldn't have said what he asked or what she replied. She was on autopilot, and breathed a sigh of relief as soon as the tour ended. All she could think about was the upcoming ritual with Nora and Tartleby and filling them in on her suspicions.

"I am afraid Ye Olde Pepper Candy Companie will have to wait for another day. Much time has passed and I need to return home."

Memnon nodded and turned his vehicle toward the Essex St. pedestrian walkway. He pulled into a parking spot to drop Anwyn off, and opened his door to climb out, but Anwyn stopped him. "No. It is okay. I can walk myself the rest of the way and I am late for my evening plans. Thank you for today, I truly enjoyed myself."

She could not climb out of the vehicle quickly enough. Without giving Memnon a chance to reply or argue, Anwyn closed the door on any protest he might make and set a fast pace toward home. She still needed to write up a summoning spell. Regret briefly niggled at her for ending such an enjoyable afternoon, but she tamped it down. Her task was not to enjoy herself. It was to stop this evil force that had haunted the earthly realm far too long. Brighid's faith in her would not be for naught.

CHAPTER TWENTY

M emnon stared at the door that Anwyn had slammed in his face. Mid-sentence, no less. That woman presented such a wealth of contradictions.

Seemingly out of nowhere, she'd come to town, bought an existing, successful business, made it more successful, and established herself very well in the most popular area of town. A feat reserved for a person with business savvy and experience. Yet, Memnon could find no record of her ever having owned a business. And with his contacts in the business world, he'd have been able to ferret out that information.

Her formal and careful way of a talking, spoke of a finishing school education. Yet, again, there was no record of her attending any of the finer schools. And, given the fact that she'd never heard of Nathaniel Hawthorne, left him wondering about her level of education, but she spoke well and was obviously intelligent.

He could lose himself in her lovely amber-colored eyes with their shimmering glow that reflected the depths of an old soul. When they came to rest on him in a fixed stare, he felt like a child swimming amidst an ocean so vast that he couldn't see an end. Yet her innocent and delightful reactions to every mundane, daily detail made it seem as if she was seeing things for the first time.

Anwyn presented an enigma. A puzzle he needed to solve. His throat tightened at the implication of getting overwhelmed by a woman. He'd never felt this way. Never been out of control or felt such a need to know every inch of her soul.

With a pounding heart, he started his SUV, shifted into gear, and headed for the condo. Maybe Seabhac could take his mind off Anwyn.

Memnon's hope for a distraction came true the second he entered the condo. He'd no sooner closed the door than Seabhac launched into a tirade of accusations.

"Where have you been? First, you slam out of here in a huff. Then, you leave me twiddling my thumbs while I await your return. What did you find out and did you bring me any donuts?"

"I went to see Cassandra, which is what I said I was going to do."

"Hours ago." Seabhac muttered.

Counting to ten to help control his frustration with Seabhac, Memnon plopped down on the couch, propped his feet on the coffee table, and crinkled the bag of donuts he held in his hand. Seabhac's eyes lit up as he reached for his favourite snack. With measured intent, Memnon held the donuts out of reach, raised an eyebrow, and stared until Seabhac sighed and rolled his eyes.

"Fine. I will hold my thoughts to myself. You may continue."

"Good." Memnon passed the bag to Seabhac and watched him devour two cream-filled donuts in barely the blink of an eye.

"I gathered some information at Cassandra's. The identity of the murder victim ties directly to Skye and Jerome's fight with the evil almost two years ago. Which also ties to Cassandra and you, considering that you dealt with the same evil force less than a year ago."

Seabhac hovered over Memnon and snapped an impatient reply as he brushed sugary dust from the front of his robes. "Gads, we already knew it was the same force. That is why I am here, if you remember."

Memnon glared at Seabhac. The arch-druid glared back and finally backed off, sat in a nearby chair, and dug into the paper bag for another donut.

Memnon continued. "Cassandra also knows I'm lying, and now she knows the dark force has returned. Hell, it wouldn't surprise me if she showed up here demanding an explanation and she'll likely have her large and imposing husband in tow as well."

Seabhac snorted. "Stop whining about inconsequential things and tell me the identity of the victim?"

"Betraying my sister's trust is hardly inconsequential. Besides, you need to be prepared to share your presence here, because it won't be a secret much longer now."

Seabhac made a dismissive motion with his hand, sending his robe sleeve sliding up his arm. For the first time, Memnon glimpsed markings on the arch-druid's arms. Some of them raised and knotted as if burned into his skin, the dark symbols wound around his wrist, up his forearm and disappeared in the shadows of the flowing sleeve. Other symbols looked to be drawn in dark blue or black ink. None of them looked familiar. They reminded Memnon of ancient symbols he would have seen in history or archaeology books.

"Fine. Fine. You may reveal my presence as it seems to be a moot point now."

Seabhac fixed his icy blue stare on Memnon, who suddenly felt warm. Between the ringing in his ears and the heavy feeling in his limbs, he wondered if he was about to faint. He opened his mouth to speak, but his brain refused to send any words to his tongue.

Seabhac spoke. "Now. Tell me the identity of the person ritually sacrificed last night."

Without thought, the words flew from Memnon's mouth. "Matthew. It was Matthew Putnam." Saying the words released Memnon from what he realized must have been a lightly induced trance.

Damned druid. "Never do that to me again. I am not some puppet for you to control."

Seabhac wiped his mouth with the back of his hand. "If you answer my questions in a timely manner, I will not have to induce you to answer me. Now we must strategize our next move."

"I thought that is what you were doing while I was gone."

"I tried." The whispered words barely registered a sound in the room.

"Pardon. I didn't hear you."

Seabhac puffed up and bellowed. "I said, I tried. And I failed. Are you satisfied now? The greatest druid of all time has failed.

His tirade finished, Seabhac deflated and collapsed onto the nearby chair. Memnon felt a tug of sympathy because in that moment, the blustering, ego-filled, powerful arch-druid looked like nothing more than an old, worn-out man. Memnon didn't like seeing him like that. He needed to do something. Fast. Getting up from the kitchen table so fast that he sent the chair crashing to the floor behind him, Memnon strode into the living room and towered over the defeated druid.

"Come on. Giving up is unacceptable. You said it yourself. You are the only one who can defeat this evil and the one solely responsible for it being here. You don't want more people to die because of your mistakes, do you?"

Seabhac's nostrils flared, and he pushed his shoulders back as he straightened his posture. "You, a human who has lived a mere speck of my entire lifetime, dares to tell me what to do."

Thunder actually rumbled outside the window and the temperature in the room raised about 10 degrees. *No way. The damned druid wasn't that powerful...was he?*

Memnon thought of his sister and the few people he'd come to know in Salem, especially a woman with red hair and blue eyes. If he had to face down the most powerful arch-druid of all time to make sure they stayed safe...he would. With a hasty swallow and trembling inside, he faced Seabhac squarely and said, "Yes, I dare."

"Humph! More guts than I gave you credit for." Seabhac smacked his hands on his knees and stood. "I suppose we best get on with figuring out how to distinguish the evil force from the strange force that it intermingles with. But how?" He paced the floor and tugged at his beard. "I have failed to separate the energies, therefore I need to find a way to see them beyond the restrictions of this three-dimensional existence."

"Is that possible?"

"Lad. Anything is possible when you are..."

Memnon put up a hand in a gesture of protest. "I know. I know...*the most powerful arch-druid that ever lived.*"

"Humph. No need for sarcasm. Yes, it is possible, but I need a powerful light to aid me. I can adapt a spell to lighten the Earth's energy and make the dark energy more dense. Though intermingled, the spell will allow me to see them individually and follow each to the source."

"Okay, so what kind of light source? Like a flashlight, fire, spotlight?"

"Think big. I need..." Seabhac snapped his finger. "I need a beacon light from one of those tall buildings that alerts ships to danger."

"You mean a lighthouse?"

"If that is the term used to describe it, then yes."

"I know there are a few lighthouses in the area, but I doubt any of them are working. Lighthouses are not in use as much these days."

"It does not need to be in use. It just needs to possess a light. I can do the rest."

"Hmm." Memnon pulled his phone from his shirt pocket and tapped away on the screen. "It seems the closest one is on Winter Island and it's not in use, but still has the beacon light."

"Good. Let us go."

"Now?"

"Of course now. Is there a reason to wait? The sooner we identify the evil and whatever other energy is out there, the more chance of saving a life and me being able to get on with mine."

Memnon pocketed his phone, grabbed the keys to his vehicle and ran after Seabhac who was already halfway down the hallway.

CHAPTER TWENTY-ONE

N ora dimmed the lights in her altar room while Tartleby poured cinnamon tea into tea cups and Anwyn lit candles while recounting her afternoon tour with Memnon.

The tour had left Anwyn with little time to prepare the summoning spell, feed Ebony—who was not happy being left alone again—grab a sweater, and walk over to Nora's store. Her new friends had already been waiting, and Nora led her and Tartelby through a heavy brocade set of burgundy curtains into a back room.

Simply laid out, the room contained an altar in the centre surrounded by thick cushions scattered on the floor. Along one wall stretched bookshelves laden with older leather-bound books and some soft cover books. While on another wall hung various dried herbs and flowers pressed behind glass and framed. Pendulums, crystals, candles, various bolines and athames rested on a small chest in the back corner.

Nora had cleared her altar of the usual items and laid it out to prepare for the summoning spell. Tartleby must have supplied the incense because it sat in the hollowed back of a small turtle, while curls of smoke wafted up from the cone-shaped incense and left a thin trail as it dissipated in the room. The scent of cinnamon tickled Anwyn's nose. Perfect, as cinnamon augmented power and helped enhance spiritual vibrations.

The candles lit the room softly as shadows and light danced upon the walls. Purple candles to increase spiritual power. Black candles to repel negativity. Combining the respective powers of the three of them might be enough, but enhancing with as many tools as possible to boost their spiritual energy would increase their chance of bringing Seabhac to them. What they did not want to do was allow the darkness to find them. The amber crystals laid in a circle around the circumference of the room would aid in turning negative to positive in case darkness came looking for them.

Nora took a seat on the cushion beside Anwyn, while Tartleby placed a cup of tea on the floor beside each of them. The spicy scent of cinnamon drifted from the tea to mingle with the incense.

"So, explain the bit about meeting the boy ghost and what he told you about his parents." Nora asked.

"It was so sad. Thomas is his name and his parents saved him by standing between him and what he described as a black, sticky hole. He is so young that I just wanted to hug him. I promised to help him, but do not know where to begin."

Nora chewed her lower lip and considered Anwyn's words. "Honestly, I think that what we are doing is all related to Thomas's missing parents. Remember your first visit to my store when a woman complained about spirits not responding during readings, and how many mediums and tarot readers were noticing a decline in various energies that used to be there?"

"Yes, I thought it strange at the time, but became distracted when I sensed the past presence of *Faerie Enchantments and Sorcerer Magick.* Our conversation from then on seemed more important. Now, I'm thinking that her observations are all part of the presence of the darkness."

"But how can that be?" Tartleby questioned.

Anwyn's hand moved to touch her necklace as she contemplated an answer. "There are ways to collect energy to empower a person. The dark force has come to Salem once in the past and two times more recently. It has failed in its task each time, so it makes sense that it would need more strength. More power. Often unbound, a spirit's energy does not sit firmly either on the earthly plane or beyond. It would be a simple task to draw in those energies and use them for its bidding."

Tartleby's face blanched. "That is horrible. I know people who have passed on...I have connected with them. But lately, there has been nothing. I just thought they'd moved on, but now..." He turned imploring eyes to Anwyn. "Can we save them?"

Anwyn's heart broke at the loss reflected, and Tartleby's eyes. She placed her hand over his and gently replied. "I am not sure. But we will do everything we can."

Nora reached over and rested a hand on Tartleby's shoulder. "We need Seabhac, then we can plan from there. Let's begin the summoning spell."

All three nodded, reached out to hold hands and complete the circle. Candlelight reflected off their faces, dancing with shadows, reflecting fear and uncertainty. Anwyn vowed she would do her best to ensure her new friends felt no more loss. She knew her future was short, but she could help have the chance to live a normal life rather than continue fulfilling a centuries old task set out by Brighid.

Anwyn felt herself relax as she focused on the candles and prepared herself for the ritual. Deep breaths. Letting loose all the knots in her shoulders. Blocking out all sound other than her heartbeat. She closed her eyes and let the scent of cinnamon fill her nostrils and wend into her lungs. Her skin tingled as the energies of Nora and Tartleby found hers within the circle. Mingling, pulsing, growing, the three energies became one. The connection forced a gasp from Anwyn. The power was earthy, spicy, flowery. An undeniable mix of ancient forces that she was about to send out to seek Seabhac. The power of three would assuredly draw him forth.

Having memorized the spell, she recited the words. Her voice sounded strange. Not her own, rather a combination of the three of them. She felt the surprise and uncertainty of the others and mentally reassured them. Kept them steady and focused.

The spell short. The words were simply a way to focus the energy and define intent, not meant actually to perform the magic.

Into a force of one from three

In all due haste, we call to thee
We summon you, Druid
We summon you here.

The last word fell into the silence and disappeared in an echo. They sat. They waited. They looked at each wondering what to expect next. Fear sat heavy on Anwyn's heart and caused it to beat erratically. Candlelight lit the tears in her eyes as she considered what would happen if this failed. So many souls rested with her. So much planning had gone into her being here for this specific purpose. She felt ready to break down with the stress.

That was when they heard the front door fly open and crash against the wall.

CHAPTER TWENTY-TWO

A locked door didn't stop Seabhac. He waved a hand and the lighthouse door swung open as if oiled and used regularly. The rust and dust everywhere attested to the fact that the door actually had little use at all.

Memnon brought up the rear, brushing Seabhac's robes away from his face as they snapped and waved behind the druid on his flight up the stairs.

"Be careful, Druid. The last thing we need is for you to fall and injure yourself before we get rid of the evil. After that...well, if you want to risk your own life and limb, that will be up to you."

Seabhac mumbled, and Memnon heard a few phrases. *...damned impertinent human...risk my life...no respect...*

Memnon almost chuckled, but the seriousness of the situation felled it before it left his mouth. Another time, and he would have had fun prodding the druid.

Dust flew up in swirling curtains of particles that caught in Memnon's nose and made him sneeze. He waved a hand in front of his face as he took the last step and stood on the platform that ran arced in a circle around the beacon lamp.

Despite the gravity of the situation, Memnon took a moment to admire the view. The sun had just set, leaving a ribbon of flaming orange light on a distant horizon. Twilight reflected on the shimmering surface of the nearby ocean and darkened the surrounding land into shadows that turned normal objects into indiscernible shapes.

Memnon shivered. Salem no longer felt safe. Heck, it wasn't safe. He'd come here last year on a business trip for a couple of days. But from the first moment he saw the house on Winter Island Rd., he'd known it would be perfect for Cassandra. He'd convinced her to come to Salem and put her interior design skills to work decorating the house for him. She never once realized that he'd bought the house for her.

Now, Memnon realized it hadn't been just Cassandra that Salem was perfect for. He felt at home here. For the first time in his life, he felt comfortable being exactly where he was. No urges to jump on a plane and visit an exotic destination. No need to take over and re-build a flailing company. He felt complete, and he knew it was because Salem was where he belonged.

Visions of a flashing amber eyes and silken auburn hair sent his stomach into a whirl of knots. A sudden urge to defeat this damn darkness and protect the people he cared about overwhelmed him. A surge of heat built within and spread to engulf his entire body. His fingertips tingled, and he lifted his hands to see a glowing light pulsing from them.

What the hell?

"When you are quite finished playing with your powers, I need you to move out of my way." Seabhac stood in front of him, with arms crossed, impatiently tapping his foot.

Memnon shook his hands and sputtered. "I...but...I'm not playing with anything. This has never happened to me." He shook his hands again as if that would stop the glow.

Seabhac raised an eyebrow. "I see. I suppose congratulations are in order, but we do not have time, so get out of my way and let me begin this ritual."

Chastised and confused, Memnon stepped away from the light and let Seabhac have access. The arch druid raised his hands, palms facing the beacon light, closed his eyes, and took a deep breath.

Not knowing what to expect, Memnon hung back by the stairs in case he had to get out of the way quickly. Sounds of traffic in the distance receded, waves rolling into the inlet from the ocean faded to a barely discernible thrum as they rolled on to the shoreline. Nothing seemed to exist other than that place and moment. The area that housed the beacon seemed to get smaller, while Memnon could have sworn that Seabhac grew larger. The druid filled the area until a single spark of light connected him to the beacon, which glowed brighter. The glow from the light spread out farther than a second ago and spilled over the window edge to flow down the lighthouse and across the ground. Searching. Separating dark from light.

The pulsing in Memnon increased. He felt a humming connection to the light and Seabhac. Afraid he might somehow interfere with the ritual, he stepped back, but Seabhac beckoned him to stay. Within the center of the beacon, Memnon watched as a ball of light cracked open and gave life to shards of light that danced about.

Just as Seabhac looked about to speak, likely to recite the spell, the druid's eyes flew open and he dropped his hands. The abruptness sucked all the air from the room and reduced the light to its natural beacon strength.

The sudden loss of connection to the light caused Memnon to stagger. Without realizing it, he'd become part of the ritual.

"Dammit, why did you do that? You're not done yet, are you?"

"Of course not. You did not hear me recite the spell, did you? But it does not matter anymore. Come. We must make haste."

Left standing with his mouth figuratively hanging open and trying to shake off the after-effects of the *almost* completed spell, Memnon took off after Seabhac, who shouted something from below. It sounded like, *close everything off,* and Memnon wondered why the druid cared if they shut the door upon leaving. Seabhac didn't strike him as the thoughtful type at all.

Shutting the door with a resounding clang, Memnon strode over to his SUV, where Seabhac already waited in the front seat, drumming his fingers on the open window frame and glaring.

Once seated, Memnon turned to his passenger. "What the hell is going on. I don't appreciate being dragged all over like some lackey and you not even having the decency to keep me in the loop."

"I do wish you would learn to speak proper English. What loop do I possess in which you want to take part?"

With a shake of his head and a mumbled curse, Memnon started the SUV and slammed his hands onto the steering wheel. Through gritted teeth, he said, "Just keep me updated about what is going on."

"Ahh, well, that I can do. We no longer needed to perform a ritual as I am being summoned."

"Summoned?"

"Yes. You know...called, beckoned. It is a simple concept."

"I understand the word. Summoned by who? How? Where?"

"The ancient, earth magic I have sensed since coming to Salem. I assume by a summoning spell. Where...I do not know. Just drive this metal beast and I will direct you as I feel led."

With a sigh, Memnon obliged. He put the SUV in gear and drove out of the parking area toward town. A glance in the rearview mirror showed him a couple of dancing spots of light up around the beacon of the lighthouse. He was about to mention them, but the abruptness of Seabhac grabbing his arm and vigorously pointing stopped him before he could speak.

"Here. Turn here."

Seabhac's voice cracked with excitement and unless Memnon was seeing things, he could have sworn that the druid's eyes glistened with unshed tears.

"Hey, are you okay?"

"Of course." Seabhac swiped at his eyes with the sleeve of his robe. "Just drive until I ask for you to turn."

The roar of the engine was the only sound for a minute or two as Memnon drove on, waiting for his next instruction. He worried they were being led into a trap and he was definitely not wanting to be the next victim of the murderous force of evil. He shot a hasty glance at his passenger and cleared his throat.

"Are you sure it's not the darkness fooling you? Somehow masking its own magic with one that you are familiar with."

Seabhac's whispered voice broke the tense silence. "I am sure. The pure, earthy quality of ancient magic is unique to each user. No one can copy it. And this magic..." Seabhac's voice cracked with emotion, "...this magic is from one who should long be dead. She was one of my greatest friends and allies, yet never feared to contradict or put me in my place. At one time, the two of us held sway over the entire land of Britannia." He laughed. "I miss her horribly."

Seabhac shot up in his seat. "This is the turn. Now. Turn now."

With little enough notice, Memnon yanked the wheel and teetered on the edge of a ditch as he made the turn. Fortunately, the defensive driving course he'd taken a while back kicked in and he kept his vehicle on the road. Barely.

"Jeesh. More notice next time, please."

"Fine, fine. Just keep driving. We are nearly there." He inhaled and sighed. "Ahh, it feels so much like home. So right."

"Well, for everyone's sake, I hope you aren't being misled."

"Bah! It is impossible to fool me."

Memnon rolled his eyes as he heeded Seabhac's pointing finger and took another turn.

"Here. Last turn."

"Wait. I can't do that. Vehicles aren't allowed on the Essex St. pedestrian walkway."

"Foolishness." Seabhac opened the door and took off up the walkway. The sound of his slippered feet slapped on the bricks.

Seeing the direction that Seabhac headed, Memnon developed a sick feeling in the pit of his stomach. So much so that he hesitated before opening his door and following. He truly believed in Fate and that everything happened for a reason and his senses screamed at him that his recent interest in a certain gorgeous, honey-eyed woman had a purpose beyond simple physical attraction.

"Damn." He climbed out of his truck, slammed the door, and took off after the disappearing druid. The cool evening air brushed his face as he loped after Seabhac. With each step, a sick feeling grew in the pit of his stomach. Relief flooded him when he saw the druid hadn't gone as far as *Avalon's Light*. Instead, he'd entered *The Magic Corner*. Memnon slid to a stop in front of the eclectic store just in time to hear the door slam against the inside wall and Seabhac yell out a name.

"Brighid?"

CHAPTER TWENTY-THREE

A voice bellowing a familiar name followed the bang of the door against the wall. Anwyn, Nora, and Tartleby exchanged surprised looks and then all three scrambled up from the cushions they had settled on for performing the ritual. The ritual that had obviously worked.

With heart pounding and knots tying up her stomach with a sick feeling, Anwyn pushed aside the curtains to face someone that she had not seen in about 2000 years. The most powerful druid of all time. The man who had influenced the outcome of battles, taught generations of druids, been an advisor for many of the tribal kings of early Britannia. The one responsible for Brighid sending her into a state of limbo so she could be here when he needed help. All because his ego would not accept help back in Avalon. Anwyn did not know if she wanted to hug him or smack a spell on him for not listening when Brighid offered help so very long ago.

As soon as her eyes connected with his and recognition dawned in those oh-so-blue eyes, she knew what she needed to do. She ran across the floor and threw her arms around him. Relief flooded through her as the arch-druid awkwardly patted her on the back.

With a shaky voice, Seabhac said. "I assume you are the one responsible for summoning me here."

After taking a step back and wiping tears from her face, Anwyn replied. "Yes, myself and two others. We have searched for you for a while but with no success."

"Let me guess, you had difficulty separating my energy trail from that of the dark force."

Anwyn nodded. "Yes. Exactly." That was when she noticed that someone else stood behind Seabhac. It felt as if a hand clutched her heart and squeezed. Her face flushed. "Oh. Memnon." Her gaze flew between the two men in confusion. "How..."

Seabhac raised a hand to belay questions. "There is much to tell, but I need answers first. Time is running short. Salem and its people are in danger. How do you come to be here? I have tried to find out what happened to Avalon and the priestesses, but to no avail."

Visions that still seemed so recent to Anwyn flashed through her mind. The pervasive smoke that sent grey clouds to cover the area. Heavy fingers that seeped into the huts and wound around ankles . Women going about assigned tasks with such resigned fear, yet cool in their resolve to not fail, although they knew their lives were forfeit. The stark sense of finality that clenched the entire realm of Avalon. Her chest heaved with the remembering of her ordeal. The ordeal of the priestesses of Avalon. The sound of a whimper reached her ears, and she realized it was her own.

The touch of a hand upon her arm drew her back to the present, and she jolted to awareness of the now. Her gaze flew to Memnon, who stood in front of her, his dark eyes searching her face. "Just breathe. You're okay. No one will harm you as long as I am here." Nora and Tartleby had also moved in to surround her protectively.

Seabhac seemed torn between wanting to offer comfort and wanting answers. "Anwyn, it is good to see you, but your presence here confuses me. How are you here? Why are you here?" His gaze flicked between Nora and Tartleby, taking them in with a look of distrust. "And who, may I ask, are these two people?"

Nora took a step forward, but Tartleby hesitated until Nora took his arm and pulled him closer. "I am Nora and this is Tartleby."

"They have helped me and are also connected to Avalon in different ways. We...all of us...are here to help stop the dark force from killing, and to help destroy it forever."

"Pardon me?" Seabhac's voice took on an ominous. "What arrogance do you possess to think that you can stop what I could not?"

Anwyn swallowed. *Oh, oh. Why is he so angered?*

"I...Brighid sent me." She may have whispered her reply, but the effect on Seabhac was definitely not quiet or contained.

"WHAT?" The druid's bellow exploded with the force of a fire spell gone wrong. A blast of heat shot through the room and all the items in the small store shook and rattled. Seabhac's anger sucked all oxygen from the room and left everyone struggling to breathe. His eyes glowed like shards of ice-blue crystals.

Anwyn grasped the crystal that lay against her chest and prayed for help from the souls within. She weakened and became dizzy, but before she could pass out, she saw Memnon grab Seabhac's arm and spin him around. Face to face, the two of them stood. Petulant anger against steady resolve. It took but a minute before the room cooled and Anwyn could draw a breath again. She immediately looked to Nora and Tartleby to make sure they were okay. Nora knelt over Tartleby, who seemed to be okay as he nodded and affectionately patted Nora's arm.

"What is your problem?" Memnon stood between Seabhac and the others. Feet apart, shoulders back, fists bunched. Ready to react.

Seabhac's hands kneaded his robe while his body quivered with pent up emotion. He replied through a clenched jaw. "I. Have. No. Problem. The one with the problem is Brighid for interfering in my life. She spouts her opinions with regularity."

White hot, steaming anger raged through Anwyn. How dare he talk about Brighid that way. The priestess who had taught Anwyn everything, given up everything, her life included, to ensure the destruction of the darkness. And there stood the druid responsible for it all, daring to insult Brighid.

The thoughts raced through Anwyn's mind so fast that she did not realize the crystal glowed around her neck. But Memnon did. With a hasty glance at Seabhac, he stepped over to Anwyn and placed his hands on her shoulders. Their eyes connected and he spoke her name.

"Anwyn."

One simple word, yet it shook Anwyn from her roiling anger. Shamed at her emotional response when so much was at stake, she bowed her head and took a shuddering breath.

"Your necklace. It glowed."

"I know."

Memnon frowned and looked lost in thought. Anwyn watched his lips as a slight smile tugged at the corner of his mouth. She liked his lips and felt sad that she would never get to feel what it was like to be kissed by those lips. She sighed for the loss of the future she would never have.

Memnon leaned closer and whispered. "You're the *Holder of the Light*, aren't you?"

"How do you know about that?"

Before Memnon replied, Seabhac clapped his hands. "If you two are quite finished with your private conversation, I would like to leave now." He pointed a finger at Anwyn and warned. "I will banish the darkness. It is my responsibility. Once I have destroyed it, you and I can sit and have a pleasant conversation about the past. In the meantime, stay out of my way."

With those words, he spun on his heel with his robe snapping behind him. As he strode through the door into the night, he yelled back to Memnon. "Hurry along, we have no time to dally."

Anwyn's heart broke. She had never considered that Seabhac would dismiss her out of hand. And so harshly. "What do I do now?"

She did not realize that she had spoken aloud until Memnon replied. "Don't worry. I think I have a plan. Obviously, the reason for you being here has bruised his ego, but it's time for him to get over himself." He turned to Nora and Tartleby. "Do either of you know where my sister Cassandra lives?"

They both nodded.

"Good. Give me half an hour, then all of you meet us there. Don't bother knocking, just come right in. Okay?"

"I am not sure..." Anwyn protested, but Memnon raised a hand.

"Trust me. Please."

Anwyn gave a hesitant smile. "I suppose I have no choice at this point. We will be there." She looked at her friends, who both nodded in agreement.

Memnon leaned over to kiss her cheek, and heat flamed through Anwyn. Their eyes met and a feeling of euphoria followed, then crashed into a familiar feeling of loss that had plagued her since coming to Salem. As she walked Memnon to the door, she reminded herself there was no future for her in Salem or anywhere else. With a bittersweet smile, she said goodbye and closed the door behind him.

Chapter
Twenty-Four

*A*s Samhain draws near, the dark force hastens in its plan *to devour souls and create terror. Bloodlust drives it. An instinct for survival guides it. While the streets of Salem fill with laughter, masked imposters playing at magic, fun-lovers, and history-seekers alike, the darkness permeates. Grows. Anticipates the destruction of this place that has plagued it for so many centuries. Always beating it down, taunting it, entombing it in a place of nothingness. This time, there will be no one left. The arch-druid still battles his internal demon...his guilt hidden within the guise of ego. The Holder of the Light, oh so young and insecure, must find her strength. And the one who is the foundation for them all, who has already set events in motion with an unheeded act of magic, will need to bring them all together. Defeating the darkness is possible. But humans...and druids...are, oh, so flawed.*

Excerpt from *Faerie Enchantments and Sorcerer Magick*

Shadows thrown from flickering candlelight danced on the apartment walls and lent a macabre scene to the ritual. Verity lit a couple of more candles and blew on the incense stick to spread the scent of cardamom in the room. She had chosen that specific scent to help with motivation, concentration, courage, and confidence. She needed all the help she could get. After all, she was about to kill someone.

The darkness choked on the cloying scent. Winding itself in her heart, flowing through her blood, insinuating itself in her mind. It whispered. *Hurry along. This ritual bores me.*

Verity brushed aside the irritating, anxious feeling that tugged at her. She needed this moment of relaxation to prepare herself.

As she'd found out last night, killing was difficult. The look on the victim's face just before plunging the knife into their body...her son's body...was one that would live in her mind for eternity. A sob caught in her throat and her heart pounded in a panic-driven beat. Her hand stilled just as she was about to pick up the ritual knife. Confusion gripped her, and she set her shaking hand down on her lap. She needed to remember, but her head buzzed with whispers like a thousand wasps humming.

He deserved it. Remember how he betrayed you? How all of them have betrayed you? And now we need to feed ourselves with another sacrifice.

Verity took a deep breath and slowed her heart. Of course, the path to her purpose became clear once again. He had deserved to die. And his death provided a boost to her powers. Now she needed another sacrifice. Anyone would do.

She frowned. Her memory was so spotty these days. This sacrifice should be a special one. One to make everyone take notice.

Yes. But plans change. Remember. Your plans are now to increase your power because something very special is coming. You need to prepare.

That's right, she remembered now. Tonight's killing was to prepare for something even bigger. How could she have forgotten?

The knife called to her, so she picked it up, enjoying the way the light reflected off the sharpened blade. The need for blood and death sat heavy in her stomach. Throbbing. Aching. Prickles covered her and her body twitched. The time needed to be now.

With guiding whispers prodding her, she left her apartment and stepped into the dark quiet of the night. Laughter from Halloween revellers sounded off in the distance.

Yes, one of them will do just fine. Pretenders. Kill. Kill. Kill.

Verity clutched the knife to her side and, avoiding the light, slithered through the shadows as she followed the sound of laughter.

CHAPTER
TWENTY-FIVE

The chill of the October night had crept into Memnon's vehicle and he turned the heat on low to warm it up a bit. Silence sat heavy between him and Seabhac. He risked a quick glance at his passenger, only to see a stony face looking straight ahead. Lost in thought.

It gave Memnon a minute to remember the softness of Anwyn's cheek when he'd kissed it. He hadn't planned on the kiss, but before he realized it, he'd planted one. Right on her cheek. Though he'd so wanted to kiss those tempting, full lips. Drawn to her from the moment they met, the urge to protect her superseded all other needs. He did not know what *Holder of the Light* entailed or what role she'd play in the upcoming battle, but he had a feeling it was a dangerous one.

"Should you not have turned back there?" Seabhac waved at the street disappearing into the distance behind them.

"Nope. We aren't going back to the condo yet."

"But we must. I need to figure out my next step."

Even to Memnon, the protest sounded weak and unsure. "No. this is no longer just you and me. Too much is at stake. We are going to Cassandra's and telling her and Samson everything. Then we can plan together."

"No. I will risk no other lives. This is my battle to fight."

"Argue all you want, Druid. My vehicle, my rules. I'm done with following you around like a puppy dog. It's time to involve anyone who can help."

With those words, they pulled into Cassandra's driveway, and Memnon stopped the vehicle right by the front door. Taking the keys, he climbed out and went around to Seabhac's side. Opening the door, he pointed to the house. "Come on. And no arguments. We've wasted enough time with your ego."

"You realize that I have the power to turn you into a toad."

"Zap away, but we're still going inside even if I have to hop there croaking all the way."

"Are you two going to stay out there all night, or come in for coffee and donuts?"

Memnon smiled and turned to see Cassandra standing in the doorway. The light from inside the house outlined her slender form as she stood with her hands on her hips. Behind her, Samson moved around the living room. He turned back to Seabhac.

"Well. Let's go."

With a heaving sigh of resignation. "Fine." The druid climbed out of the truck, snapped his robes around himself, held his head high, and seemed to glide to the house and up the stairs. He leaned over and gave Cassandra a quick hug.

"My dear. How have you been?"

Memnon blew a derisive breath. "Sure, her you're nice to." He leaned over to kiss his sister on the cheek. "To repeat the druid, how are you?"

Cassandra waved them in and closed the door. "I was fine until I had a vision. We've been waiting for you to show up. Both of you."

"And you remembered my taste for that hot brew and the sweet treats you call donuts." Seabhac sat on the edge of a chair and chose one of his favorites from a plate of donuts. He bit into the chocolaty goodness and moaned with delight.

"Of course I did." She glanced at Samson, who came from the kitchen carrying a tray with coffee, cups, cream, and sugar.

His face reflected his don't mess with me, Chief of Police look. When he placed the tray on the table, he did so with a resounding thump that sent coffee sloshing over the edges of cups.

Cassandra rested a hand on Samson's arm. "Relax. Let's find out what's going on before getting upset."

"Too late." Samson said. His voice low and threatening. "We've had one ritual murder and if history repeats itself, there will be more." He thrust a finger at Seabhac and demanded. "What have you done now? It's the darkness. It's come back, am I right?"

"You are correct."

Samson turned his blazing gaze to Memnon. "How are you involved in this? And why the hell didn't you come to us sooner? Or did you just find out the druid was back?"

Memnon swallowed. "Umm, no, he showed up at the condo yesterday looking for you. He found me and I brought him here right away, but for some reason, he decided not to involve either of you and that he could take care of it himself."

"Not myself. I decided you were the foundation or the link to help defeat the evil. It was unnecessary to involve Cassandra or Samson this time."

"You don't get to decide what information to share or not share with me, Druid. My job is to protect the people of Salem. And Cassandra. You should have come to me right away. You didn't, and now someone is dead." Samson glared at Seabhac. "Now how do we prevent another murder and how do we destroy that damned stubborn dark force that keeps disrupting my town?"

Before Seabhac could answer, the front door opened and Memnon jumped up and motioned for Cassandra to stay seated. "It's okay. I know who it is. I asked them to come."

Anwyn stepped into the living room and said. "Is it okay? You did say to come right in." Nora and Tartleby stood by her side.

"Yes, please come in and I'll introduce you." Memnon took Anwyn's arm and led her forward, but before he could make any introductions, Cassandra stepped forward and hugged Anwyn.

"No introductions needed. I remember you, Anwyn. And of course, Nora. But I do not know who you are." She looked at Tartleby questioningly.

The small man bowed with a slight incline of his head. "Tartleby at your service."

Cassandra's eyes sparkled. "Oh, so polite. It's nice to meet you, Tartleby. Come in and sit. Would anyone like a coffee or donut?"

"Enough social prattling." Seabhac stood and took a step forward so he could look Memnon right in the face. He stabbed a finger toward the visitors. "Why are they here?"

Memnon grit his teeth and vowed to remain civil in his sister's home. "I asked them to come."

"Yes, you mentioned that already. I repeat my question. WHY ARE THEY HERE?"

The power of the druid's voice boomed through the room and raised the already palpable tension to explosive. As they didn't know what had transpired up to that point, Cassandra and Samson looked on in confusion. Samson's face hardened as anger and frustration slowly took him over. Anwyn, Nora, and Tartleby had experienced Seabhac's outburst and likely didn't want to prod him into another one. Memnon, on the other hand, had suffered enough of the druid's petty ego and temper tantrums.

"Why? Because you've battled this evil force more than once and been unable to destroy or contain it. Why? Because it already brutally murdered one person this time around and it won't be long before the next ritual sacrifice. Why? Because people I care about are involved. Again. Why? Because your over-inflated ego won't let you admit you can't do this alone. Why? Because you've spent the last 36 hours searching for the *Holder of the Light,* and in your arrogance, you totally missed the fact that she is standing right here in front of us."

Anwyn clutched her necklace and her face drained of all color. Seabhac's face hardened as he strode over to her and pulled her hand away from the necklace.

"What trickery is this? You cannot be the *Holder of the Light.* You are nothing but a novice priestess living in a time that is not her own." A sneering curl of his lips accompanied the intended insult. He made a move to grab the necklace, as if wanting to yank it from Anwyn's neck. Instead, he received a shock that sent him flying back and almost took him to the floor. A look of surprise crossed his face, but he recovered.

"How dare you attack me." Seabhac protested as he stood and ran his hands down his robes.

Her voice quivering, Anwyn replied. "I did nothing. The necklace protects itself."

"But, how..." Seabhac struggled to make sense of everything.

Memnon enjoyed seeing the haughty druid put in his place and would have let him reason things through himself, but Samson broke the tension.

"Okay, enough. Everyone to your corners. I want to know what is going on and I want to know now."

The deep, authoritative voice of the police chief garnered instant attention and Nora and Tartleby sat down on a nearby loveseat while Anwyn and Seabhac looked on in confusion.

"To your corners? What is it with you humans and your blasted way of speaking?" Seabhac mumbled.

"It means to back off and sit down while someone explains what exactly has been going on. From the minute of your arrival would be good." Samson turned his attention to Memnon. "You explain. Everyone else be quiet."

"Anwyn, you can sit over here beside me." Cassandra patted the couch beside her. Samson sat on the other side of Cassandra while Memnon remained standing with his hand on Anwyn's shoulder, hoping to reassure and relax her. Seabhac paced and mumbled.

Memnon gathered his thoughts and spoke. "Honestly, all I know is what I already told you. Seabhac showed up at the condo yesterday, looking for you. He made me promise not to tell either of you and he set about looking for the dark force himself, but also sensed another energy. A strong enough force that he couldn't separate it from the darkness. We were out searching last night." He looked at Samson and explained. "That's how I...we...ended up at the murder scene. Seabhac led us there because he sensed the darkness."

He took a breath and continued. "So, Seabhac spent today trying to locate the darkness, while I did a bit of exploring and searching myself."

"Yes, your exploring entailed spending the day sight-seeing." Seabhac stopped his pacing long enough to glare at Anwyn. Memnon noticed Cassandra's interested look at the woman sitting beside her.

"Yes, well, you just had to do everything yourself, so what did you expect me to do? Anyway," he continued before the druid could interrupt him again. "Seabhac needed to magnify his energy, and I thought of the light at the Winter Island Lighthouse, so we headed there. Before we could complete the ritual, Seabhac took off. I followed, and we ended up at *The Magic Corner*, where we found Nora, Tartleby, and Anwyn. It seems they had just performed a summoning spell directed at Seabhac. Turns out that Anwyn is a priestess from Avalon...somehow here in this time, but don't ask me how. And she is the *Holder of the Light* that Seabhac has been searching for." Memnon shrugged. "That's all I know."

Samson opened his mouth to speak, but Cassandra put her hand on his knee and shook her head. She turned to Seabhac and asked. "Obviously, the evil escaped your care, and in less than a year. If we couldn't destroy it before and it escaped you so easily, what do you propose we do this time."

"*We* do nothing. It is my responsibility alone. And you are mistaken about the timeline. Ainevar and I took the evil to the Netherworld and contained it. Time moves differently there, so for us, it has actually been about 200 years since we left Salem. Now, if I have answered enough questions, I need to leave. There is much to prepare."

Before anyone could speak, Anwyn stood up and stared at Seabhac. "Stop. Just stop. You show blatant disrespect for these people who battled at your side less than a year ago. People who risked their lives to help you contain the evil." Her voice faltered, and Memnon encouraged her with a nod. Her eyes softened for a moment, then she returned her attention to Seabhac.

"And your contempt for Brighid's carefully laid plans is beyond comprehension. Dozens of novices and priestesses of Avalon willingly sacrificed their lives to ensure Ainevar's escape and to allow me to be here to help you succeed in the final battle with this dark evil. Do you not understand? Avalon, Brighid, everyo ne...DIED. It was your ego that made that a necessity in the first place. Brighid tried to warn you. Tried to reason with you. But you would not listen. And Avalon is gone. Brighid is gone. And that IS your responsibility more than any dark force."

Tears ran down her face to mingle with the pain of loss etched so clearly in lines of despair. The room was silent other than the sob that caught in Anwyn's throat. Nora and Tartleby moved to comfort her, and Memnon stepped aside to allow them to wrap her in a hug.

Seabhac's face whitened and his mouth opened and closed. It was the first time Memnon had seen the druid at a loss for words. Before anyone could question Anwyn's horrific explanation of past events, a sizzling flash filled the room. The ensuing white light cast out the shadows from every corner and left everyone blinking to regain their vision.

CHAPTER
TWENTY-SIX

"**S**he is not wrong, my love. You hold more responsibility for whatever happened in Avalon than you do for the dark force."

The lilting tones of a familiar voice accompanied the bright light. A voice that Anwyn remembered well from her days in Avalon. A voice from one who she respected and look up to as a paragon of beauty, intelligence, and virtue.

"Ainevar." Seabhac finally spoke. With a hearty bellow of joy, he ran to her side and enveloped her in a hug. Not a tight hug, though, as the size of Ainevar's belly and the book she carried did not allow close contact.

A moment of confusion ensued as Cassandra moved Seabhac aside so she could share a hug with the woman who used to inhabit her body as a spirit.

Anwyn noticed how the two of them could have been twins with similar hair color, height, facial structure. Their story was one that she wanted to hear once this was over. Then she sighed in frustration. Once again, her thoughts wandered to a future that did not exist for her.

With bittersweet emotions, she stepped in to hug her mentor tight and whispered. "I have missed you so much." The reunion lasted but a moment as the gravity of the situation took hold. Smiles faded to hardened resolve, hugs receded into awkward stances as everyone looked at each other, waiting for whatever came next. More than one interested look fell to Ainevar's rounded belly.

"I know I'm stating the obvious," Cassandra said. "But you're pregnant. How? I mean, I know *how,* but I didn't think it was possible."

"We did not think so either." Ainevar smiled at Seabhac, who put his arm around her shoulder and held her tenderly. "Who knows what the Goddess has in mind, but here I am. The size of a large watermelon."

Seabhac laid his free hand on Ainevar's stomach. "Why are you here, love?"

Ainevar moved from Seabhac's protective embrace and stepped toward Anwyn, her blue eyes fixed in a hypnotic stare at the crystal necklace. With each step forward, the room warmed. Once Ainevar stood directly in front of Anwyn, the necklace sent a tendril of light to touch the cover of the leather-bound book. The glow from the necklace encompassed the book and gently faded.

"I brought the book because it compelled me to do so." Her gaze softened as she looked at Anwyn. "I assume you are the *Holder of the Light* and this," she gestured to the necklace. "Is the *Light of Many Souls.*"

"Yes." Anwyn replied. "Does it mention that in the book? I assume that is *Faerie Enchantments and Sorcerer Magick* you hold in your hands?"

"Yes, and yes."

Anwyn reached out to touch the book. Seabhac moved to prevent her from doing so, but Ainevar stopped him with a look and cautioned him.

"Leave her be, Seabhac. The book reaches out for her and as much as it may pain you, you are not alone in this fight."

Anwyn hesitated, half expecting the druid to smite her with a look. But he obeyed Ainevar's caution and dropped his hands to his side. Satisfied that she was safe from his anger, for the moment at least, she laid her hand upon the book.

A stifling sense of being alone threatened to drop her to her knees. An overwhelming understanding of the vastness of the universe crept into her soul, and she realized it was a brief look at the time she had spent in the limbo of nothingness. It lasted a mere moment, and then a sense of euphoria enveloped her. A feeling of the familiarity of home and family.

Brighid.

A sob escaped her lips, and she looked pleadingly at Ainevar for comfort.

"You are safe, child. Brighid watches over you, as do all the souls who gave their lives. You are where you need to be."

"What foolery is this?" Seabhac waved his hand dismissively. "There is much to do and as pleased as I am to see you, Ainevar, your attention is better spent taking care of yourself and our babe." His voice softened. "I implore you to return home and have a care. I will deal with the evil here and return to you both shortly."

Ainevar laughed. "My sweet stubborn druid. No, I shall not return home until I have done what I came to do. Anwyn has her tale to tell and you will listen." She fixed a steely blue gaze on Seabhac, who puffed his chest. They stared, and the room became heavy with tension. Literally. Anwyn felt the pressure, and by the look on the faces of the others, they felt the same.

"Seabhac." Ainevar spoke. Her voice a husky growl.

"Ha. Fine. I shall listen. Then you return home." Seabhac gestured to a chair. "Sit, woman, before you fall over. You have a babe to think about, you know."

With a snort, Ainevar sat. "Tell me something I do not know." She sighed in relief as she sank into a comfortable lounger.

"Refreshments, please." Seabhac ordered as he sat on a chair beside Ainevar and snapped his robes into place.

Cassandra rose and bowed Seabhac's direction. "Your wish is my command, oh, mighty one."

Seabhac nodded. "Now, see, there is a woman who respects my power."

Samson laughed. "You really don't know women very well, do you, old man?"

With Nora's help, it only took Cassandra a couple of minutes to refresh coffee, cold drinks, and bring out more donuts.

The knots in Anwyn's stomach grew with each moment until everyone had settled, and Ainevar turned to her with a nod. "Tell your story, child. And leave nothing out. We need to hear it all."

So she did. She told of the chaos of women and girls preparing to die, crackling fires, choking smoke, and the resigned fear on the faces of the acolytes and priestesses she respected and loved as family. Her voice cracked when she recited the events in Brighid's tent and the request to complete an unknown task she needed to commit to before learning the details. The presentation of a box of jewels and coins to help her at an unspecified time in the future. And, breathlessly, she related the purpose of the necklace, as well as Brighid's admonishment to run for the cliffs and to drink the sleeping potion only when the necklace glowed and she felt the presence of all who had given their lives so their souls could reside in the necklace.

She told of the great fear and desolation standing on the clifftop with the wind whipping around her and knowing everyone she loved was about to die while she lived. Her last thought was one of Brighid's face as she yelled the last words Anwyn ever heard from the High-Priestess.

ANWYN. RUN. Do not look back.

Tears fell freely, and she forced a sob back down her dry throat. She took a sip of water and peered at Seabhac from under her lashes as she set the glass down.

"I floated in nothingness for so long. Unaware. Not living, yet not dead. My last memory was of drinking the potion on a stormy clifftop. Then, I awoke standing in front of a storefront that was for sale. I knew naught how long had passed, where I was, who I even was until my head cleared. I held a box in my hand and wore clothing very different from what anyone else wore. It took only a couple of minutes for the fog to lift and I knew what I had to do. I bought the store and began my search for Seabhac."

Anger prompted her next sentence. "Brighid spoke many truths that last day. She said that your ego would not allow you to listen to her. She tried to help you with knowledge you struggled with, yet had been part of her abilities for years. Your plan to send Ainevar away with the book and knife would fail. She knew that, yet you would not listen." Anwyn shot a look of accusation at Seabhac, who shifted in his chair and looked away.

"No choice remained for her, but to arrange events such as she did. Your obstinance and your ego were your undoing and continue to be so. Yet she has planned for the evil to be defeated."

Anwyn clutched the necklace for warmth and reassurance. "Since coming to Salem, the necklace has grown stronger. It now contains the souls of all the witches murdered during the Salem witch trials. They willingly joined the souls of the priestesses of Avalon."

With a smile, she waved a hand at Nora and Tartleby. "We also have my new friends who have waited, prepared, and sacrificed for this day as well. Their story is theirs to tell, but they are as much a part of Brighid's plans as we all are."

It was at that moment, she realized that during her tale, Memnon had moved to sit on the arm of the chair beside her and his hand rested on her shoulder in a gesture of support. A warm buzz of energy sizzled down her spine, and she moved closer to him to enjoy the satisfying feeling of comfort.

The room full of people sat silent, and Anwyn wondered if she had talked too long or possibly upset them with her story. It was Cassandra who spoke first.

"You remember nothing about your time in the Netherworld? When I was there, I was aware of time and even had a muted sense of the earthly realm."

"Brighid had no knowing of how long I would be there. The Netherworld can drive a person insane in a short time, so the potion she gave me put me in a suspended state."

"So, when you woke up, your memories of Avalon were as fresh as if they had just happened?" Cassandra questioned.

"Yes."

With tear-filled eyes, Cassandra stood up and came over to pull Anwyn up from her chair and engulfed her in a hug. "You lost everything and everyone. With memories that felt as if they had happened that day, you awoke in a place so different it had to be terrifying, bought a store, built a business, made friends, and found Seabhac to fulfill your task." She held Anwyn at arm's length. "Anwyn, you astound me. And I am so very sorry for your loss."

Anwyn fought to keep from folding to the floor in a blithering mass of tears. She had kept so much inside since coming to Salem, and now she had friends who understood her pain.

Ainevar's voice broke into the teary moment. "We are all very sorry for your loss, Anwyn, but now we must plan, together." She nudged Seabhac's arm. "Agreed, my love?"

Seabhac sighed and faced Anwyn in contrition. "I am truly sorry for what transpired in Avalon. In more ways than you can ever imagine. But it does not change the fact that this is my battle to fight. No one else's."

Anwyn felt the blood leave her face and give way to an anger that swelled from deep within. Anger built to a rage and flared into an uncontrollable inferno. The necklace vibrated so much that she thought it would pound a hole through her chest. The book, still held by Ainevar, jumped from her hands and smashed to the ground, its pages flipping wildly until they came to rest on a page that glowed.

Finally able to speak past her anger, Anwyn practically spat the words at Seabhac. "How dare you dismiss all those lives as if they were nothing. Brighid was correct. Your ego is massive and will be the end of us all."

Seabhac's eyes flared and an icy cold filled the room to battle the heat generated by the necklace. From the corner of her eye, Anwyn saw Memnon and Samson direct everyone to a corner of the room, where they stood in wide-eyed dread. She fought the cold that filled her limbs and pushed through the miasma that filled the room. Fueled by her anger and loss of all the people she loved, she made her way to Seabhac. Lifting her hand, she put every ounce of emotion that had built from that day in Avalon and she channeled it into her hand and smacked him across the face with all of it . The druid's head snapped back and his feet left the ground as he flew across the room to smash into the wall.

Then there was silence.

The cold and heat disappeared.

Everyone waited.

Anwyn waited for reprisal and Seabhac looked ready to do exactly that as he stood and lifted his hands.

"Stop." Ainevar commanded. She knelt down and read the pages where the book had opened.

"Seabhac. I know why you are so adamant about doing this yourself, as does the book. I think it is time that you stop being so damned stubborn and accept help." She lay a hand on her stomach. "We will not stay here and watch you die." She handed the book to Seabhac, who took it reluctantly and read the entry.

No one had moved yet. Once she had released her anger and excess energy, Anwyn felt better. More able to deal with the situation without exploding as she had. Though that transgression came more from the influence of Brighid through the necklace than from herself.

Seabhac came to the end of the journal entry, and his shoulders sagged. With a sigh, he sat in a nearby chair and put his face in his hands. When he read out loud the one sentence, fatigue and sadness replaced his usual bluster and arrogance.

"The arch-druid still battles his internal demon...his guilt hidden within the guise of ego."

"Why do you feel guilty?" Memnon asked. "You told me yesterday that the Fates set you on that cliff as a balance for the energy. You also said that for you to be responsible for the dark force would make you the Creator of All, which you're not. So, why the guilt? Come to think of it, why were you on that cliff?"

Seabhac stood and faced Memnon, his face darkening with each question Memnon shot his way. Dark turned to thunderous, and Anwyn feared the druid might suffer a fit of apoplexy right on the spot. Instead, he collapsed in the chair, his face resigned.

"I was there to cheat death. Vespasian, the druid-killer, had hunted me for months and somehow avoided all my spells. That cliff was about to become my tomb, so I begged the Heavens to let me live on in spirit as a protector of this journal." He motioned toward *Faerie Enchantments and Sorcerer Magick*.

"I touted that only druid power could keep it safe and as I was the most powerful druid of all time, they had no choice but to let me live. Even if just in spirit. That arrogant claim signaled the beginning of the evil force we now battle. The Heavens darkened. The ground beneath me trembled. Jagged flashes of light streaked across the black of the night. Highlighted by the lightning and black, roiling clouds, I saw Vespasian...so did the evil. In the next flash, a dark bolt struck him. It brought the darkness to physical form. The same form that bounces from person to person and destroying anything good in its path. The Heavens fulfilled my request, but I had no inkling that so many innocents would pay the price. All of it is my fault."

Silence signaled the end of Seabhac's confession, and everyone shared uneasy glances. The shrill ring of Samson's cell phone cut through the tension and Samson excused himself to go answer it in the kitchen.

Anwyn understood Seabhac's reasoning for feeling guilty. She also knew there was no time to pander to his ego.

"Nonsense." She said. Her voice came across loud and self assured, though her hands shook at the thought of arguing with the druid. "You are no more responsible for the evil's presence than you are for the clouds in the sky, or the tides of the sea. The evil existed, and the Universe sent it to you because your abilities superseded those of anyone. Your sarcastic, mocking self analysis of being the most powerful druid ever is actually a statement of fact. If a lesser human had to deal with this darkness, they would not have curtailed it and by now the evil intent that it wishes to instill upon the world would likely have spread everywhere. You may think you had influence enough to taunt the Universe into reigning evil upon the world, but, in actual fact, the Universe decided you would be a worthy recipient of the evil. Do not let your arrogance assume any other scenario."

"Bravo. You have certainly learned much wisdom since your early days in Avalon. I could not have stated it better myself." Ainevar smiled at Anwyn, then turned her attention to Seabhac. "She is correct. Let your ego go. The book itself writes that you must put your ego aside and work together. Anwyn is the *Holder of the Light,* the necklace entrusted to her holds the souls of many who gave their very lives to ensure a positive outcome to the final battle and it holds the souls of the witches who already died at the hand of the evil force. Do not dare to put yourself above all that others have sacrificed. If you do so, you are not the man I thought I loved."

"Hey, sorry to interrupt, but I have a question." Memnon interjected. "On that cliff, before the evil possessed Vespasian, you couldn't have known how important your journal would become in this battle. I mean, at that point it was merely your journal, so why was it so important to save?"

"Humph! Merely my journal is enough of an insulting description of a book that held all my knowledge. But, the book is so much more." He glanced about the room, his gaze resting on the faces of each person as if weighing them up. "No one knows what I am about to reveal, and it must remain a secret. Understood?" He waited for nods and murmurs of agreement before continuing. "The book not only holds my knowledge, which is plenty enough," he shot a withering glance at Memnon, who shrugged. "But it also holds all knowledge since the beginning of time. The history and recounting of the world and all its civilizations."

Nora gasped, her face losing all color. "What? And I had it in my shop in nothing more than a glass case. Oh, my god. I think I feel sick."

"No worries." Seabhac assured. "It is well-protected and only the *Guardian of the Knowledge,* which is me, knows how to access the information."

"That seems rather short-sighted." Memnon threw up his hands in disbelief. "Here you are thinking about taking on the evil by yourself and leaving all that knowledge lost if you die. What the hell."

Seabhac waved a hand dismissively. "That is moot now, as I have decided to work with Anwyn and her necklace to end the darkness that has threatened Salem for so many centuries. Before it spreads and wreaks havoc in other places."

Ainevar relaxed her shoulders and Anwyn lifted her hand to hold the crystal in a silent acknowledgement of relief.

A short-lived relief as Samson stepped into the living room from the kitchen and uttered the words they all dreaded. "There's been another murder."

CHAPTER TWENTY-SEVEN

"**T**his one is at Winter Island Lighthouse."

Memnon and Seabhac shared a look. "The lighthouse," Seabhac mumbled. "That makes no sense. Yet there is no such thing as coincidence." Seabhac rubbed his chin as he paced the floor.

"What are you talking about?" Samson asked as he gathered up his jacket and keys.

Lost in thought, Seabhac didn't reply, so Memnon answered for him. "Remember? We were at the lighthouse earlier this evening."

Samson snapped to attention. "Damn, that's right. What the bloody hell did you do out there?"

"Nothing. We didn't perform the ritual that Seabhac intended because he heard the summoning sent out by the others." Memnon inclined his head toward Anwyn, Nora, and Tartleby.

"Not true." Seabhac said. "Something happened. When your hands glowed, you opened a portal of light and let in the souls to help with the ritual."

Memnon shook his head in confusion. "I did no such thing."

Seabhac rolled his eyes. "Those shards of light were souls summoned to aid the ritual. They came at your behest. Obviously, you did not close the portal, and that is what would have drawn the evil to that spot. It likely soaked up the souls and used their energy for the ritual."

"No. That can't be right. I don't have any power other than minor visions and slightly heightened senses when it comes to reading people's energy."

"Bah! You obviously have no idea." Seabhac shook his head. "What is it with this modern world when a person's powers are ignored and not put to use."

Samson put up a hand. "Okay, fine. None of that matters now, as we have another murder and I need to go." He leaned over to kiss Cassandra and headed for the front door.

Seabhac stepped in beside Samson. "I am going with you." He nodded to the rest of the group. "I suggest the rest of you go get some sleep. Memnon, make sure they make it home safely."

"Wait a minute." Anwyn protested. "After everything that has gone on tonight and you are still going out on your own. I thought we agreed to work together?"

With a deep sigh, Seabhac turned to her and talked as if addressing a child. "I am merely going to track the evil. As it has already killed tonight, there is no worry about another death. You need rest so that tomorrow we can go after and destroy it for good this time. I, on the other hand, do not need to sleep."

"Oh. That makes sense." Anwyn put her hand to her face to cover a yawn. "And it is a good idea."

Memnon watched Anwyn yawn and fought the urge himself. The day had been long and eventful, so everyone could use some sleep. "Come on, I'll drive the three of you home and make sure you're settled before going to get some sleep myself."

"If you're coming with me, Seabhac, let's go."

"Yes. Fine. I will just say goodbye to Ainevar." He put his hands on either side of her face in a gentle, loving way. "You go home and take care of yourself and our babe. I will be there as soon as possible. I promise."

"I will go, but only for the babe. Otherwise, I would fight at your side, my love."

"I know. But I think we have enough warriors to defeat the evil and end the battle permanently. Do not forget to take the book with you. "

He leaned down to kiss her as she picked up the book and shimmered into nothingness. For a split second before settling into his normal grumpy look, Seabhac's face shone with the soft look of love. The vulnerability of the druid surprised Memnon, but he also felt envious at the bond that Seabhac and Ainevar shared. A love literally tested by time.

He glanced at Anwyn, who had her head bent in quiet conversation with Nora and Tartelby. Her hair gleamed with red-gold highlights and hung in thick waves almost down to her waist. The delicate features of her face reflected worry and tiredness. Yet even the mask of stress on her face couldn't detract from her ethereal beauty.

Damn. I think I'm falling hard.

The extra beat in his heart backed up his thoughts. With a sigh, Memnon shook himself from his reverie long enough to say goodbye to Cassandra and direct the others out to his vehicle. They had taken a taxi there so they could hitch a ride back in his SUV.

The short drive was a silent one. Each person lost in thought. Anwyn's insides felt as if they had twisted into knots. Standing up to Seabhac and decrying his actions had been a desperate move, but he had left her no choice. Lives counted on him getting over his ego and too many people had already sacrificed to ensure destruction of this rampant evil. Of course, she had not realized the guilt driving Seabhac's insistence on such lone wolf tactics.

She gave a quiet sigh and snuck a peek at Memnon so patiently and easily steering the metal vehicle among the crowded streets. Despite the lateness of the night, people filled the streets and stores, taking full advantage of Haunted Happenings. It seems as if Samhain had become a busy celebration in this future time. Not as reverently celebrated as in Avalon, but more of a time for dressing up and merry-making.

As if sensing her attention on him, Memnon turned and gave her a quick smile. Her stomach felt as if it had fallen a great distance. She gasped a quick breath to steady herself and turned back to watch the road, hoping he had not noticed the effect his dazzling smile had on her.

Memnon was fortunate enough to find a parking spot fairly close to the Essex St. pedestrian walkway.

"A cup of tea and bed sound heavenly about now." Nora said as she closed the SUV door behind her.

Tartleby nodded. "That does sound delicious. I could walk you back to your place and we can have a cup together before I head home?"

Nora and Tartleby shared a smile. "I would appreciate the company." She glanced uneasily from Anwyn to Memnon. "Do you feel up to a cup of tea, Anwyn?"

Tempted, but also tired, Anwyn shook her head. "No. I am exhausted, so bed is my next logical stop. Besides, Ebony will be hungry and lonely and likely pounce on me in retribution for daring to ignore her for so long."

"Okay. Good night, then. I'm sure Memnon will take care of you."

Anwyn noticed the glint in Nora's eyes and the hint of an underlying meaning in her parting words. Her face flushed. Was her interest in Memnon that obvious? Waving at her friends, Anwyn started walking, hoping Memnon would not notice her blushing face. Just the mere thought of him taking care of her in the way Nora had insinuated made her breathless. And uncomfortable for many reasons.

"Hey. Are you okay? You're practically running for home."

"Oh, umm, sorry." She slowed her pace and took a calming breath.

The walk to her place was short and silent. Anwyn did not know what to say, as everything that Memnon knew about her had changed in the last couple of hours. What would he think of her now? Not that it mattered, as once they destroyed the evil, her life would be over. Her mind whirled with thoughts of her life ending, while her body warmed with the wondering of what it would be like to be kissed by the man who now stood in front of her.

"Do you want me to come in and check around?" Memnon asked as he reached up to tuck a stray curl behind Anwyn's ear. Her skin flamed when his fingertip touched her cheek. She swallowed and tried to look away, but his dark eyes drew her into their depths.

"I will be fine. Do not bother yourself." Even to herself, her voice sounded shaky.

"It's no bother. You know, I found you fascinating before, but now I have to add amazing to that original impression."

Anwyn turned and fumbled with the door handle, desperate to get away from this man and how he made her feel. Nothing in her upbringing or training prepared her for dealing with the sensations a man like this sparked inside. He stood close enough behind her that the heat of his body wrapped around her in comfort. His breath tickled her ear and the butterflies in her stomach fluttered ferociously. Finally, the door opened and Ebony made her usual dash out the door in greeting.

Memnon was quick to scoop up the kitten and cuddle her under his chin before handing the wriggling black ball of fur to Anwyn. "I think you're right. She needs some attention."

A brief sense of envy flashed through Anwyn. What would it be like to be snuggled so close to Memnon? She would never know and there was no sense pondering the impossible, so, keeping her hand on the doorknob, she hardened her resolve.

"Thank you for seeing me home. I'll be fine from here."

Memnon quirked an eyebrow and fixed her with a stare. In what seemed to be slow motion, he leaned forward. Anwyn's heart beat fiercely and panic flared in her chest. He was going to kiss her, and her body refused to move. She wondered what it would feel like to be kissed. During her training, there had been no time to explore physical relationships between men and women. She always thought there would be time for that later.

And now, those very kissable lips moved closer to hers. But at the last second, Memnon tilted his head to the side and kissed her on the cheek instead of the lips. Disappointment dropped a rock into Anwyn's stomach.

Before Memnon backed away, he whispered in her ear. "When this is over, you and I have a lot to talk about. Now lock your door after me and go get some much needed sleep."

In barely a blink of an eye, Memnon disappeared into the dark of the late night and left Anwyn leaning her forehead against the locked door. She sighed. Unfortunately, there would be no talking once this was all over. And that thought hurt her more than she could have imagined.

CHAPTER
TWENTY-EIGHT

Memnon gripped the steering wheel and cursed himself for being such a gentleman. Damn, he'd wanted to kiss her so badly, but something had made him behave and kiss her cheek instead of tasting those luscious looking lips. Ugh! On one hand, he cursed this entire situation for keeping him from spending the time getting to know Anwyn. On the other hand, without the presence of evil and the irritation of babysitting Seabhac, he'd never have met Anwyn. And the thought of never having heard her voice or being able to look into her lovely golden colored eyes was unacceptable. Learning of her history and reason for being in Salem fascinated him, but the woman herself fascinated him even more.

Forgetting his destination for a moment, he almost missed his turnoff. He cut the corner short and his rear tires went up and over the curb. Muttering a curse for his lack of attention, he refocused on driving. He'd decided to head out to the lighthouse because someone needed to keep an eye on Seabhac. The stubborn druid was not well-known for his diplomacy or for keeping a low profile. Samson would be too busy to babysit, so Memnon figured he'd keep Seabhac out of trouble.

Besides, after Seabhac's comment about him leaving a portal open and possibly being responsible for the location of the murder, if not the murder itself, Memnon had to find out what was happening. What he could do to help.

Even from a distance, flashing lights and voices carried across the camping grounds and parking area as he approached the lighthouse. Yellow police tape separated the rocky walkway leading to the lighthouse from the mainland, while police cars and the coroner's van filled the parking area. Flashing lights lent an ethereal quality to the dark night. Voices drifted across the water and filtered into the distance.

Memnon climbed from his SUV and headed toward Samson's familiar voice. Even this far from downtown and this late at night, people crowded around gawking. Halloween revelers dressed in inventive costumes added to the otherworldly feel of the ritual murder site. A few reporters also wandered about trying to find a way in or a police officer with loose lips.

Nodding at Jaks, who stood guard at the cordoned off entrance to the lighthouse walkway, Memnon lifted the police tape and ducked under. Not only a police officer, Jaks was also a friend of Samson's and Cassandra's, so gaining access to the crime scene was easy for Memnon.

He left the grumbling reporters behind and found Samson at the base of the lighthouse. The police chief was just pulling a sheet up over the body while a photographer took photos of the wall of the lighthouse. Blood patterns sprayed out across the weathered white wall and left drip marks as it slowly ran down the wall to mingle in the rock and dirt below. The stark shape of a spread-eagled human body showed white in the middle of the red blood.

Fighting down nausea, Memnon cleared his throat and asked. "Is it anyone we know?"

Samson's face reflected anger, frustration, and the stark look of despair. "No. I don't know him, but that's not the point. My job is to protect the people of Salem and obviously I can't do that one thing. Damn!"

"Hey. None of this is your fault. This evil has been around for centuries, so you can't pressure or blame yourself like this. It's not as if battling an ancient evil that birthed from the heavens in a single flash of lightning is a normal part of your job description."

The corner of Samson's lip lifted in a half smile, then hardened into his business-like police chief look. "Yeah, well. I do take this personally and whatever it takes, this evil is going down." Samson stabbed his finger toward the water where Seabhac stood in a trance with his arms raised upward. "You get him on track, find that evil S.O.B. and destroy it. Do whatever it takes. I have work to do at the station, but keep me updated if you find anything tonight. Otherwise, we'll talk tomorrow."

Memnon nodded, but Samson had already stalked off to bark orders at some nearby police officers. He turned his attention to Seabhac, who stood by the water at the foot of the lighthouse. The druid was now chanting or casting a spell with his arms raised upwards and eyes closed. Memnon climbed carefully down the rocks and stood quietly while Seabhac finished his chant.

"I did not think you would stay away. You are too curious for your own good." Seabhac lowered his arms and turned to climb the rocks back up the lighthouse.

Memnon followed him, being careful about where he stepped as the lights set up by the police didn't quite reach this far.

"What did you expect after you told me I was responsible for the murder?"

"No. I said you opened a portal and let in spirits that attracted the evil to this spot. The murder would have happened, regardless. Just in a different location."

"That doesn't make me feel any better. I didn't even know what I'd done. How could I be so unaware?"

"No matter now. There are other concerns to contend with." Seabhac waved his hand, the brisk breeze coming off the bay snapping his sleeve against his arm. "The evil is powerful and I sense a more sinister intent within its energy than I have felt in the past." His voice dropped to a whisper. "It knows this is the final battle, and it knows the fight is no longer mine alone. It will prepare. We must find and destroy it before it becomes stronger. I have ascertained its general direction. Since you are here, we can search together."

"What you mean is that I get to be your chauffeur."

Seabhac waved dismissively and set off at a quick pace toward the SUV. Memnon sighed and followed. He'd wanted to have a look at the portal and maybe get a feel for what he'd done and how he'd done it. Obviously, that would have to wait. He still had trouble believing he possessed powers to open a portal to another dimension. How could he have lived his entire life and not seen any sign of that ability?

"It is likely that the minute you stepped within the ethereal boundaries of Salem, your powers came into being. They lay mostly dormant until then." Seabhac waited at the SUV, tapping his foot impatiently.

"Stay out of my mind."

"You had a question. I answered it. Salem is steeped in magic, history, death, life, magic. The place throbs with power that multiple witches and magical practitioners have fed into over the years. Now, can we please go before I lose the already thin thread of evil that I sense?"

Memnon didn't reply. He was too busy thinking about Seabhac's words and wondering what other powers he might possess. Just another thing to focus on once this final battle thing was over. He climbed into the driver's seat, started the SUV, and drove into an uncertain darkness with a powerful druid at his side. When had his life gotten so strange? Oh, yes. When he'd come to Salem.

So much blood. It covered her arms, ran down her hands and stained her clothes in a red display of spots and blotches. Her heart pounded in fear. She didn't remember how she came to be covered in blood, and she certainly had no idea where she was. Her brain hurt and, try as she could, she couldn't clear the fuzz.

You did what you needed to survive. Feel your strength now. Your power has never flamed so hot. The reach of your magic can surpass even the most arcane of witch bloodlines. The ritual sacrifice at the lighthouse gave you the ability to exact revenge on all who have wronged you. One more sacrifice will solidify your place in Salem. All will kneel in your presence. Worship you. Fear you.

Yes. She remembered. How could she have forgotten her driving need for revenge? The fight for her rightful place at top of the hierarchy of Salem's witches?

Verity breathed deeply. Blood heated and raced through her veins, giving her a surge of strength. This latest sacrifice merely empowered her for the battle ahead. The portal created at the lighthouse gave her access to more souls to drain when the time was right. Yes, the final battleground had been chosen. She had hidden the portal to make it look sealed, but when needed, she would cast away the veil, hiding it and suck the souls into herself to defeat those who opposed her.

And the druid. Do not forget our purpose is to destroy him.

"Yes. The druid must die."

A muffled sound from the shadows drew Verity's attention. With an arrogant look of disdain, she looked at the figure held captive with swirling bonds of dark magic. "Oh, don't worry, Ainevar. You will be there to see the ultimate destruction of your beloved."

Fear lit soft blue eyes and Ainevar struggled against her bonds. Deep, warped laughter filled the room and Verity sat down to listen to the whispers.

CHAPTER TWENTY-NINE

C louds obscured the near full moon and left the town in shadows that created a dark shroud over everything. By three in the morning, even the most ardent of partiers had deserted the streets and headed for a soft bed to catch some sleep before waking up to do it all over the next day.

Memnon slowed to a stop at a red light and perused the deserted streets. Spooky. That was the word that described it best. Store windows and streets decorated with skeletons, pumpkins, spider webs, even witches in stereotypical pointed black hats, long black robe and wart on the end of a hooked nose. He wondered if such decorations ever ticked off actual witches. Face it, the old hag with the wart on her pointed nose was not a complimentary rendition.

Either way, for the sake of all the residents and visitors to Salem, Memnon truly hoped they could stop the evil before it murdered again. Then he remembered what he'd forgotten to do at the lighthouse.

"Damn. I meant to close the portal at the lighthouse. We should go back."

"It is unnecessary."

"Oh, did you close it? I thought only the person who opened it could do that."

"It remains open, as only you can close it. But the evil cloaked the portal, likely hoping to come back later to feed off the spirits circling around." Seabhac pointed to a side street up ahead. "Turn there, I think we are close."

Wheeling the SUV around the corner, Memnon frowned and asked. "Is it a good idea to leave the portal open? I mean, if the evil gets strength from feeding off the spirits, shouldn't we close the portal to weaken the evil?"

"I do not plan on letting it feed on any more spirits. But, with the portal open and providing a feeding place, at least we know the evil will show up there again. It gives us a place to fortify and prepare."

"Makes sense. But if that's the plan, why are we driving around town looking for the evil, if we already know it's going to show up at the lighthouse again?"

Silence greeted his question and a quick glance at the druid showed a face scrunched in concentration. He almost appeared to be in pain. Finally, Seabhac replied. "We search because I feel a rift in the space-time continuum."

"Forgive my lack of knowledge, but wouldn't that mean some kind of rip or rupture between dimensions?"

"Yes." Seabhac's voice was low and gravelly. Filled with emotion.

"Oh." Memnon's brain raced with possibilities, but only one came to mind and the grave look on Seabhac's face meant that was the thought on his mind as well.

"Hey, don't worry. We'll search all night if we have to. Failing that, you said the evil will return to the lighthouse. We'll greet it with all the power at our disposal. Hell, you, Anwyn, and the necklace hold more power than has ever existed in one place, so victory is a given."

Seabhac almost smiled. "Roaming the streets is getting us nowhere. We will return to the condo where I will follow up on my suspicions and you can get some sleep. You will need it for the final battle."

"I'm fine. We can keep searching. I mean, what if..."

"No. You need your sleep, and I need to focus. Back to the condo."

"Fine." Memnon couldn't imagine what Seabhac would do if his suspicions proved correct. Hopefully, the fact that Ainevar left for another dimension shortly before Seabhac sensed the rift was just a coincidence. One look at the granite look of despair on Seabhac's face showed the druid didn't believe that any more than he did.

CHAPTER THIRTY

A single ray of dawn beamed through the blackout curtains and lit a narrow beam on the altar. Verity cursed and reached over to yank the curtains closed. Darkness fell heavy and welcoming to her tired eyes. She'd spent the night weaving magic. Solidifying her plan to destroy those who stood in her way. Fired by revenge, guided by whispers, she'd set her plan in motion. Now, as morning showed its light, she realized that this human body needed sleep.

She grasped the table's edge and stood with a groan. Pins and needles prickled her legs, and she cursed the limitations of this body. Once she defeated Seabhac and that bitch from Avalon, she could easily dispense with the rest of those who opposed her. Then, she could wield ultimate power and revel in her immortality. No more pain, no more hiding in dark places, no more kowtowing to that damned druid.

A rustling sounded from the corner and Verity snapped at her prisoner. "Be quiet. There is nothing you can do." A self-satisfied laugh rumbled from deep in her chest. "I have arranged it so that your trail leads directly to that Anwyn wench. Your lover will accuse her of your disappearance. As long as they fight among themselves, I can complete my rituals, then kill them before they can destroy me."

She yawned and stretched. "Tonight is the final battle and I am ready. I am afraid you will never see your lover again."

Verity walked over and gave a tug on the ropes tying Ainevar in place. Of course, magic imbued the rope to keep the sorceress in place. "Well, you may see him once more. But it will be from the upper level of the lighthouse. I want to see the look on his face when I push you to the rocks below. The pain on his face as you and his unborn child crash to the ground and lay there broken and twisted will feed my power. He and that bitch have no chance against me."

Ainevar stared at Verity. Challenging. Taunting. There was a light in her eyes that shouldn't be there. The whispers in Verity's mind screamed until they throbbed.

She knows something. She knows something. She knows something. She knows something.

Exhaustion made Verity weak. She needed sleep. Stumbling to the bedroom, she assured herself that she'd thought of everything. Nothing could go wrong. With a sigh, she dropped onto the bed and fell into a near hypnotic sleep.

It felt as if his head was being shaken off his body. Memnon struggled to waken from the sweet dreams that had filled his sleeping hours. Silken waves of thick auburn hair had wrapped him in ecstasy. Honey gold eyes sparked with life and teased him with unfulfilled promises. Ahh, heaven on earth.

And, now, he woke to be confronted by an aged and flushed face of a druid yelling at him to *stop being lazy and get his hind end from the bed.*

With an effort, Memnon shook the dreams from his mind and sat up. "Stop, dammit. I'm awake. What is so important that you had to interrupt my dreams?" He glanced at the bedside clock. "And wake me up at 7:00 in the morning?"

"Time does not matter when Ainevar and my child's lives are at stake. Come. Hurry. I have ascertained their location." Seabhac strode from the bedroom to leave Memnon to get ready.

With his heart pounding, Memnon sprang from bed and pulled on jeans, a long-sleeved t-shirt, and warm socks. He ran his hands through his hair and joined Seabhac in the living room.

"Are you sure we should go on our own? I thought that tonight at the lighthouse was when it was all going down."

"Yes, well, plans change. I followed Ainevar's energy, which ended up here in Salem rather than home in the Netherworld. I recognized the destination." Anger infused Seabhac's face. "I will have answers or I will let loose my full wrath and not care who pays the price. And do not even think to get in my way or I will turn you to dust."

His words made little sense. Filled with curiosity and a growing sense of unease, Memnon grabbed his jacket and followed Seabhac out the door.

Anwyn woke to the warmth of the sun on her face and realized she had slept later than normal. In Avalon, waking up to meditate as the sun rose was common practice. But, considering the late hour she had finally slipped into bed and the nightmare filled dreams that had plagued her sleep, it was not surprising she slept late.

Ebony lay snuggled under her arm with her wet nose pressed against Anwyn's cheek. She allowed herself a moment to enjoy the peace, but a pounding on her front door followed by someone yelling for her to open up abruptly shattered the peace.

She scrambled from bed and grabbed a robe to put on as she rushed down the stairs. Before she reached the door to open it, it flung open and crashed against the wall. A very pissed off looking druid and a confused-looking Memnon stood looking at her. His eyes raked her body and she self-consciously pulled her robe tighter about her body.

"What is wrong? Why are you here so early? I do not remember making plans to meet so early." She looked questioningly at the two men.

Seabhac's face reddened and waves of anger rolled from him and filled the room with a choking, heavy miasma. Anwyn's heart pounded as she tried to think of anything she could have done between last night and this morning to anger him so much.

"Where is she?" Seabhac's voice rumbled through Anwyn.

She shivered and turned pleading eyes toward Memnon, who shrugged and gave her a worried look.

Then, in a move so fast, Anwyn barely had time to blink, Seabhac grabbed her throat in one hand and lifted her off the ground. Panic set in as she could not breathe and his hand felt as if it was going to rip her head from her shoulders. Through a haze of pain, she heard Memnon yell and jump forward to grab Seabhac. With pleading eyes, she beseeched him to save her because she sensed Seabhac's mood and he was out for blood and death. Her death.

A struggle ensued, but no one was a match for Seabhac and his unexplained rage. Spots danced in Anwyn's vision and she felt herself losing consciousness. Terrified for her life, Anwyn silently pleaded for help.

That's when all Hell broke loose.

CHAPTER THIRTY-ONE

"Stop struggling." Verity stomped over to Ainevar and slapped her across the face. "I don't have the time or energy to deal with you constantly draining me."

A triumphant gleam lit Ainevar's blue eyes, and a quiet chuckle leaked out past the cloth tied across her mouth.

IDIOT! Think before you speak. Now she knows she can affect your power. Since you do not need her until nightfall, spell her to make her sleep for the day. You will need to kill to replace what she has drained.

"Yes. I need to kill." Verity mumbled. "But doing the ritual during the day is dangerous. There are too many people around."

I care not about the ritual. Power is what you need. Killing is how you get it. Find anyone alone in a parking lot, alley, or side street, and kill them. Leave them where they fall. Your exposure will be minimal. Once you feel quickened, return here and to make final arrangements for tonight.

Verity took a potion from a nearby shelf and turned to Ainevar. "This will make you sleep." She curled her lip. "I truly hope the potion does not harm your unborn child."

The sudden look of fear and pleading in Ainevar's eyes sparked a snort of laughter from Verity that echoed off the walls and belied the truth of her comment.

"Sleep tight, bitch. I'll be back stronger than ever and then we shall see who is the most powerful."

The potion took effect quickly, but not too fast. That brief second before Ainevar succumbed to unconsciousness, Verity glimpsed a flash of taunting certainty in the eyes of her captive.

Verity's mind exploded. No longer a distant whisper, the ubiquitous voice in her head boomed. She clutched her head and fell to the ground on her knees.

She knows something. She knows something. What did we miss?

"I. Don't. Know. Stop screaming." She pleaded for relief.

The voice ceased, but the seething rage and frustration whirled about her head. Fired her blood and need for revenge.

Driven and needing to regenerate her flagging energy, Verity picked up her favorite knife and taunted an unconscious Ainevar. "With your lover and Anwyn fighting each other, there will be no one to stop me. It will be my supreme pleasure to wipe that self-satisfied look off your face."

Verity slammed the door and left to find her first victim.

Memnon's heart clenched in fear at the pleading look on Anwyn's face. The damned druid was choking her to death. Her eyes closed and her body went limp and he sensed her slipping into darkness. Before he could move, Cassandra ran through the shop's open door, waving her arms and yelling. "Seabhac. NO!"

At that moment, Anwyn's necklace shot a focused stream of light that hit Seabhac mid-chest and sent him flying back against the wall so hard the painting and mirror on the wall shook.

Nora and Tartleby pushed into the store behind Cassandra and ran over the Anwyn who leaned against the wall, barely conscious. Memnon also raced over to Anwyn to ensure she was okay, while Cassandra confronted Seabhac. Looking like an avenging Valkyrie with her hair in wild disarray over her shoulders and down her back and her blue eyes lit with intent, Cassandra stood between Seabhac and Anwyn.

Seabhac scrambled up from the floor, straightened his robes and manhandled Cassandra out of his way.

"How dare you strike me down. That proves you are guilty." He pointed a finger in Anwyn's direction.

"No." Cassandra stamped her foot and grabbed the sleeve of Seabhac's robe, effectively stopping him from moving.

"I have not trusted her from the beginning. Now Ainevar is missing, her trail leads here, and that novice priestess attacked me."

Memnon left his sister to deal with Seabhac as he helped Anwyn to the nearest chair to sit. Red finger marks stood out on her white neck, and Memnon knew that bruising would follow shortly. His nostrils flared in anger and his allegiance to Seabhac paled compared to the protective instinct he felt for Anwyn. Anger welled within, and he stood to face Seabhac. The light touch of Anwyn's hand on his arm stopped him from acting on his anger.

Cassandra waved a hand for him to stay back, and she turned to Seabhac. "She is not guilty. You are being deceived by a false trail. I saw it in a vision and I know the identity of the murderer. At least, who the evil has possessed."

Seabhac narrowed eyelids and pinned Cassandra with a heated gaze. "Why should I believe you?"

Cassandra slammed her fists on her hips. "How dare you question me? I nearly died last year dealing with this same evil. I would think that earns some iota of trust from you and it seems you're forgetting that I lived with Ainevar's essence inside me for most of my life. If anyone other than you has any kind of connection with her, it would be me. Right? I say she is not here."

A flash of light from Anwyn's necklace preceded a minor explosion that whooshed against Memnon and sent him back a couple of steps. Before he could move, a woman appeared where he had just stood beside Anwyn.

"I would listen to her, Druid. She speaks the truth. And Anwyn did not blast you...I did. You came close to killing one of my priestesses and you of all people know how I protect those under my care."

Words spoken in a soft, melodious tone by a woman who was translucent and shifting like a dream you can't quite remember upon waking. Her presence filled the room, yet to touch her or get a genuine sense of what she looked like was like grasping at wisps of smoke. Memnon swore he felt his heart expand and fill with grace, love, and compassion. Her mere presence brought calm to the room, yet her admission to blasting Seabhac showed her steely and protective side.

Memnon noted that Seabhac stood dead still, pale as moonlight. Even trembling a bit.

"Brighid." The druid whispered her name with respect and a touch of fear.

"Seabhac." She bowed her head in acknowledgement, then turned to Anwyn. "My sweet Anwyn. How fare you?"

Anwyn immediately dropped to a knee and bowed her head. "I am doing well, Priestess."

"Nonsense. You are scared, confused, and feeling very alone."

Anwyn flushed. Feeling the overwhelming urge to protect, Memnon moved closer to her and laid a hand on Anwyn's shoulder.

Brighid laughed. A sound resembling water gently trickling over rocks in a mountain stream. "Stand up, my child." She reached out to Anwyn, who took her hand and stood. "You have done well. I see you have gathered new souls to strengthen the necklace. That you have done so affirms my decision to send you into an uncertain future rather than someone else."

With a raised eyebrow and speculative look at Memnon, she said. "I also see you have gained your own protector. Very handsome and loyal by the looks of things."

"No, he is not...we are not..."

Brighid lifted a hand for silence. "It was not an admonishment, child. I am happy for you."

Avalon's priestess turned to look at Nora and Tartleby, and tears filled her eyes. "I recognize you both. The essence of your ancestors is vibrant within both of you. I am beyond pleased to see you both and know that I did not misplace my faith when I made my choices so many years ago."

Nora and Tartleby seemed too much in awe to speak, but both bowed their heads in acknowledgement of Brighid's words.

"Enough." Seabhac spoke. "Why are you here Brighid?"

"I sent a vision to Cassandra with the truth and to help calm you down, but by the time she arrived, you were already attacking Anwyn. You forced me here to protect her. I understand your concern for Ainevar, but you must focus on destroying the evil. That is the only way to save her and your child."

"You sent me the vision?" Cassandra asked.

"Yes. You needed a reason to use your powers again. After last year, you have been afraid and denied your innate abilities. I merely helped you access that which shines within you."

"Oh." Cassandra frowned. "I hadn't realized that's what I was doing, but, looking back, I can see that I've been hesitant to access my powers." She smiled at Brighid. Her face beamed with renewed belief in herself. "Thank you."

Brighid bowed her head in acknowledgement, then pinned her steely gaze on Seabhac.

"Seabhac, do you have a plan?"

"Yes. I plan on destroying the evil once and for all."

"Do not be snarky. It does not become you, Druid. I did not reshape destiny or ask my priestesses to sacrifice their lives to assuage your flippant ego."

"MY ego." Seabhac bellowed. His rage heating the room to an uncomfortable temperature.

Memnon could have sworn he felt the floor shake and the walls vibrate. But Brighid did not back down. If anything, she raised her energy and pushed it at Seabhac in a pulsing mass of roiling intent. Pressure built as the two battled it out silently. Memnon's ears hurt, and he was about to step in and put a stop to the battle of egos, but Anwyn moved first. Moving across the floor in the soft, gliding way that Memnon loved to watch, Anwyn stepped between Seabhac and Brighid and raised her hands out to her sides, palms facing each of the offenders.

"Stop. Fighting each other will only allow the evil to win in the end. We need to work together. Brighid, what you have achieved is truly amazing. Your foresight and planning have come together centuries later and will probably be what wins the battle. Seabhac..." She turned to the druid, her eyes soft and comforting.

"Let go of your guilt. It will destroy us all if you let it. You have been told more than once that none of this is your fault. The universe sent the evil to you because you were the only one strong enough to control it over the centuries. Even Brighid, with all her power and planning, could not do this alone. We have to work together."

Respect and admiration for Anwyn shot through Memnon. To step between two of the most powerful beings ever born, in the middle of an argument no less...well, awesome and brave didn't even begin to describe that kind of nerve. But it worked. Brighid and Seabhac both settled and drew their energy in, so the room didn't feel as if it was about to explode.

Tears filled Brighid's eyes, and she cupped Anwyn's cheek with her hand. "I knew I had chosen wisely all those years ago." She looked at Seabhac and challenged. "So, Druid, are you in this with us, or for yourself?"

Seabhac snorted. "Of course we are in it together. I am stubborn, not addlepated."

Her face lit with a soft smile. "Yes, you are most definitely stubborn. But also brilliant, honorable, and powerful. I feel the evil building its strength and fear it will take another life or two before this evening. Cassandra, I showed you the infected person. Warn your husband, the defender of the law, and have him to try to prevent her from killing another person of Salem. Tonight will be the end...one way or another. Do not let my planning and all the lives sacrificed be in vain."

With a sigh, Brighid morphed into a wisp of mist and drifted back into the necklace. Silence followed her disappearance until Memnon cleared his throat and spoke.

"Seabhac, I think you owe Anwyn an apology."

The druid pressed his lips into a thin line and crossed his arms. Memnon faced him down with a pointed stare until Seabhac finally blew a breath out through his lips and relaxed his stance.

"Fine. My only excuse is that Ainevar's disappearance muddled my better judgement."

Memnon raised an eyebrow. "That's an excuse, not an apology."

"Give a druid a break. I have centuries of ego to deal with." No one moved. The quiet in the room magnified so that even the creak of floorboard seemed like a gunshot. Seabhac heaved a sigh. "I suppose this is as good a time as any to tame my ego. So, Anwyn, I apologize for accusing and choking you. I should have known that any initiate of Brighid's would be honest and not go around kidnapping people."

Anwyn moved her hand to her now bruised throat. "It is fine. I understand your concern clouded your logic."

"Good, so we are now all friends again." Memnon turned to his sister. "Cassandra, who has the evil possessed this time?"

Cassandra's eyes rounded. "Oh, I couldn't believe it when I had the vision. It's Verity."

"What!" The exclamation came from everyone in the room, accompanied by shocked expressions of horror.

"You mean she killed her own son?" Nora asked. "How horrible."

"I'm sure the evil has squelched any intent or moral restraints Verity might have had. If she is even aware of her actions, it will be on the most base level." Seabhac explained.

"Could we appeal to her to fight the evil within her?" Anwyn asked.

"No, we cannot. No mortal is powerful enough to fight this force. It has lived for centuries and gathered strength every time it shows up. It is much more powerful than ever. That is why we must work together with every source of power at our disposal.

I see that now. I have tried to battle and contain it myself many times, but failed each time. My refusal to accept my limitations resulted in lives lost."So what is the plan?" Memnon asked. "Does knowing the identity of the possessed person change our plans at all?"

Anwyn and Seabhac shared a look. A faint glow lit the area between them and a calm settled into the room that hadn't previously been there.

Anwyn answered Memnon. "It changes nothing. The zenith of the full moon's power is tonight, and the source of light that will amplify all our powers is the lighthouse beacon. So the time and place remain fixed."

Seabhac nodded in agreement. "In the meantime..."

The musical tones of Cassandra's phone interrupted what Seabhac was about to say. With an apologetic look, she moved to the corner of the room and answered the phone. Even at a whisper, her voice carried to the others. She hung up and turned to look at them with a pale face. It didn't take a genius to guess what the call had been about.

"Samson had a call about a body in a downtown alley. Throat cut, blood everywhere and a huge upside down pentagram drawn with the victim's blood. No other signs of a ritual and the body wasn't positioned like the others have been."

"According to Samson, the ritual aspect of the murders was more to instill fear and set a mood. Right now, I would guess that the evil...Verity...is more concerned with just storing up on power and strength. She will know that tonight is the night." Cassandra frowned and asked. "How will we lure her to the lighthouse tonight?"

Anwyn spoke. "We do not have to. The purpose of using the beacon is to enable us to send a power pulse a larger distance than we would be able otherwise. Kind of like an amplifier. If the evil is anywhere within miles, we will destroy it. At least, that is the idea. Am I correct, Seabhac?"

"Yes. Quite so." He inclined his head toward her in acknowledgement. "Now, time runs short. Nora, can you assess the constellations and moon cycle and determine the optimum time to meld our powers and send them out, then let us know so we can assemble at the lighthouse in plenty of time. Cassandra, if you have not already done so, let Samson know to keep an eye out for Verity. Warn him it would be certain death to confront her, though he may deter her enough to prevent another victim."

He looked at each person in the room. "Tonight, we battle an evil that has left a reign of terror, darkness, and death in its path for centuries. Prepare by cleansing your mind of any doubt. Fortify your aura with meditation. Strengthen yourself in whatever way works for you and make sure that you deal with only white light energy. Failure is not an option."

"I will update Samson and we will both be there later tonight." Cassandra gave a weak smile and left.

With subdued goodbyes and the promise to contact everyone with a more specific time once Nora did some calculations, Nora and Tartleby left together.

The door shut on a subdued trio, each lost in their own thoughts. Memnon gave a sigh of relief that Brighid's actions ended such a volatile situation without further incident. He glanced at the developing bruises on Anwyn's neck and flushed with anger at Seabhac, but he realized that in similar circumstances of thinking his wife and child were in danger, he may have acted the same.

Anwyn reached down to pick up Ebony who was winding herself around Anwyn's ankles and meowing. She snuggled the kitten under her chin and spoke in soothing tones. A sharp stab of envy struck Memnon, and he looked away to hide the emotion. That's when he noticed Seabhac looking very perplexed and tilting his head as if listening for a distant sound.

"Seabhac? Everything okay?"

The druid tilted his head again and parted the curtains on the front window to look out to the street. With a shake of his head, he dropped the curtain and turned to look at Memnon and Anwyn.

"Do either of you feel that vibration?"

Memnon shook his head and looked at Anwyn, who shrugged.

"Strange. It is there and then not. Sometimes almost a whisper in my ear, then changes to a humming in my chest. I feel it. Hear it. Sense it. So strong and then gone. I do not understand."

"Do you sense danger? Would it be the evil trying to control you?" Anwyn asked.

"No. It is a warm and comforting feeling. Yet there is fear within its cry, a prick of urgency in the vibration. As if calling to me. Bah! I need to find the source of this strangeness. I must go."

With that statement, Seabhac stormed out of the store, his robes billowing behind him. Memnon ran after him, but once he got outside, Seabhac had disappeared, leaving only a shimmer of mist in his wake.

CHAPTER THIRTY-TWO

S eabhac's hasty departure left Memnon and Anwyn standing on the cobblestones outside her shop, staring at each other in confusion.

"Well, I guess he won't be needing a ride wherever he was going." Memnon broke the awkward silence.

"No. I suppose not." Anwyn smiled. "I suppose you must leave to go find him?"

Part of her hoped he would stay for a few minutes. The other part reminded her that this would be her last day in Salem. Her last day alive. Whether the evil won or not, she had no future, so acting on her burgeoning feelings for Memnon was not logical. It would be best if he left and she got on with meditation and cleansing her aura.

"Honestly, I wouldn't know where to begin. He was acting more strange than normal, so he could be anywhere. I guess I should go back to the condo and wait for him. I can do some meditation."

"Yes, of course." She said the words and bit her tongue to leave it at that, but her foolish emotions made her offer. "Or you could stay for lunch. I mean, we must keep up our strength."

"There is nothing I'd like better. Are you sure it's no bother? I mean, I don't want to keep you from preparations for tonight."

Anwyn's heart flipped and her mouth went dry. He was staying. Oh, oh. Did she even have food to make him for lunch? Her brain did a quick tally of what she thought was in her cupboards and fridge. She might be okay.

"Not to worry. The necklace is my main preparation and I will meditate later to build the energy and connect to the souls in the necklace. For now, I am hungry and need some food. Will a grilled cheese sandwich and tomato soup be okay with you?"

Memnon's smile lit her heart. "That sounds perfect."

Dear Goddess, he was so handsome. She deserved at least an hour where she could pretend her life was normal. An hour to enjoy the attention of a man who found her attractive. She would create a memory to carry with her into the afterlife...or wherever destiny led her after she fulfilled her purpose here in Salem.

While she opened a can and buttered bread, Memnon played with Ebony. The kitten seemed quite taken with him, and Anwyn admitted she was as well. He had no qualms about sitting on the floor and having Ebony crawl all over him. Anwyn laughed when the kitten curled up in Memnon's lap and went to sleep.

With the sandwiches made and grilling in the frying pan and the soup heating, Anwyn pulled a couple of plates and bowls from the cupboard and placed them on the table.

"You amaze me." Memnon said from his place on the floor.

"Me? Why?"

"I cannot imagine being taken from your time and placed here, so far in the future, from everything you're used to, and accomplishing as much as you have. I guarantee that if I suddenly found myself back in your time, I'd be lost. A total basket case."

"Well, I am not sure what a basket case is, but you are a strong and intelligent man. I do not doubt you would cope just fine."

She flipped the grilled cheese sandwiches and ladled soup into a couple of bowls, which she set on the kitchen table. By the time she added spoons, crackers, ketchup, and salt to the table, the sandwiches were ready. Savoury scents of tomato and toast filled the kitchen as they sat to eat. Ebony followed Memnon and curled herself on the floor by his feet.

"This is nice. A satisfying lunch eaten in the company of an amazing woman. It brings a sense of calm amid so much chaos." Memnon squirted ketchup on the plate beside his sandwich and crumbled crackers into his soup.

Not sure how to reply, and a bit embarrassed, Anwyn bit into her grilled cheese. "Mmm. This is honestly one of my favorite things to discover in this time period. Grilled cheese." She moaned again and took another bite.

"Wait. You have a bit of butter...just here." Memnon reached over and brushed a finger at the corner of her mouth.

His touch sent shivers through her while her breath caught in her throat. Butterfly wings fluttered in her stomach and reminded her of the early days of spring, with its familiar ache of anticipation and hope for the cycle of new life. The intensity of his dark eyes fixated on her as he traced the outline of her mouth with his fingers. She shivered. He leaned closer until his lips touched hers.

Hesitantly.

Questioningly.

Without thought, she sighed and leaned into his lips. She ached for more. She craved the fulfillment of something she did not even understand.

Memnon cupped her cheek with his hand, and warmth spread through her like a fire. His tongue touched her lips and parted them enough to dart in and touch her tongue. She moaned as an electric charge shot through her. Lunch was all but forgotten as the kiss deepened. So much to feel, Anwyn could barely experience it all. Hot, cold. Hard, soft. Prickles, warm flushes.

Being raised in Avalon meant that her exposure to men was minimal. She had devoted her entire life to her studies and becoming an advanced priestess. There had been no chance or thought to kissing a man, let alone feel so overwhelmed. Body and soul throbbed for more.

Why not? She deserved this last self-serving act before disappearing into a void or moving on to whatever waited for her after death. Just as she was about to suggest moving to the bedroom, Memnon pulled away from her.

He closed his eyes and took a deep breath while standing and then moving across the room.

A rock dropped in Anwyn's stomach. At least that is what it felt like. Followed by a feeling of cold water washing over her body.

"Oh," she whispered. In a swift move meant to cover her disappointment and embarrassment, she picked up the dishes and moved them to the sink.

"No. It's not you. My goodness, woman, I can barely keep my hands off you."

Hope soared within Anwyn, only to drop as she remembered her limited time here.

"We just need to get past this final battle and then we'll have time to get to know each other. This feeling between us is too precious to rush. Too powerful to disappear."

Memnon walked up behind her and rested his hands on her shoulders. His touch offered warmth and comfort. "Do you agree, or am I way off base here?"

Without turning around, Anwyn said. "Yes, too precious for sure." She said nothing about disappearing because that is exactly what she would be doing. But she was not brave enough to tell him that. There would be time later. And, if not, she would spare them both a wrenching goodbye.

Using every bit of strength she possessed, Anwyn turned and smiled at Memnon. "I suppose you should get back to the condo to see if Seabhac ever found what he was looking for. I need to do some preparations for tonight."

Memnon looked at her, his brow furrowed and eyes concerned. "You're okay? You do understand I am just putting off going any further in our relationship...I'm not rejecting you. A man would have to be insane to reject you."

Under normal circumstances, Anwyn would have admired Memnon's solid and fair morals, but nothing was normal about this relationship. She almost wished he would just take advantage of her so she would have that memory to carry with her. On the other hand, if he was that kind of man, she likely would not be so drawn to him. Fates, what a mess.

So, despite her major disappointment and the knowledge they would never have the chance to complete what they had started, she smiled. "I understand and respect you for caring."

"Awesome. I swear that tomorrow will be different. A new beginning." He kissed her cheek and, with a wave, left her standing in the middle of her kitchen.

Ebony sat in the middle of the floor and meowed a long, mournful sound. The kitten lifted a tiny paw and waved it at Anwyn, begging to be picked up. With tears in her eyes, Anwyn snuggled the kitten close, letting the purr and feel of soft fur ease the sick feeling in the pit of her stomach.

"Well, little one, let's light some candles and purify ourselves and the necklace. We have an evil force to kill and a life to leave behind."

Ebony meowed and tapped her face with a paw.

"No worries, I will leave you with Nora. I promise she will take care of you." Tears filled Anwyn's eyes and her heart filled with pain. "It is okay. It really is." She tried to convince herself.

CHAPTER THIRTY-THREE

L aden with coffee and donuts, Memnon walked up the two flights of stairs to his condo. All the way home, he'd struggled with emotions ranging from elation to fear and realized that he needed to get it together or he'd be useless that evening when they face the evil.

But that kiss. It had almost done him in and he'd had to fight every instinct he had to not pick Anwyn up and carry her to bed where he could make passionate and sweet love to her. But considering her past, he assumed she had never made love. When the heck would she have had time? So, keeping in mind how his feelings for her had grown in such a short time, he knew he wanted to take his time and woo her.

After tonight. That's when both their lives could start. The moment he had seen her standing in her store with her blue eyes and long auburn hair , his heart had flamed to life. He realized he'd been living his life in neutral, and Anwyn would be the one to kick it into full gear.

But first, they needed to defeat the evil force, and that scared the crap out of him. Now that he'd found someone he wanted to share his life with, he didn't want some faceless evil ending it before it could even start.

Damn you Fates for being so fickle and playing with our lives.

Turning his key in the lock, he opened the door and entered the condo. Silence greeted him as he walked to the kitchen to place the coffee and donuts on the table.

"Seabhac." He called out. "Are you here?"

His voice echoed through the rooms with no answering voice.

"Hmm, wonder what he's up to." He took a sip of coffee, moaned in appreciation, and followed it up with a bite from a Boston Cream donut. Just as he reached for a second donut, the front door opened and Seabhac bellowed out a hello.

"In here." Memnon answered.

A disgruntled looking Seabhac entered the kitchen, his nostrils quivering as he sniffed out the coffee. "Ahh, you are saving me from having a complete and utter breakdown from frustration. I guess I shall keep you around."

"Gee, thanks." Memnon handed Seabhac his coffee and opened to box of donuts for the druid to peruse. "Why are you so frustrated?"

Amidst slurps of coffee and bites from his donut, Seabhac replied. "Remember that feeling that I mentioned earlier? An insistent, but faint prod? It will not stop poking me, but I cannot find its source. I feel it is important, yet it eludes me."

"You're sure it isn't the evil messing with your mind?"

Seabhac frowned. "If *messing with my mind* means what I am guessing, then no, it is not the evil. This entity or force is trying to help. I am sure. But I cannot make a connection. It feels as if there is a veil separating us and I am unable to break through."

Memnon's cell phone rang, effectively interrupting speculation about the source of Seabhac's feeling.

"Hello."

"Hi, Memnon. It's Nora."

"Hey, Nora. What's up?"

"I did some constellation calculations and figure that 11:41is the optimum time to do our ritual tonight. I don't know what Seabhac has planned, but I assume we need to be there earlier than that to set up a protective circle."

"Likely. Wait a sec, while I ask him." Memnon covered the phone with his hand and asked. "We need to be ready by 11:41, so what do you need to do to prepare? How long do we need?"

"I need 15 minutes to cast a circle of protection. Please ask Nora to bring some candles. Blue, black, and white would be preferred.

And have her ask that little man to prepare tea for afterwards. Peppermint or lemon would be best to help re-energize us."

Memnon relayed the requests to Nora, and he heard her mumble to Tartleby, who must have been standing close by.

"Okay, candles and tea are no problem." She paused. When she spoke, her voice wavered. "I suppose having tea ready will help us focus on the after of it all. Assuming we make it out alive."

"We will, Nora. Don't think any other way."

"Okay."

"Come on, say it like you mean it." Memnon encouraged her.

"Fine." Nora's voice rang firm. "Dammit, we will be fine. With all the power on our side, how can it work out any other way?"

"Exactly. So, we will see you at the lighthouse around 11:00 tonight. And stay positive. It is the only way we can succeed."

"All right. See you there." Nora replied and cut the connection.

"She has doubts?" Seabhac asked.

"Hell, we all have doubts."

"Hmm. Take your own advice and do some meditating to keep your thoughts on the positive path. It truly is the only way to overcome this evil."

"I will. I just have to call Cassandra and fill her in on what's happening. Hey, what is the purpose of the different colored candles? I always figured that a candle was just a candle and just used for atmospheric reasons."

"You really know nothing about magic, do you? I find that most unusual considering how much of it races through your blood."

Memnon shrugged. "I don't feel magic. I mean, I have always been able to sense people's intent and get a feel for the right decisions to make. That's how I have been so successful in business. But, I've never gone beyond that."

"By not pursuing your abilities, you deny your very heritage. You need to take time to learn about yourself. As for the candles, blue is for peace and protection, black is for protection and warding off negative energies, white will help with purifying and cleansing away old energies. Put them all together in a circle and add our energies and we will have a truly powerful circle to keep the evil from us long enough to meld and direct our energies."

"So you do have a plan once we get there, right?"

"Basically. But often magic has a mind of its own and we must be fluid and willing to adapt. So, I have no plan set in stone, just a general idea of how to start."

"That doesn't sound encouraging."

"Bah! I am not here to coddle to your insecurities. We will protect ourselves, meld our powers, use the lighthouse beacon to increase our power tenfold and send it out toward the evil. That is enough to know. Anything else that happens will be up to the Fates." Seabhac's face softened. "The very first words my mentor spoke to me have maintained me through centuries. *Trust and Believe*. One of the most important edicts by which to live your life."

"Trust and believe. In what? Myself, the universe, karma, other people?"

Seabhac just smiled and said. "Do not forget to phone your sister and inform her of the plans for tonight." With those words, he closed his eyes and drifted into meditation.

Memnon grumbled about grumpy old men and moved to the other room to call Cassandra so he wouldn't disturb Seabhac.

She answered on the first ring.

"Hey, sis. It's me."

"Memnon, hi."

"Oh, no. What's wrong?" Memnon knew his sister better than she knew herself at times. Since the accident that had killed their parents, his main purpose had been to care for her and make sure that her burgeoning powers and visions hadn't gotten her in trouble. It hadn't been until last year that he'd felt confident enough to pass the major worry for her welfare over to Samson. But she was his sister, and he'd always worry about her. The tone of her voice warned him that something had happened.

"I am at the police station. I had already told him about Verity on the phone at Anwyn's store, but wanted to make sure he didn't confront her on his own. He realized it would be suicide and neither he nor his officers can fight the evil, but he thought that staying close to her would deter her from killing again." She paused and then spoke in a hushed tone. "It didn't."

"How many?"

"Just one more, but that makes two so far. Samson has the entire force patrolling the streets and urging people to stay in groups and inside. He had thought about just shooting Verity, but he worried the evil would possess someone else and we wouldn't know who. Or it's possible that the evil would protect Verity's body, so a bullet wouldn't harm her. We just don't know, so leaving things status quo is the plan for now."

"Okay. We are meeting tonight at 11:00 at the lighthouse. We'll take care of this permanently."

"Oh, I also called Skye and Jerome. They are driving back to be there tonight as well."

"Is that necessary? I mean, they have a baby to think about now."

"All the more reason to help. If the evil wins, Salem is in danger and who knows how pervasive the evil will be. Forging all our powers to defeat this evil once and for all is the only way to ensure a safe place for their child to grow up."

Memnon sighed and shook his head. "You're right. I just hate the thought of them risking their lives and possibly leaving a child with no parents."

"Stop thinking like that, Memnon. Seabhac said earlier that staying positive is vital to helping us remain strong. We will defeat the evil tonight. Nothing else is acceptable."

"I know you're right. I better let you go. Take care and rest up for tonight. We'll need all our strength."

"You as well. See you tonight, big brother."

The connection went dead, and Memnon placed his phone down. That was it. Nothing else to do until tonight. Nora, Tartleby, Anwyn, Cassandra, Samson, Skye, Jerome, Seabhac and himself would all be at the lighthouse at 11:00 to prepare to battle the evil. Of course, Anwyn and Seabhac were the powerbrokers in the group, but the rest of them would add a boost enough to destroy the evil.

Turning his thoughts to Ainevar and Seabhac's unborn child, he sent a silent prayer to the universe that they were still alive.

Verity dipped her fingers in the blood she'd collected from her last victim and traced lines and symbols on her face and arms. Their meaning was unclear to her, but an unseen force led her hand as she drew swirls and lines that took shape into what looked to be Celtic symbols, or maybe ancient hieroglyphics.

Each swipe of finger upon flesh heightened the sense of frustration that had built since returning to the earthly plane. Such power should not be confined within the shell of such a weak, disposable shell.

Verity pressed harder and dug in with her nails until her arm bled and mingled with the blood of the murder victim. She bared her teeth and let the rage flame through her body.

Such a potent force direct from the universe deserved its own body, and not a human one. Taking over Vespasian's body on the clifftop so long ago should have been temporary. It should have been a simple thing to take its own shape and present itself to the world as a conqueror. Yet, that arrogant druid plagued every move and every plan. Enlisted others to thwart and entrap to the point of having to run and hide just to survive.

Verity's head pulsed with centuries of failure. Her heart raced with the fuel of denied wrath. Smacking her palms on the table, she strode over to an unconscious Ainevar and slapped her across the face.

Spit sprayed from her mouth as she screamed at Ainevar. "It is the fault of your druid. All of it. Tonight he dies. Tonight, revenge will be mine. Seabhac, along with all his conspirators, will die and their powers will transfer to me. The victor."

She raised her hand to slap the now semi-conscious Ainevar again, but a stab of light hit her hard enough to lift and send her flying across the room and slamming into the wall.

Dazed, Verity stood. She'd used a binding spell on the woman's powers. Ainevar shouldn't have been able to use them against her.

"How did you do that?"

Obviously still dazed, Ainevar mumbled a reply. "I did nothing."

"LIAR."

Ainevar shrugged and let her head fall forward on her chest, but Verity grabbed her hair and yanked her head back up. "We have only a few more hours before everyone you know will die. I know they are planning something at the lighthouse, but I will be there to prevent them. The druid and priestess do not possess magic enough to destroy me. I have grown too powerful."

"Your hubris will be your downfall and I, for one, cannot wait to see you die forever."

Ainevar smiled, which only incensed Verity to greater anger. She grabbed a nearby lamp and threw it across the room to smash against the wall. As the shattered pieces fell to the floor, Verity sneered at Ainevar.

"Don't worry, you'll be coming with me to greet your lover. Then we'll see who survives the night."

Verity pulled a knife from a sheath strapped to her waist and held it against Ainevar's belly. "You will behave, or I will cut your baby from your body and gut the whelp in front of your eyes. I'll watch you both die and then use your blood to enhance my magic. Maybe even use it to help kill your druid."

Fear sparked in Ainevar's eyes, but only lasted a moment. A look of knowing and surety replace the fear and the voices in Verity's head screamed.

She hides something. She hides something. She hides something. She hides something.

Verity dropped the knife and slammed her hands to her ears. "Stop. I can't stand it."

The voices subsided and Verity drew in a breath. She stabbed a finger at her captive. "Tonight I will see the arrogance wiped from your face as you see Seabhac's death. Finally, I will have freedom to reign in the world as I should have done from the beginning."

With those words, Verity settled on the floor, crossed her legs, and chanted in a haunting tone. The ancient words lent an eerie mood to the room and foretold the coming battle.

CHAPTER THIRTY-FOUR

A crisp chill in the night air hinted at the coming winter while the moon cut through a gossamer-like mist to illuminate the area around the lighthouse. Darkness fell upon the rocks and water, seeming to muffle all sound and still all movement. There was no wind. Not even a wayward breeze.

The lighthouse rose from the wavering mist and reached toward the sky. The intermittent beacon light blazed across the water as a warning to seafaring vessels. Though, in these days of technology, the beacon was more of a reminder of days gone past rather than an actual deterrent.

The sound of a car door slamming echoed across the distance from the parking area. Memnon placed the last candle and stood to see who was arriving. So far, just he and Seabhac were there. He had laid the candles while Seabhac cast a circle and chanted in an unfamiliar and archaic language.

Car lights pierced the night and another couple of cars arrived. Quiet voices melded with the sound of water gently lapping against the rocks. The full moon shone across the water and bathed the near glass-like water in a soft shimmer. Memnon took a moment to appreciate the beauty of the night, but approaching voices drew him from his reverie.

It looked as if everyone was here, but Memnon's eyes automatically picked out Anwyn in the group. Ethereal was the best way to describe her. The moon outlined her delicate shape and her red hair glowed in defiant glory. Fiery. Graceful. Age-old wisdom captured within amber eyes that currently rested on him. His body vibrated, and he was sure it wasn't the spell that Seabhac was working on that was the cause.

Anwyn, Nora, Tartleby, Cassandra, Samson, Skye, and Jerome came to a halt outside the circle of candles that signified the safety of the circle. With Seabhac and himself, the circle would protect nine of them. If Memnon remembered correctly, nine was a completion number, signifying the end of a cycle. It also held mystical properties that had to do with being able to multiply and single digit number by nine and adding the ensuing numbers adds up to nine. Every time. Memnon wasn't versed enough to understand what all that meant, but it was a strong number and that was enough to know for tonight.

"Please remain outside the circle until I complete the ritual and then I will open a way in for you." Seabhac cautioned the group.

"What can I do to help?" Anwyn stepped forward and asked, but Seabhac motioned her to wait.

"Your time will come soon enough. I am just casting a circle of protection for now, then I shall explain what we are doing."

Anwyn nervously rubbed her necklace and a shadow of fear crossed her face. Memnon rushed to reassure her.

"You'll be fine. The necklace will guide you."

"I suppose. It is just that there is so much at stake. So many lives. I truly do not know what I am required to do."

"I am sure that Brighid didn't go to all the trouble to leave you in the dark when you need guidance the most."

"Hey, Memnon. Good to see you again." Jerome walked over and shook his hand.

"Thanks. You as well. I'm surprised you and Skye came. I mean, with the baby and all...it could get dangerous."

Jerome's face darkened. "We dealt with this evil and thought we'd destroyed it, only to have it return. This time we make sure its death a permanent one. The fact is that if it wins, Salem won't be safe for our child. If we lose, Skye's parents will take the baby and move far away from any influence this evil might have. Either way, there is no choice but to fight."

"I understand." He waved at Skye, who stood talking with Cassandra and Samson. She waved back and smiled. Her long dark hair alongside Cassandra's white-blond hair made for a contrast in beauty.

"Hey." Jerome growled. "Put your eyes back in your head. Besides, from what I understand, you're interested in a certain red-haired woman."

Before Memnon could answer, Seabhac motioned everyone over to the circle. The tension in the surrounding area took an immediate spike and faces paled in nervous anticipation.

Once the group had assembled, Seabhac mumbled a few words and used his knife to cut the shape of a door on the edge of the circle. He stepped back and allowed them access. Once they all huddled in the circle, he took his knife and reversed the direction he'd just cut. To anyone else, it would look silly, as if he was cutting the air. But Memnon knew he was providing an entrance through the bubble of energy that should now protect them from the evil should Verity show up.

A cloud passed across the moon, temporarily casting darkness over the entire landscape. They all stood silently within the circle. Each one likely pondering the coming events. Hoping to make it out alive. As moonlight returned, a collective sigh of relief sounded among them.

Seabhac nodded to each of them and spoke. "Thank you all for being here. We have in common the shared experiences of dealing with this evil in various ways. People have sacrificed their lives and plans laid centuries ago to prepare for the ultimate destruction of this evil. Tonight, we fight this final battle for the future of Salem. We cannot lose, as the price to be paid for such a loss is too great."

Memnon searched the faces of the assembled group and saw nothing but determination and the strength of friendship. People willing to die for the safety of others. Pride filled him and he realized that even if he died that night, he was fortunate to have known such people.

"In about four minutes, the moon will be at zenith. We will join hands and concentrate on creating a single pulse of energy. Order does not matter, except Anwyn and Memnon must join hands and stand closest to the lighthouse. Anwyn's right hand holding Memnon's left. I will explain why in a moment. Anwyn, you will not call on the power of the necklace until I say. We will all call only on our own power to start. Am I understood so far?"

Everyone nodded.

"Good. As soon as I feel we have built as much of a force as possible, I will say 'Now'. Anwyn and Memnon immediately release your hands. Memnon, remember the portal you opened earlier?"

"Of course."

"It is there. Verity thought to hide it, but I have made it visible again. See the shimmer?" Seabhac pointed to a barely noticeable shimmer beside the lighthouse.

"Yes. I do."

"When I give the word, you reach out with your left hand and call for the spirits that are at the portal. As you created the portal, they will answer your call."

"Are you sure? All I have to do is call for them?"

"Yes, and yes. You will take them in with your left hand and out your right, still concentrating on melding your energy with the collective energy of the circle. Each of you will take the spirts in your left hand and pass them through to the person on your right, sending your own energy with them."

"Understood?"

Samson replied. "Yes, build our energy, take the portal spirits in the left hand and out to the person on the right."

"Good. By the time it reaches Anwyn, things will get interesting. Anwyn, a force beyond what a normal person could handle will hit you hard, but the necklace will protect you. It is up to you to assimilate all that force and send it into the necklace to meld with all the spirits you hold there. When it gathers and builds within the Light of Many Souls and you feel magic at its most optimum, you throw your right hand toward the beacon and let loose."

"Let loose? How? I do not understand."

Tears filled her eyes, and the uncertainty in Anwyn's voice tugged at Memnon. He wanted to protect her. Damn it, she shouldn't have to be dealing with this kind of evil. None of them should. He silently swore that if they made it through tonight alive, he would do everything in his power to ensure she lived the life she deserved.

Seabhac raised a hand. "Do not worry. Brighid created the necklace to guide you, did she not?"

"Yes."

"Then follow what it leads you to do. You will know when the time is right to release all the pent up magic. All of us, the spirits of the witches, priestesses, Brighid, souls from the portal...the beacon light will magnify all of it and throw it out to cover miles. The evil will not stand a chance against that kind of power."

"Nora, if you would please light the candles, it is time to begin."

Once lit, the flickering candle flames cast dancing shadows and set an eerie mood. Everyone reached out to the person beside them to hold hands with Memnon and Anwyn closest to the lighthouse as directed. The warmth of Anwyn's hand spread through Memnon like the warm comfort of a fire in the hearth. His heart lifted and filled with a certainty that they would make it out alive.

"A caution. Do not let go of the person beside you. We must not break the circle no matter what. When I instruct Anwyn and Memnon to release hands, the rest of us must remain connected. If Verity shows up to fight, do not let her distract you. Everything rests on us building the magic, then relaying it from Memnon to Anwyn, through the necklace and toward the beacon light. Am I understood?"

Fear and tension rose a notch as everyone in the circle nodded. As they closed their eyes, a breeze fluttered the candle flames and set some dry leaves rustling across the rocks. Hearts pounded and breathing rasped as a dead calm settled over the group. The protective circle lit in an unearthly glow.

Time passed as the moon rose above the circle. Memnon experienced a tingling rush of blood and focused on the pulsing power. It felt amazing and surprisingly he recognized the individual powers building around and within him.

Cassandra's, of course, he'd felt his entire life, so that was easy to pick out of the swirling mass of energy. Jerome and Samson emitted assertive, in-your-face solid energy, while Skye's was just a powerful, but more gentle in how it melded rather than pushed. Something about the ethereal quality of it reminded him of wildflowers in a summer meadow. Anwyn's pulsed with substantial force and made Memnon think of loamy earth, sun baked cedar, and lily-of-the-valley flowers.

He squelched the urge to breathe deeply, to inhale her essence. Focus. He needed to focus and wait for Seabhac's signal to access the portal. Swirls of the various energies filled him, gave him strength, and made him feel as if he was floating.

A desperate shout of anger from Seabhac dragged him back to reality and his instinct was to let go of the hands he held, but Seabhac's admonishment stopped him.

"Do not let go. No one drop hands. Keep the circle connected." The druid's voice rose over a rising wind as he yelled the words. The top of the lighthouse held his attention while grief etched his face in a mask of fear.

Memnon looked up and wished he hadn't. Verity stood at the edge of the widow's walk, her arm around Ainevar's throat and a knife at her belly.

Gusts of wind whipped around the lighthouse, blew the leaves and dirt into mini dust devils that twirled around their feet. Grey clouds filled the sky and covered the moon.

"Stop what you are doing, Druid, or I will kill your woman and your child."

Tears streamed down Seabhac's face and he hesitated briefly, almost dropping his hands. But his voice rang out loud and true.

"Do not let go. We are almost there." His blue eyes pinned on Ainevar and Verity as his voice bellowed. "You will die this night. I give you my word on that, Devil."

"Then all those you love will die as well." Verity gripped the knife tighter and readied it for the killing plunge into Ainevar's belly.

CHAPTER THIRTY-FIVE

"Seabhac?" Anwyn's voice cracked amidst the ever volatile weather. The urgent looks on the faces of the others reflected horror and hesitation.

"DO NOT BREAK THE CIRCLE." Seabhac screamed. Agony seeping through his voice with every word.

As if in slow motion, Verity plunged the knife toward Ainevar. Seabhac paled, closed his eyes and chanted as if casting a spell. He opened his eyes and widened them as the knife literally bounced off Ainevar and flew over the edge of the lighthouse to clatter on the rocks below.

"Nooooo!" Verity screamed and reached for Ainevar, who had escaped her grip.

Verity lunged toward Ainevar with murderous intent in her eyes. Before she could reach the sorceress, an unseen force lifted Verity off her feet and threw her back.

Anwyn looked at Seabhac, wondering how he had managed such a feat while devoting himself to building the energy in the circle. He looked just as surprised and perplexed as the rest of the group.

Verity made another attempt to reach Ainevar, but pinpricks of sparkling lights created a barrier that Verity couldn't penetrate. Her scream of rage reverberated across the water. Lightning streaked across the now black sky. Leaves and other debris snapped and jumped in the building wind.

Memnon stood on one side of Anwyn and Seabhac on the other, so she heard Seabhac when he whispered.

"Fates above. I know what that tingling is that I have been feeling all day."

"Now is not the time, Seabhac." Memnon cautioned.

"Oh, now is definitely the time. We have unexpected help." Elation lit the druid's face, which softened for a moment, then took on a determined, predatory look as he increased his chanting.

It was almost time. Anwyn's entire being filled with elation and pulsing, invigorating power. She saw the same sense reflected in the faces of those in the circle. Their faces alight with flames from the magically sustained candles. Determination etched into each of their faces.

Regal.

Loyal.

Bonded.

Determined.

Powerful.

All words that described these people. Tears threatened at the thought of never getting to know them better. To stand together in the face of potential death for the greater good and benefit of those who would never know the sacrifices given to protect them. These people amazed her. Love surged in her heart.

That is when Seabhac yelled out one word. "NOW!"

Reacting to the stark command, Memnon and Anwyn let go of each other's hands.

Memnon reached toward the whirling portal and called out. "Come to me now."

Misty shapes flew from the portal and shot straight for Memnon. His body jerked and his hand vibrated and glowed as it seemed to suck in the mist. The portal grew and moved closer to him as the spirits continued to flow between the otherworldly realm and Memnon. His head snapped back and his body wavered between solid and insubstantial. As the mist moved from person to person, each of them glowed in an ever-increasing luminosity.

"Hold on, Memnon." Seabhac yelled above the increasing din of the storm. "You are now the anchor, just as I predicted. Do not let us down."

Memnon's face mirrored the herculean effort he exerted in sustaining the connection. Sweat broke out on his forehead and his neck muscles knotted with the effort.

Seabhac gasped when the moving force of energy hit him. The druid sagged and Anwyn worried he would fall to the ground, but Seabhac clenched his teeth. "Do not falter, Anwyn. It is up to you and the necklace now. Aim for the light."

"But Ainevar stands between me and the light."

"Yes. Do it. Aim directly through her to the light. Trust me."

And then the energy grabbed her left hand, and she nearly passed out. Roiling, seeking, growing, the magic-induced energy filled her to the point where she thought she would explode.

The necklace jumped and heated on her neck and flashed so brightly that it blinded her. A sucking sensation followed as the spirits joined the gathering force. Hot tears flowed down her face as Anwyn felt the energy and thoughts of all the young girls and women she had known in Avalon. Bittersweet feelings of nostalgia almost undid her resolve, but Seabhac tugged at her hand.

Pain and jubilant power mingled together. Pushing through her, it searched for an exit. Focusing her thoughts and ignoring the overwhelming sense of losing herself, she mentally directed it to her right hand. As it passed through her, the emotions of hundreds of spirits assaulted her. She grit her teeth and fought to keep control.

"Do not give in. Fight to keep control. You are so close." He whispered in her ear.

Her body shook. Thunder cracked and boomed above so loudly that the ground beneath her shook. Verity screamed and launched herself at the railing, throwing streaks of sparking flames at them. Anwyn heard someone cry out in pain, but could not look. She was so close.

Her arm ached as she held it extended, palm facing up toward Ainevar and the light. Pressure built and when it finally released, the whoosh boomed louder than the thunder. A massive ball of swirling, whirling light forms shot at Ainevar. Weak and exhausted, Anwyn immediately fell to her knees and most of the others in the circle did as well.

What followed was impressive. Ainevar lit up as the energy engulfed her body and then focused on her belly. The glowing ball bathed Ainevar until it gave one huge pulse and flew at the beacon light.

BOOM. The light exploded and sent out a massive blanket that expanded with a whoosh and filled the landscape to the horizon in either direction. Just a split second of light and then it was dark again. The storm disappeared as if it had never been. Silence settled around the group. Raspy breathing and the rustle of clothing as they moved. The ones who had collapsed picked themselves up.

Every eye turned to the lighthouse. Anxiety was palpable. Had it worked? Anwyn's stomach clenched when she saw Verity still standing at the railing. They had failed.

"Oh, no, Seabhac. We failed." Her whispered words sparked the others to move closer until they huddled together in resignation.

Seabhac raised a hand. "Wait. Watch."

Verity looked down at them with a sneer of triumph. "You have failed, Druid. Even with your reinforcements, I am too powerful for you. I grow weary of our constant battles, so this will be the last one. I will kill you, all your conspirators, your woman..."

Verity coughed. Her hand flew to her throat as foam frothed from her mouth. She coughed again, but this time blood speckled the foam. Then her eyes and nose ran with rivulets of blood that fell to the ground. She screamed in rage.

Her body pulsed with lumps appearing and disappearing intermittently all over her body. She grabbed her stomach and hunched as she staggered to the railing. Morphing into a beast and back to human again, she screamed. "What have you done to me?" Her black eyes blazed as they turned to the people standing below. Her expression changed suddenly to one of astonishment.

"Nooooooo!" Her scream ripped through the night as she lurched forward and fell over the rail to the ground. A crunching thud followed her descent.

A black cloud rose from her body, snapping with black and red sparks. It rose above Verity's broken body and swirled in a funnel cloud. Higher and higher until it was almost out of sight, then it exploded into tiny particles that drifted into the heavens.

The release of pressure in Anwyn's chest brought such relief. She sighed. "Is it over, Seabhac?"

"Not quite."

CHAPTER
THIRTY-SIX

He beckoned to the others, who came over to hear what he had to say. White faces, each etched with exhaustion, stared hopefully at Seabhac.

His gaze touched on each of them and softened with tears as he considered the motley group who stood before him. He cleared his throat and spoke.

"You are all amazing. I am proud to count you among my friends and applaud your warrior souls that have finally defeated this evil."

"So we have killed it for good this time?" Skye asked, with just a hint of uncertainty in her voice.

"Yes. The essence that made up the evil's living force now rolls around the universe in so many tiny pieces that it can never reassemble and murder anyone again."

Skye moved into Jerome's arms and buried her face. "Thank goodness we will see our daughter grow up." Her shoulders shook, and a sob escaped her. Jerome comforted her as he closed his eyes and his lips moved in silent prayer.

Cassandra and Samson held each other close, as did Nora and Tartleby. Anwyn smiled because it looked as if her two friends would now have a chance at love and to live a normal life. No more sacrifices from either of their families. Memnon moved to stand beside her and rested a hand on her shoulder as he whispered in her ear.

"Are you okay?"

Tears filled her eyes because she did not know how to reply. She did not know what happened to her now, but not wanting to ruin the triumphant mood, she nodded.

"Wait." Anwyn frowned. "Seabhac, you said it is not quite over. What is wrong?"

"Nothing. But this battle depleted the soul energy in all of you and needs to be replenished or you will suffer health problems and eventual death."

"Wait. What? You could have mentioned that to us earlier. And what's the difference between soul energy and just, well, regular energy?" Memnon asked.

Seabhac snorted. "You all came here to fight a battle that would likely end in death, so I did not think that depleting your soul energy would be a major problem. And soul energy is exactly what is sounds like. It goes much deeper than the energy of your aura. If you deplete it, your soul withers and has difficulty moving from one life to the next."

"Great." Samson snorted. "So what do we do about it, Druid?"

"You all go to Tartleby's store where he has rejuvenating tea ready to brew and I will do energy work on each of you." He glanced at the lighthouse where Ainevar had appeared at the doorway.

"Now, begone with your questions. I have my own business to attend. I will see you shortly at Tartleby's."

He left the exhausted group of people and strode to Ainevar and engulfed her in his arms. The air around the couple shimmered, and Anwyn would have sworn that she saw will-o'-the-wisps dancing around them.

"Okay, let's get this done." Samson said. "And if you don't mind, Seabhac can work on me first as I will have a lot of explaining to do and paperwork to fill out."

They filed toward the vehicles. Cassandra, Samson, Jerome, and Skye in one vehicle. Nora, Tartleby, Anwyn, and Memnon in Memnon's SUV.

When Anwyn looked back, there was no sign of Seabhac and Ainevar. The lighthouse and surrounding area looked desolate in the moonlight.

CHAPTER
THIRTY-SEVEN

Anwyn watched the room full of her friends chatting and laughing while they drank their lemon or peppermint tea. Relief and exuberance filled the room as they made plans for the future, or even tomorrow, knowing they'd destroyed the evil forever.

She ran a finger across the crystal, still on a chain around her neck. It no longer felt the same, and neither did she. This waiting was torture because every minute she spent watching others be happy, drove home the fact that she had no future. She wanted to go now before her heart broke anymore than it already had.

The problem was that she did not know if she would poof into nothingness, or collapse to the floor dead. When she thought of Memnon seeing her die, she knew she could not stay. It was better if she just left and awaited whatever fate befell her. She had already snuck Ebony into Nora's store and written out some legal papers dividing her store and box of coins and jewels between all her friends. Everyone who had helped defeat the evil. They deserved it.

Seabhac had set up a room in the back to do energy work on people. So far, he'd done Samson, Cassandra, Jerome, and Skye. Samson had left to do damage control at the office and Memnon was currently getting a treatment from Seabhac. Now was the ideal time for her to slip away. Pretending to use the bathroom, she snuck around to the side door and quietly crept into the night. Her heart broke a bit with every step she took.

Not sure where to go or what to do, she wandered and enjoyed the peace of the early morning. Because of the lateness of the hour, few people wandered the streets, but there was the occasional reveller intent on enjoying the Halloween atmosphere, no matter the hour.

With a sigh, she turned to head back to her own store to await her fate, but almost walked into a wall of mist forming in front of her. The ethereal mist formed into a familiar and beloved shape.

"Brighid." Anwyn's heart thumped with elation at a familiar face. "How are you here? I thought you would be gone with all the other spirits in the necklace. Used up and moved on after the battle."

"I have one last chore before moving on, child."

"Can I help you with anything?"

"Why yes, you can. Why are you wandering the streets alone when you should be celebrating with the others? What you have all accomplished is stellar. You should be proud."

"I am, but...it hurts too much."

Brighid smiled and touched a finger to the necklace. "It is now empty of souls, but it is beautiful nonetheless. It is now up to you to fill it again with love and magic."

Anwyn frowned. "I do not understand. How can I do that when I am to die?"

"Oh, child. Your life is just beginning. You accomplished what I asked of you. What the universe asked of you. Now you get to live out your normal life span. Except it will be in this lifetime rather than your own."

"But, how? Why did you not tell me? I was so sure that my life would end once this was over."

"You had to give of yourself completely. Remember I told you that when I offered you this task. No expectations. No promises. Your acceptance had to come from a place of complete selflessness."

"I remember." Bubbles of joy burst through her. "That means this life is mine now. I can stay. Everyone I have befriended can remain my friends." Anwyn threw her arms around Brighid and hugged tightly. "I am so happy."

Suddenly, a thought struck her, and she pulled back. "Oh, no. That is not fair. What of all the others who sacrificed their lives? Why should I get to live while they died? And what of you? Oh, Brighid, I do not know if I can bear the guilt."

"But you gave your life. Willingly. You let me put you in a sleep state for centuries and you offered your life to destroy the evil. It just so happens that the Fates gave your life back to you. Be happy. Live to help others so this is not a wasted gift."

"Will I ever see you again?"

"Probably not." Brighid's form faded as she spoke her last words. "You shall be far too busy living your life to care about me."

Anwyn gazed sadly at the spot Brighid had just stood. "I will never forget you, My Lady." She whispered into the still night.

Feeling sad and elated, she returned to Tartleby's where the others were finishing up their tea and energy booster from Seabhac. Nora noticed her first and came over to hug her.

"I have a feeling that you will want to take Ebony back with you when you return home?"

"What? How did you know?"

"I understand the unspoken price that binds you to a task such as yours. You could not have expected to live in order to commit a selfless act. And you couldn't know the outcome or that would have negated your selfless act."

"Well, you certainly knew much more than I did." She laid a hand on Nora's arm. "Thank you for everything. I am proud to call you friend, and thrilled to have the chance to get to know you better."

"There you are. You disappeared for a while and I was wondering if you were okay." Memnon came to stand beside them.

"I am great. Better than ever." Anwyn beamed with all the happiness that she felt inside.

"Have you had your energy boost yet?"

Seabhac must have heard the question because he called out from across the room. "She does not need one. Her soul is ancient and powerful. She will be fine."

Anwyn laughed and touched the crystal around her neck. "The *Light of Many Souls* has now been drained and nothing more than a pleasing bauble. I am afraid I have returned to my own limited powers."

"Ha. Shows how little you know." Seabhac said as he walked over to join them. "Why do you think Brighid chose you for this task? It was not because you were an average priestess, I can assure you?"

Ainevar joined them and placed her hand on Seabhac's sleeve. "If you had remained in Avalon and progressed along your path, you would eventually have taken Brighid's place as head priestess. Your very soul throbs with earth energy, and as you settle into your new life, you will find your strength. Trust me." Ainevar's soft smile warmed Anwyn.

"Now, I think it is time for us to retire, my love." Ainevar place a hand on her belly. "Our child is restless, and I am exhausted."

"The child." Memnon exclaimed. "That is the tingling you felt all day. The unexpected help that you mentioned in the circle. That is why you told Anwyn to aim through Ainevar. To use the magic of your child."

Seabhac laughed. "Yes. It seems our son is already a powerful druid."

"Daughter." Ainevar said.

Seabhac rolled his eyes. "Either way, we must leave." He reached out to touch the book held by Ainevar. "We must also take *Faerie Enchantments and Sorcerer Magick* somewhere safe. It served its purpose with helping defeat the evil in the past, but the knowledge this book holds is too much for humans , I am afraid."

"Will we see you again?" Anwyn asked.

"Once the babe is born, we will return for a visit. I want our child to meet you all." Ainevar smiled fondly at each of them as she and Seabhac disappeared into a whiff of smoke.

Anwyn smiled. "Despite his gruffness, I am going to miss Seab-hac."

"Hmm, like a damned headache." Memnon said, though the look on his face softened his words.

"I think it's time for us to leave as well." Skye said, and followed it with a yawn. She leaned over and gave Anwyn a hug. "I look forward to getting to know you. As soon as we return from my parent's place, that is."

"I look forward to it more than you could possibly know." Anwyn exclaimed, so excited to be planning for a future.

Jerome gave her a quick hug. "Cassandra, are you coming with us." He sent her a pointed look.

"Yes, that sounds good. No sense in making Memnon drive me all the way home when you live right next door." She smiled at her brother. "I'll see you tomorrow. I mean, later today, I suppose. It's already getting light out." She hugged her brother and whispered. "I want details."

Once it was quiet and settled in the store, Nora and Tartleby started cleaning up. When Anwyn offered, Nora shooed her away. "No, you go home and get some sleep. I will help Tartleby. Memnon, I assume you will see her home. And don't worry, Anwyn, I'll bring Ebony back to your place later."

Memnon fixed a fiery gaze on Anwyn. "Great. It will give us time to talk."

The orangey yellow of the sky signalled dawn as the sun rose above the horizon. The people of Salem already stirred the sounds of the day beginning. Memnon reached out to take Anwyn's hand in his and her heart beat quicker than normal. His hand was warm and solid feeling. Neither of them spoke until they arrived at her door and Memnon cleared his throat.

"So, we saved Salem and rid the world of a terrible evil. Not bad for a night's work."

Anwyn laughed. "The night was just the culmination of so much. So much planning and sacrifice." Her eyes clouded over.

"Hey, don't be sad. We did a good thing."

"Yes, and so many people paid the price."

Memnon pulled her into his arms and just held her close. His chin rested on top of her head and his heart beat against her cheek. It felt wonderful, and Anwyn did not want to move...ever. She wanted to ask him a question, but feared the answer. Before she could say a thing, Memnon spoke.

"So, I have decided to stay in Salem permanently."

Anwyn's heart soared. But she calmed it down. Just because he was staying did not mean he was staying because of her.

"Oh. Your sister will be happy."

Memnon laughed and stepped back so he could look her in the face. "I hope Cassandra is not the only one who is happy."

"I also am happy. Very much so." Anwyn threw her arms around his neck and held tight.

"Whew. That's a relief. A guy doesn't like to assume anything, but I was hoping you'd want me here."

The streets were getting busier and Anwyn wanted peace, so she unlocked her door and motioned Memnon inside. She loved her store and home and still could not believe they belonged to her now. And all the jewels and gold.

"Oh, my. I just thought of something." Excited, she turned to Memnon. "What are you going to do here? Can you run your business or have you thought of another task to fill your days?"

"Another task?" Memnon chuckled. "I am selling my business, but I haven't yet decided what I'm going to do with my time."

Anwyn clapped her hands. "I have an idea. As long as you are agreeable, of course."

Memnon narrowed his eyes and crossed his arms. "Go on."

"You do not know it, but I am rich. Very rich."

"How wonderful for you, but what does that have to do with me. I won't want to be a kept man and you don't need to offer me money to be with you."

"No, silly. I have an idea. When I came to Salem, the number of people who play at magic with no idea what they are doing astounded me. There is no reverence, no true understanding of nature, energy, or true connection to one's self. I have also seen some who have innate abilities and no idea how to access or use them. I want to open a teaching place to help the people who truly desire to learn. I would also like to guide those whose ancestry goes back to times when magic was part of one's soul. Magic still exists in some of these people, even though they are just playing at it for now. I cannot do this alone. I need help."

She looked expectantly at Memnon, who was silent. Her heart dropped, and she wondered if she had been too forward. Relief flowed through her when Memnon's face lit with a smile.

"I love it. But on one condition."

"I need to hear the condition before agreeing. Last time I agreed to something unconditionally, I ended up battling an evil force and almost dying."

Memnon laughed. "I get it, but this is a simple task. I want to be your first student. I have spent most of my life downplaying my abilities for various reasons. Now, I want to explore them. Seabhac seems to think I have all these powers that I know nothing about."

"If I teach you, you will help me set up a school and teach?"

"Yes."

"Wonderful. Now can I ask something of you?"

Memnon reached out and gently pushed a stray piece of hair from her cheek. He smiled. "You can ask anything of me, Anwyn. Don't you know that?"

There were those darned butterflies in the stomach again. And her knees felt weak for some reason. She needed sleep. That is what was making her weak.

"I would ask that you teach me about this time. My home and everything I know is so far in the past, and I know nothing about now. Or even history and events leading up to now. I have missed so much and feel quite awkward most of the time."

"Awkward?" Memnon's laughter might have embarrassed her, but the words that followed melted her. "You are grace and beauty combined. There is nothing awkward about you."

"Oh. Then it is a deal." She put her hand out to shake as that is what she learned people of this time did to seal an agreement.

"Yes, it is. But a handshake won't be enough. A kiss is the only form of deal sealing I will accept from you."

Memnon leaned down to kiss her, and the moment his lips touched hers, Anwyn knew her destiny was here with this man. Fates above, he was an amazing kisser. She sighed and melted into his arms.

A sigh settles over the land as a centuries old battle ends. What started on a clifftop across an ocean, ended in a place haunted by its own history. Life given with selfless intent gave way to blood taken in ritual sacrifice. Soaked in blood and fear, the land cried out, and the universe ached with the pain of many lost souls. Now, humans and druids alike live on with hope for the future and dreams filled with magick. As always, this book shall hold the knowledge and accounting of all that transpired...until, once again, a need arises.

Excerpt from *Faerie Enchantments and Sorcerer Magick*

Afterword

I hope you enjoyed reading this book and would appreciate if you could leave a review. Reviews help an author with future sales and marketing, so it's a great way to support and motivate the authors that you like. You can find me online at these places:

Website:

https://cathywalkerauthor.com
FB Author Page:

www.facebook.com/cathywalker.author

Author Bio

Books have fueled my imagination since reading the Black Stallion series when I was younger. Never thinking that I could actually write a book, I sat down and began writing anyway. I now have multiple published books and more on the way. All of them with a theme of myths, legends, romance, or fantasy.

I am fortunate enough to live on a farm filled with animals to love and care for. Every morning my dogs, cats, goats, and horses greet me at the barnyard. Spending time with them helps motivate me to write.

Printed in Great Britain
by Amazon

60268552R00134